Love
Next Door

OTHER TITLES BY HELENA HUNTING

ALL IN SERIES

A Lie for a Lie
A Favor for a Favor
A Secret for a Secret
A Kiss for a Kiss

PUCKED SERIES

Pucked (Pucked #1)
Pucked Up (Pucked #2)
Pucked Over (Pucked #3)
Forever Pucked (Pucked #4)
Pucked Under (Pucked #5)
Pucked Off (Pucked #6)
Pucked Love (Pucked #7)
Area 51: Deleted Scenes & Outtakes
Get Inked (crossover novella)
Pucks & Penalties: Pucked Series
Deleted Scenes & Outtakes

CLIPPED WINGS SERIES

Cupcakes and Ink
Clipped Wings

Between the Cracks
Inked Armor
Cracks in the Armor
Fractures in Ink

SHACKING UP SERIES

Shacking Up
Getting Down (novella)
Hooking Up
I Flipping Love You
Making Up
Handle with Care

STAND-ALONE NOVELS

The Librarian Principle
The Good Luck Charm
Meet Cute
Felony Ever After
Little Lies (written as H. Hunting)

Love
Next Door

HELENA
HUNTING

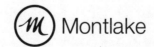 Montlake

This is a work of fiction. Names, characters, organizations, places, events, and incidents are either products of the author's imagination or are used fictitiously.

Published by Montlake, Seattle

www.apub.com

Amazon, the Amazon logo, and Montlake are trademarks of Amazon.com, Inc., or its affiliates.

ISBN-13: 9781542029308
ISBN-10: 1542029309

Cover design by Eileen Carey

Printed in the United States of America

This one's for you, Grandma Nell

CHAPTER 1
THEM'S THE BREAKS

Dillion

I toss another empty can in the garbage bag. There has to be an entire case's worth under my freaking bed. My ex-boyfriend used to drink diet soda in the middle of the night because he didn't like the taste of water but couldn't afford any more fillings in his teeth—as if diet soda is any better than the regular stuff.

It was a weird habit I no longer have to worry about since he doesn't live here anymore. And in two days, neither will I. We didn't part on bad terms—it was an amicable breakup. In fact, I'm less upset about the breakup than I am about the fact that the company I was working for over the last few years closed, and I'm now out of a job. Which is probably a pretty strong indicator that the relationship wasn't meant to last. Still, it sucks to be down a job, a boyfriend, and, in two days, an apartment.

What I'm trying to get to, and failing at, is the suitcase that's been stored under the bed for more than two years. At this point, with the sheer number of random cans I've come across, I'm certain of two things—the woman who used to clean our apartment every other week *never* cleaned under the bed, and I most likely will not want my suitcase once I'm able to get to it.

I put mission get-the-suitcase-while-cleaning-under-the-bed on hold when my phone rings. I debate ignoring the call. I'm not entirely sure I want to speak with anyone, especially since I've been procrastinating and left cleaning and packing until the eleventh hour.

I sigh when it reaches the third ring and finally pick up. It's just my dad. I wait for some kind of latent disappointment or sadness that it isn't my ex, Jason, to follow, but there isn't any. Jason made a choice when he took the job back in his hometown in Connecticut, and I made mine when I decided not to follow.

"Hey, Dad, what's up?"

"Hey, kiddo. You doing okay?"

He knows about the recent bumps in the road of my life. I left out the part about needing to find a new apartment because I felt like the breakup and losing my job were enough for him to worry about. He still thinks I'm coming for a visit in a couple of days, which honestly was the plan until the apartment I'd hoped to move into turned out to be infested with bedbugs. "Doing great. Is everything okay? You don't usually call me at"—I check the clock on the nightstand—"ten on a Thursday morning."

"Uh, well, Billy had an accident."

My heart is suddenly in my throat. My younger brother has never been particularly good at staying out of trouble's way. "Is he okay?"

My dad is quick to reassure me. "He's a bit banged up, but he'll be all right."

Just because Dad says Billy's all right doesn't necessarily mean it's completely true. My dad has always been good at downplaying situations. Making it seem as though things aren't as bad as they truly are. Like two years ago, when he and my uncle were struggling to make ends meet with the family construction business and hiding how close they were to being bankrupt. I didn't find out about that until well after the fact, when they were back on track and no longer in the red.

When I asked him why he hadn't said anything, he told me he'd been afraid I'd think it meant I needed to come home and help out. At the time, Jason and I had just moved in together in a cute one bedroom in Wicker Park. I genuinely don't know what I would've done if he had told me, and I'm grateful that I didn't have to find out.

"What kind of accident was it? Please tell me it wasn't on-site. And what exactly does 'a little banged up' mean?" I put my phone on speaker, toss it on my unmade bed, and pick up a stack of folded clothes before riffling through them to make sure they're not from my "frequent wear" pile. Those will go in my suitcase, if it's deemed useable once I get it out from under the bed. I determine nothing in the pile is going to be worn in the next couple of days, so I toss them in a box labeled CLOTHES.

I need to do something with my hands to keep me from entering stressed-out-pacing mode.

"It wasn't on-site; he was in a car accident. He was on his own, and no one else was involved, but he broke his ankle and totaled the truck." My dad's words are clipped, almost rehearsed.

Billy works with my dad and my uncle. They own the only construction company in town and handle everything from snow removal in the winter, to lawn maintenance in the summer, to renovation projects and framing all year long. In the past few years they began subcontracting out some of the trades because the rich city dwellers on the north side of the lake have started hiring them to make their mansions even bigger than they already are.

I drop down on my bed and fold and unfold a pair of socks repeatedly. "How severe is the break?"

"The doctor says it'll be about six to eight weeks in a cast."

Eight weeks seems like a long time. And it's only mid-June. This is their busiest time of year. "Is it his right or his left ankle?"

3

"It's the left."

I breathe a sigh of relief. "So he can still drive."

"Well, not quite." I can practically feel my dad pacing the room on the other end of the line. It's a habit we have in common.

"What do you mean 'not quite'?"

"His license has been suspended." My dad sighs. "He, uh, wrapped the truck around the McAlisters' mailbox because he was drunk, so he's been charged with a DUI."

"Oh my gosh. What the hell was he thinking?" The question is rhetorical. I can already guess what must have happened. He went out with his friends, got carried away, and drove his drunk ass home but didn't manage to make it to our driveway before he hit something. This isn't the first time this has happened—although the last time, we never could prove he was drunk since it wasn't until the next morning that we found his truck parked in the ditch, between two trees. Luckily he never injured anyone—not that it's any better.

"Apparently he wasn't. I don't think he realized how drunk he was. He tried to walk the rest of the way home after he hit the McAlisters' mailbox but ended up sleeping in the ditch. The McAlisters found him in the morning when they went to take old Rufus for a walk."

I run a palm down my face. I can only imagine the gossip. The McAlisters live about fifteen houses down the road from us. We've known them our entire lives. Billy dated their youngest daughter back in high school for a very brief period, and my dad built their garage a couple of years ago.

Everyone knows everyone else's business back home. That's what living in a small town is like, all the Nosy Nancys with ears to the ground, salivating like hungry dogs over the newest piece of gossip. And now my family is a prime target.

"How long is his license suspended for?"

"Looks to be about a year, but Bernie said he might be able to get it reduced to six months." Bernie Sawyer is the town lawyer. Yes, it's kind of hilarious that his last name rhymes with *lawyer*. He lives in a huge house that is basically the dividing line between the summer homes and the permanent homes on the lake. He and my dad have been friends since they were kids.

"That's still a long time. Even when he gets his cast off, someone is going to have to drive him around. I guess it's good it's not snow season, huh?" My hometown of Pearl Lake is on part of a snowbelt, which means winters are long and there's an endless amount of white powder to contend with. It's great for tobogganing, skating, and skiing and not so great for driving.

"It'd be better if we weren't in the middle of a huge renovation project."

"But you still have Aaron, right?" Billy might not be able to do the heavy on-site stuff, but they have Aaron Saunders, who is close in age to my brother. Aaron mostly handles the plumbing and electrical work, but he can also fill in for Billy.

"Yes, but he's already working overtime. It looks like I'm going to be back on-site for the next few months."

That puts me on alert. "Who's taking over the paperwork if you're back on-site? Please don't say Mom."

"Not sure I have much of a choice." He chuckles, but there isn't any humor in it.

"There has to be another option, Dad." A couple of years ago, my dad had the great idea to hire on my mom to do some of the bookkeeping. Except it didn't go well, and I had to come in and clean everything up over the Christmas holidays so it wouldn't be a complete cluster come tax time. After that he had to hire someone else to come in and help out, since he couldn't juggle every aspect of running the company.

"There isn't one, unless you're looking to move back home for a few months instead of visiting for a few days."

I laugh, but it's flat. I love my family, but I worked my butt off to get a scholarship to a college in Chicago. Away from Pearl Lake and all the things it doesn't have to offer, like anonymity and opportunity.

I spent four years earning my bachelor's in business administration. I worked two jobs, aced all my exams, and walked out of college and straight into a job with a sweet paycheck. For a while, I felt like I had succeeded. Gotten out of Pearl Lake and fulfilled my dream of living the city life in Chicago, which everyone back home refers to as "the city," as if it's the only city there is. To me, it was. Yet now I'm currently still jobless, and in two days I'll be homeless as well.

To me, moving home means I've failed. It means facing all the people I left behind and have basically avoided for the past decade. It means going back to where everyone knows everyone else's business. But I honestly don't have anywhere to stay in Chicago that isn't an Airbnb, and I don't have the kind of money to sustain that.

I must take too long to answer because Dad fills the silence. "Did you manage to get another job out there in the city?"

"No, I haven't found anything yet." I've applied for a bunch of positions, but none of them are what I really want to be doing—and to be honest, I don't even know what that is. I have always been singularly focused on getting a job so I can continue to live the city life. Only I never stopped to ask myself what it was I wanted to do as a profession. And now that I'm in a position to find a new job doing something I love, I'm a bit lost.

"What is it exactly you'd want me to be doing for you, if I agreed to stick around for a while?"

"Same kind of thing you did last time. Help manage the books, field calls from customers, set up deliveries, make connections with the other companies in town. I know it's a lot to ask, but I could really use your help, Darlin'. Just for a few months, until Billy is back on his feet." My family and friends have this habit of saying my name in a way that sounds like Darlin' instead of Dillion.

I look around my half-packed bedroom and consider what's left of my life here. I have no job and no boyfriend. All the people I've worked with have either had to take jobs elsewhere or were part of a couple, putting me on the outs. Sure, I'll get the occasional text message or invitation to go out for drinks, but they are proximity friends, not the kind I would reach out to after Jason and I broke up.

I have a couple of girlfriends from college I still talk to, but I spent most of my time studying and working, trying to get ahead. I've realized that as much as I love the city, I built a life in a bubble that consisted mostly of my boyfriend and my job, and with both of those gone, there's not much left for me to hold on to.

Besides, my dad asking for help is a big deal. We've always gotten along well, and I know how much work the project-management side of things can be, especially since it's such a small business. I don't want my dad to end up in the same position he did two years ago—not when I can actually do something to help. Even if it means leaving the city behind.

"Okay, Dad, I'll come home."

CHAPTER 2
SMALL-TOWN WOES

Dillion

Two days later I'm behind the wheel of a rented U-Haul, driving the contents of my apartment back to the town I grew up in and swore I'd never live in again. I remind myself that this is temporary—that I'm only going to be here as long as my family needs my help, and then I'll move back to the city. I'll have time to job hunt without the pressure of taking just *any* job. At least that is what I'm telling myself.

I pass the old, worn sign that marks the beginning of Pearl Lake. YOUR DREAMS ARE A BOAT RIDE AWAY is written underneath in fancy cursive with a small, wilted-looking garden surrounding the base of the sign. The summer's barely begun, and we're already having one of those nasty heat waves. The grass has taken on the hue that's typically referred to as "August gold," everything dry and brown and brittle. We obviously need a good dose of rain soon, or there won't be any bonfires happening on the beach. The trees lining the sides of the paved road are lush and green and full. Sporadic driveways create breaks in the tree line, with sleepy little cottage-style homes tucked inside them. It's the opposite of Chicago, and every time I visit, I can't wait to get back to the hustle and bustle of the city.

I turn onto the main road leading into town, shifting gears as I climb the steep hill, gravel spitting under my tires. When I reach the top, I downshift and take a moment to appreciate the view of the lake. It's completely unobstructed at the highest point. The beautiful, clear, deep-blue water is surrounded by the same lush trees and evergreens. To the right are massive estate-style lake homes rising up above the landscape. Their presence is a reminder of all the things I aspired to as a teenager. I wanted to be on the other side, to have all the things they did.

Sandy artificial beaches lead into the water; boathouses and expensive water toys are tied to docks; trampolines and floating mats dot the water. Jet Skis and speedboats cut lines through the lake, toy-size in the distance. For the people on that side of the lake, their time here is an escape from their busy lives rather than their normal. I envied their ability to leave Pearl Lake when I was young.

The left side is far less opulent. A span of beach, with darker sand and fuller trees, fills up one corner, and the rest is lined with trees, with small narrow docks and tin boats dotting the water. And smack in the middle is Bernie's house, the great divide between the rich and the moderately average townies, which is what the locals called themselves.

I exhale a breath as I head down the steep decline, veering left toward the downtown area so I can stop and pick up my mom on the way to the house. I timed the trip so I'll arrive right as her shift ends.

I turn onto Main Street and pass the eye roll–inducing stores frequented by the more affluent members of the community—high-end furniture stores and water-toy rental places; a couple of nicer restaurants owned by city people; Indulgence, the overpriced ice cream and chocolate store I always secretly wanted to go to but couldn't bring myself to because it would mean that I was taking business away from Corbin's convenience store, which was owned by one of my dad's friends.

I pull into the town parking lot and back my monster of a moving van into one of the spaces at the edge. I'm slapped with muggy June air as soon as I open the door and hop down onto the pitted pavement.

A group of teenagers from the rich side of the lake are draped across the ancient picnic table beside the equally ancient food truck. The same one I used to work at when I was their age. It was probably one of my most and least favorite jobs. I smelled constantly of stale french fries that summer. But it was a job, and money in my bank account. It was also the last summer I spent in Pearl Lake.

A teenage girl with long blonde hair pulled up into a high ponytail leans out the window while one of the summer boys flashes his perfect straight-toothed smile at her. Memories, some fond, some not, bubble to the surface.

Those summer boys were always so polished. Entitled and privileged, aware they had more and were better off than those of us who grew up in a small town, isolated and insulated. And in some ways, I bought into their narrative—their arrogant demeanor made my friends swoon. Local boys either cowered or puffed out their chests and looked down at those rich kids because they had more money and never had to work to earn it. Not like the townie kids, whose parents ran the local shops, catering to the people who came here for a few weeks or months of the year and then left everything behind again.

We were servants of the affluent. We lived outside the snow globe of entitlement. Close enough to shake it up, watch the chaos we caused, and then set that pretty picture-perfect world aside to collect dust until next season.

I pass the food truck and cross the street, heading for Tom's Diner, where my mom has worked for as long as I can remember. As a teen I used to pick her up from work all the time. Never my brother, though, because he wasn't very reliable, and half the time he didn't have car privileges. Seems like not much has changed.

I brace myself as I peer through the frosted glass, taking in the tables and people sitting at them. The diner is mostly frequented by older townies or the summer teens from the rich side of the lake. Townie teens tend not to eat there, favoring the food truck for the cheaper food and the lack of adult and parental supervision.

I open the door, the bell above me tinkling softly. A few heads turn as I step inside the air-conditioned diner and let the door fall closed behind me, the puff of hot, humid air following me in. I shiver as the heat is eaten up and absorbed by the cool blast coming from the vent above my head.

"Darlin'!" my mom exclaims from her spot behind the counter.

She wipes her hands on her apron and slides behind one of the other servers, who is punching in an order at the computerized register. It must be an upgrade since I was last here. The girl at the computer turns toward the door, her expression registering shock as her gaze slides over me. She's vaguely familiar, and it takes me a few moments to realize she's Claire, the youngest sister of one of the girls I used to hang out with in high school but lost touch with after I moved to the city. More like ghosted on my part, which makes being back here that much more challenging.

Familiar faces line the counter, townies who eat at the diner on a regular basis, some of whom come for breakfast and don't leave until the same time my mom's shift ends in the afternoon, drinking coffee and using the place like it's their own personal living room, not an actual diner.

"My baby is home!" My mom throws her arms around my neck, and I stumble forward a step. She's several inches shorter than me, and I'm wearing heels—admittedly not the best choice for driving a U-Haul, but old habits apparently die hard. They're also a bit of rebellion, signifying my reluctance to return to the place I only ever planned to visit for holidays.

Other than being several inches taller than her, I'm pretty much a carbon copy of my mom. We have the same unruly, curly blonde hair, pale-green eyes, button nose, and full lips. We both have overactive metabolisms, which means keeping meat on our bones is basically impossible.

She grabs my hand and drags me toward the counter, lined with red vinyl-covered stools, and pats the top of a free one. "Sit down, I'm just cashing out. Can I get you anything? A cup of coffee? How about a slice of pie? The Fetterlys dropped off a batch of their strawberry rhubarb custard pies. You know the ones with the crumble topping? How 'bout a slice of that?"

As much as I want to say no, because I'd rather get the heck out of here and away from all the familiar faces and the inevitable gossip, the Fetterlys' pie is the best in the county, winning awards every year at the fall fair. Besides, I sort of feel like eating my feelings.

"Maybe you could pack me up a slice? I had lunch on the way here." It's not a complete lie. I ate an entire bag of trail mix on the drive from the city. It's more that I don't want to get sucked into conversations with people I haven't seen in years who will want to talk about what happened with my brother and ask questions about me.

"Sure, of course. Just coffee, then." My mom slips back behind the counter and quickly sets a mug down by the stool, the only one not yet taken. She pours a steaming cup of fresh coffee while I drop down next to Rudy Dunn, who also happens to own the food truck across the street. Or at least he did.

My mom tops up his coffee and then goes back to cashing out.

"Well, if it isn't little Dillion Stitch. Ya done growed up, didn't ya?"

"Seems that way. Still running the food truck?"

"Sure am. Got my niece working there this summer. Brings in all those teen boys from the other side of the lake. Same as that summer you worked the truck. Gotta keep a close eye on things, but can't say it's bad for business, ya know? She's nicer to look at than this old mug." His grin is missing a couple of teeth at the edge of his smile line.

I return the smile. I remember exactly what it was like when those summer boys would show up in their flashy cars, or on their new ATVs.

They'd hang out near the picnic table, flash their flawless smiles, and flirt shamelessly. They were always trying to hook up with the local girls, almost like it was some kind of game for them. But when they showed up on our side of the lake for parties, it was their turn to learn their place in this town.

One time I kissed a summer boy on the beach to get back at my on-again, off-again boyfriend, who had decided we needed a break.

It had been the kind of kiss to sink into, at least until someone had made a "trailer trash" comment. That didn't go over well. At the time, townies didn't like it when one of the summer boys took advantage of their own or, worse, point out how much less they thought of us. Fights happened, and townies didn't care about broken noses or scars. I'd left the beach as soon as the fists started flying, not wanting to deal with the embarrassment or humiliation. I'm not sure how much has changed in the years I've been gone, based on who was sitting by the food truck when I passed it.

Rudy and I make small talk—mostly me asking questions about his family, his boat, what kind of fish he's been catching so far this season—in an effort to keep the topic off Billy and me.

Claire passes by with the coffee two minutes in and gives me a stiff smile. "Can I top you up, Dillion?"

I cover the top of my mug with my hand. "I'm okay, thanks. How are you?" I'm struck by a sharp pang of guilt. All these people I spent my childhood with I left behind, sloughed off like snakeskin. I never looked back, either, desperate to escape small-town life.

"I'm good." Claire holds out her left hand and splays her fingers, a small diamond glinting in the light. "Got engaged to Tommy Westover last month. We're gonna get married next summer in my parents' backyard."

"Oh wow! Congratulations! That's wonderful." I remember Tommy Westover. He graduated the year below me, played football for the school team, had two older brothers.

"Thanks." Her smile is softer now. "He's managing the hardware store. Took over 'cause Harry wanted to go down to part time, being retirement age and all. I might start doing the books or something after we're married." The bell at the kitchen window dings, and she glances over her shoulder. "Anyway, it's nice to see you, Dillion. Maybe we'll see you around, if you're in town for a while."

I swallow down the awkwardness and smile. "Absolutely."

She nods and turns to the kitchen window, balancing plates along her forearms so she only has to make one trip.

Thankfully my mom is finished cashing out, which means we can skedaddle before I run into any more blasts from the past. I follow her out the door, and when we get to the U-Haul van, I realize as my mom hops into the passenger seat that once I return it, I won't have a car. I'm used to living in the city, where I didn't need to own one. Hopefully my dad will have a work truck I can use.

"How was the drive down? Traffic okay?" Mom smooths out her skirt and crosses her legs. She clasps her hands in her lap, and I assume it's to avoid fidgeting. My relationship with my mom hasn't been particularly easy. I love her and she's a great mom, but my life goals and hers are not the same. She's never once been to Chicago, happy living in her little bubble where nothing ever changes. We get along well enough, but she doesn't understand my desire for more. She likes the simple life, and I like the city.

"Once I was out of the city, it was smooth sailing. How are things? How's Billy?"

"Oh, you know your brother; he'll be fine. It's not like anyone was hurt."

I glance briefly at her. "He was driving drunk, Mom."

"It was two in the morning. The only thing he was at risk of harming was a deer and himself."

"He drove into the McAlisters' mailbox! What if it had been their house?" Leave it to my mom to downplay a drinking-and-driving accident.

Mom scoffs. "They're fifty feet back from the road; he'd have had to hit a lot of trees on the way through to make that happen. Anyway, he's learned his lesson. It won't happen again, especially since he can't drive for the next few months."

"Dad said Bernie was going to try to get it down from a year to six months."

"It'll be reduced. And he'll be able to catch a ride in to work with your dad until all of that is sorted out. Anyway, enough about that." Mom doing what she does best when it comes to my brother—deny, avoid, and change the subject. "Did Claire tell you she's marrying the youngest Westover boy? He's such a nice young man. And they're having the wedding in the Bells' backyard. At least that's the plan. They're going to have a pig roast. Don't you think that's lovely?"

I leave the Billy conversation alone for now. I'll be seeing him soon enough, and hopefully my dad will have the full story. "It sounds great, Mom."

"I'm sorry things didn't work out with that Jackson boy you were dating. It's too bad we were never able to meet him."

"His name is Jason, and we just had different life plans, is all." I bite my tongue so I don't say what I want to, which is that they could've met him if they'd come up to visit even once. I never brought him home because . . . well, there wasn't anywhere for him to stay in our little three-bedroom house, and he went home to his family during the holidays. They at least made the effort to come see us in the city a few times.

"Mmm." My mom nods and does some more skirt smoothing. "I honestly half expected the two of you to get engaged. You'll find the right person, someday." She pats my arm and gives me a small smile.

"I'm sure I will." And whoever that someone is, I doubt I'm going to find him in Pearl Lake.

We pass familiar driveways lined with tin mailboxes, some prettily decorated, others seeming like they're about to fall off. Our driveway has a mailbox that looks like a miniature house. My mom repaints it every year with a new design. This year's is a cute white home with a red roof and flower boxes lining every window.

I turn down the gravel drive lined with trees and pull up to the old, worn-down house that's more like a typical cottage for this side of the lake. My dad constantly has a project on the go, a renovation he's trying to tackle in his spare time, which admittedly he's never had much of. Based on the scaffolding that surrounds it, he's repointing the brick on the chimney. The wood siding has been restained on the right side but is still aged and faded on the left. I love it and loathe it in equal measure.

"Your dad cleared a space in the garage for all your things, and he'll help you unload when he gets home tonight. I'm sure you want to return the van so you're not paying all those rental fees." My mom hops out, her tennis shoes hitting the gravel with a low crunch.

I gingerly step out, my heels highly impractical for small-town, rural living. I resign myself to the fact that I'm going to have to put these in storage with the majority of my stuff. I also have to get my head around living with my parents again. At the age of twenty-eight.

"Your dad renovated the kitchen this spring! I can't wait to show you!" She motions for me to follow her. I drop the keys into my purse and don't bother locking the truck. No one steals from their own community around here.

I follow my mom into the house. The front foyer is small, a closet to the left, a small bench to the right. Past that is the kitchen.

"Well?" She smiles brightly, her excitement obvious. "What do you think? Doesn't it look great? Obviously it's not all new stuff, but they did this renovation on a cottage on the north side—you know, where all the rich folk live." She waves a hand in the air, like the explanation is silly. "Anyway, the owner said your dad could take whatever he wanted. Can you believe it? The kitchen was almost brand new!"

The cabinets look like they're maybe a few years old—white Shaker style with simple lines. It's a huge improvement to the nineties-era kitchen I grew up with. The highly modernized kitchen is beautiful, but it also showcases how dated the rest of the house is. Still, I can recognize why she's excited by it. "It's great, Mom!"

The dining room, which is beside the kitchen, boasts an eighties-style table and wooden chairs with a geometric pattern—designs that have been made popular again thanks to the show *Stranger Things*. Beyond that is the living room, where my brother lies stretched out on the black leather sofa that's so worn in places that the wooden frame peeks through.

He takes up the entire couch, his long, lean frame barely fitting the length, with his casted leg, propped up with a pillow, dangling over the edge by about six inches. He's currently watching an episode of *Garage Wars*, nursing a beer. On the coffee table next to him is the remote and a bottle of prescription pills.

I bite my tongue, because coming in guns blazing, trying to parent my brother three seconds after I've arrived, is only going to cause problems I don't need. Especially if I have to live in the same space with him for the foreseeable future.

"Billy! You know you're not supposed to drink while you're taking medication!" Mom drops her purse on the kitchen table, mouth curving down.

He tips his head back, shaggy blond hair falling away from his forehead. He has a big gash that's taped up with a fly bandage, and dark shadows line his eyes. "It's fine, Ma, it's a light beer. Oh, hey, Dillion," he calls out from the couch. "I forgot you were coming down for a few days."

"Didn't Dad tell him?" I mumble as I arch a brow at Mom.

"Didn't Dad tell me what?" Billy may be irresponsible and make poor decisions, but he does have ridiculously good hearing. Even with the TV on and the door partially closed, he can listen in on someone else's conversation.

"Darlin's staying for longer than a few days."

"Really? Why? You got vacation time you have to take or something?"

"Uh, no, I'm coming to help out." Of course my parents didn't tell him.

He props himself up on one arm, grimacing with the movement. "Help out with what?"

"With the business."

Billy frowns. "You're kidding, right? You can't even lift a two-by-four without rolling an ankle."

That's not even remotely true. I used to help my dad all the time. Did I love lugging two-by-fours? Nope, but I had serious biceps for one summer, until I realized I could work in the service industry and make four times as much money behind a bar as I could building one. "Dad has to supervise the big reno project on the other side of the lake, so he asked if I'd come help in the office."

"How you gonna do that when you're working in the city?"

"I'm not anymore. At least not for a few months. Once you're on your feet and you have your driver's license reinstated, then I'll move back to the city."

His eyes flare, and a slow smile creeps across his face. "Is that why you were out there messing with the trailer, Ma?"

"The trailer?"

Mom's eyes light up, and she claps her hands. "Let me show you! I spruced it right up! Still needs some TLC, but I think you'll like it." She grabs my arm and guides me back toward the front door.

Billy waggles his eyebrows and flops back on the couch, his attention returning to *Garage Wars*.

Mom leads me out the side door, onto the covered deck. It used to be a sunroom, but now it's full of winter gear and old, half-broken chairs and projects. "What's all this stuff?"

"Oh, you know your brother, always looking for treasures. Once he's back on his feet, he'll be able to fix some of this stuff up. There's a whole set of chairs that he wants to have re-covered, and a table that he's planning to refinish."

It looks more like a relocated dump, and I have my serious doubts that my brother plans to do any of those things, but again, I keep it to myself, not wanting my negativity to rub off on my mom or make her feel bad. Half of me believes I might be veering into overreacting territory, and I can admit it's in part due to the circumstances and the fact that I'm back here after promising myself I wouldn't return. But I'm worried about the way our mom likes to brush things off, and the fact that Billy is loafing on the couch, drinking beer days after being in an accident caused by drinking and driving.

And now I'm being herded around the side of the house, past the shed, to where the trailer has been parked for the better part of a decade. It's been set up, and the awning, which is full of patched holes and a few that still need mending, is strung with white lights. A set of camping chairs are perched to the right of the door.

The exterior hasn't changed since we bought the thing probably twenty years ago, back when I was a kid. My parents had bought it with the plan to take us camping, but we already lived on a lake, and neither of their schedules was ever particularly conducive to taking more than a couple of days off. Even when they did get a week here or there, they preferred to stick close to home.

So when I was a tween and wanted to get away from my annoying little brother, me and my friends Tawny and Allie, and sometimes Sue, depending on whether we were on the outs or not, would have sleepovers here.

"Let me show you what I've done. I didn't have much time, so a few things still need to be taken care of." She pokes at the hole in the screen door before she opens it and ushers me in.

I probably haven't stepped foot in here since I was eighteen. My high school boyfriend, Tucker, used to sneak over some nights, and we'd have super-quiet sex on the floor, which was the only surface that didn't squeak.

I shake that memory like I'm trying to erase an Etch A Sketch design. It appears as though very little has changed since my teens. Everything looks exactly the same, but older, worn out, and full of moth holes. It's probably not a stretch to believe that rodents have made a home in here at some point.

Directly in front of me is a small table, with benches covered in brown fabric on either side. To the right is a tiny sink and a hot plate; below that is the bar fridge. Past that is a door leading to a small bathroom with a toilet and sink—no shower, which means I'll need to use the one in the house.

To the left is the pop-out with the bed. It's a queen, and the comforter is the same one that's been in my room since I was probably fifteen years old. Even my stuffed dog, Fluffy, who used to be white and is now a matted gray, is perched on the pillow.

"I know it needs work, but I hung new curtains! Do you like them?" She tugs at the end of a hot-pink curtain with a geometric pattern on it that makes me feel like the entire trailer is sitting in the middle of a very wavy ocean at dawn.

"They're great, Mom." I try my best to inject some enthusiasm into my response.

"There's a tear in the canvas over the bed that I've patched with tape until I can get it sealed, but it's been dry lately, and there's no rain in the forecast, so you should be okay for a few days. And the bathroom works; I made sure of it. Your dad hooked up the water and everything." Her smile is expectant and strained.

Next to the seventies- and eighties-era brown theme, the curtains are hard to look at. But I can see that she's gone to a great deal of trouble to get this place ready for me, and she most definitely has done her best with the limited amount of time she's had.

"You didn't need to go to all this trouble, Mom."

"I thought you might want your own space, especially with Billy being stuck in the house and on crutches. We moved him into your old bedroom because it's bigger, and easier for him to get around in, you know, since his bedroom is so small, and I didn't think you'd like that cramped space, so I got this all ready for you. The heater works, too, so you don't need to worry about being cold or anything if you're still here when the weather starts to turn. You know how cold August nights can get near the end of the month."

I nod my agreement and swallow down my panic over being here long enough to need the heater. At the very least, I'll be here through September, based on what I know about Billy's injuries, anyway. "It's perfect, Mom. It'll be great."

"And you can use the indoor shower whenever you want, but you have your own little place. I think maybe when you go back to the city, I might make this my girl cave when I need a break from the boys." She smiles mischievously. "Especially when your dad and your uncle have been into the beers. The snoring is too much."

I chuckle. "I remember."

She gives me another hug. "I'm sorry about Jason. He seemed nice."

"He was. He still is. He just wasn't the one. Better to know that now, I guess."

"Mmm. Everything happens for a reason, doesn't it? If that company hadn't gone under, then he wouldn't have moved, and you wouldn't have ended up back home with us." She gives my hand a squeeze. "I know this isn't where you thought you'd be, Darlin', but it's where you're supposed to be. I feel it in my bones. I'll leave you to settle in."

She lets herself out, and I allow myself to deflate. My mom has always been a firm believer in things like fate and karma. She has her tarot cards read all the time by some batty lady who lives in the next town over. She used to take our neighbor Bee with her every once in a while. They dragged me along once. The lady told me she couldn't read me because I was blocking her energy, whatever that means.

I can't see any reason for me to be back here, other than fate and karma are having a good laugh at my expense.

CHAPTER 3
HOME SWEET HOME

Dillion

I head back to the U-Haul van and grab my suitcase so I can do what Mom suggested and settle in. I shouldn't be surprised that Billy has my bedroom now. His is tiny, barely able to fit a double bed and a dresser, whereas mine has a closet. The room hasn't technically been mine in almost ten years, when I moved to the city for college.

And Mom has a point about privacy. There isn't much in the house. My parents have a bathroom to themselves, but I'll be sharing the shower with Billy, so this is definitely preferable.

I check the fridge, more to see if it's cool than anything else. I'm surprised to find a six-pack of beer. And it's cold. I free one from the plastic ring and crack the top, bring it to my lips, and tip my head back.

After I moved to Chicago, I stopped drinking beer out of cans. I stopped doing most things that reminded me of home, wanting to remove myself as much as I could from small-town life. I drop down on the sofa and sigh. The curtains are a lot to handle in such a compact, brown space. I reach over and pull them open so I can look at something that feels less like a bad acid trip.

Beyond the trees is Bee's cottage. My heart aches at the sight. I miss her. She was such a huge part of my life growing up, and even after I moved away for college, we stayed close. She helped me in ways I could never forget, so the fact that I couldn't make it to her funeral gutted me. I'd been overseas at a conference when I got the news, and I wouldn't have made it back until after the funeral was over. It was better that I'd missed the funeral, though, because if I'd met Bee's family, I probably would have said things I shouldn't.

Apart from one of her grandsons, she didn't have much good to say about them, and she was particularly disenchanted with her son-in-law. I think she blamed him for her daughter's death. Her daughter, Adelaide, had passed when Bee's grandchildren were very young due to complications during an elective surgery, one Bee said she hadn't wanted but felt pressured to go through with. According to Bee, her daughter had an allergic reaction to the anesthesia and suffered a fatal heart attack. She was only in her thirties. Bee called it a waste of a beautiful life. I couldn't fathom what it would be like to lose your child, no matter how old they were.

Losing Bee felt like losing a family member, and I don't feel like I've had much of a chance to mourn her properly. She passed in her sleep—a brain aneurysm that took her swiftly and painlessly. At least she didn't suffer.

I decide I should do the thing I've been avoiding for the past six months, which is check on Bee's place. I was hoping that by the time I came home, her grandson would have finally gotten his priorities straight and cleaned it out.

My dad checks on the place every week. Rodents love abandoned homes, and the pipes can seize and the septic system can take a real shitter—pun totally intended—if no one is around to make sure things are working properly. But since I know Dad's been busy, I wonder what state I'll find it in.

I push up off the couch, and a flash catches my eye. I pull the curtains open farther and frown as I take in the sports car sitting in Bee's driveway. It looks expensive, like something an out-of-towner might drive.

Donovan Firestone, Bee's favorite grandson, is from Chicago, so that might make sense. Ironic that we've been living in the same city and he spent all his summers growing up next door, and yet we've never officially met. He was the sole recipient of her entire estate, which includes the cottage next door, its contents, and all the land that goes with it. To the left of her cottage is a huge plot of undeveloped land, which also belonged to Bee. I've been communicating with Donovan since her passing. This has consisted of a few emails back and forth regarding the estate and me checking on things until he had the time to come out this way to do it himself. Despite what Bee has said about him, he hasn't proven to be much better than the rest of his family.

Donovan hasn't seemed particularly concerned about the property, although it's hard to read someone's tone in an email. After the will was shown to the family and it was revealed that I was the executor, he called me with some questions about the property. He wanted a better idea of how many acres she had, as well as how much of that was water front-age, and if I could tell him the value. It was an unexpected blow—I was still processing Bee's death, and all her beloved grandson cared about was how much the property was worth. Apparently Bernie, who had prepared Bee's will, got a similar call, only this time asking about sub-dividing the lot and how easy it would be to parcel it off or develop it.

It irked me that this guy who had spent so many summers at Bee's was so quick to look at trying to squeeze money out of the land by developing it. That maybe he didn't care about the cottage, like Bee had suggested and I'd believed. I might not have spent time with Donovan, but in a lot of ways I felt like I knew him, because of the stories Bee would tell me and my observations from a distance. He was always helping Bee out, working on the cottage when he was here in the sum-mers. From what I'd seen and heard, he had genuine affection for his grandmother.

25

So now, the idea that he'd try to parcel off the land or knock down Bee's cherished cottage is frustrating. Of course it would drive the value up. But it would also have an impact on everyone else's property value on this side of the lake. Most people would think that was a good thing. But the locals don't want to pay hefty property taxes because some out-of-towner like Donovan gets ideas in his head.

And maybe he's already realized that, and that's why he wasn't in a rush to come out here. The will hasn't even been put into probate, and in the last email, he said he didn't expect he'd be able to come out this way until summer.

Wanting to see if I'm right about who's scoping out Bee's cottage, I root around in my purse for my key chain, which includes a key to my parents' house and one of Bee's spares. Sadness wells and chokes me up for a moment. I'm aware there's a distinct possibility that this grandson of hers won't want her place, and he'll sell it.

I hop out of the trailer, close the door behind me, and then cut through the narrow path that connects our properties. It's filled in over the years from disuse, trees bowing toward each other and small shrubs growing heartily under their protective canopy.

I get hit in the face with a few branches and sputter when I walk through a cobweb and nearly eat the freaking spider. I stumble over a root as I wipe my hand over my face and nearly face-plant into the dirt.

When I open my eyes, I'm face to face with Bee's cottage. I take a moment to breathe through the sudden tightness in my chest. I'm not a sentimental person. Not really. I don't get attached to places or things. I try not to fall in love with buildings or spaces, because life is fluid and you can't have roots and wings at the same time.

But as I stare at the old, beautiful, run-down cottage, a million wonderful memories come flooding back. When I moved away for college, Bee made me handwrite letters to her. Once I tried to send a typed one, and she mailed it back. When she passed, she took a piece of my heart with her, and I'm feeling that hole now more than ever. Other than once a year for the holidays, I didn't see her much after I moved away for college, and I realize now how selfish that was. I didn't want to feel tied to this place, so I avoided it and everyone in it. I created distance when what I should have been doing was spending as much time as I could with her.

The front porch is in quite a state of disrepair, and once again I'm reminded that my heels are ridiculously impractical around here. I'll be trading them for flip-flops, flats, and running shoes.

The age of the cottage is starting to show. The exterior is in need of fresh stain; some of the boards on the front porch are soft and beginning to rot through. If I had to guess, I'd say there are probably a few chipmunks living under there. A pair of rocking chairs sit in the corner, a table between them, the layer of dust and dirt making it clear they've gone unused since Bee passed. We used to sit out here and play cribbage in the evenings, drinking unsweetened iced tea in the summer or hot chocolate with marshmallows and whipped cream in the fall.

I knock on the front door and wait for someone to answer. After a good thirty seconds I knock again, then move to the window and peer through a gap in the curtains. Everything looks the same inside—a mass of organized clutter.

Maybe it's not her grandson like I thought. Or maybe he sent a developer to look at the property. I figure it's probably a good idea to let myself in and check things out, knowing that Bee wouldn't want a stranger rummaging around her place. I slide the key into the lock. It's always been a tricky door, so I lift, jiggle, and twist to the right until I hear the faint sound of the lock clicking. The door creaks on its hinges as I push it open and step inside the dimly lit space.

Twenty-year-old wallpaper covers the majority of the open space, and it always takes me a moment to gather my bearings, since it's a heavy visual assault, at first anyway. The colors are muted with age and sun. Blue teapots are now nearly gray and pink peonies the palest of peach. The living room is a mishmash of eclectic furniture, purchased from the town flea market; nothing matches, not even the chairs around the dining room table. A layer of dust covers nearly every surface, making it an untouched shrine to Bee.

The wall to the right is covered with old framed photos, some black and white, some color. There's a distinct line through the center of half of them, where the sunlight from the window cuts across it at midday, bleaching the pictures on the top half of the wall.

I move across the room to stand in front of the framed photo collage until I'm casting a shadow over the pictures. Mostly they're of Bee's family. My gaze catches on a picture of Bee with Donovan. He was always wearing a ball cap, half his face hidden in shadow, making it impossible to get a clear picture.

I took it on the sly with the camera on my phone while I was working in the food truck, the summer before I left for college. They were picking up deck boards at the hardware store. Bee was trying to climb into the bed of the truck while wearing a dress, and Donovan was trying to stop her. It encapsulated everything about her as a person and the love between them.

Despite being close to Bee, I always kept my distance when her favorite grandson was with her for the summers. I had Bee ten months out of the year, and I knew how much she looked forward to seeing him, so I gave them privacy. So, other than seeing brief glimpses here and there, we never crossed paths.

I touch the corner of the frame to straighten it. Then I step back to make sure the rest of the pictures line up properly as well. Which is when the sound of water running registers. I glance toward the kitchen, but the sound isn't coming from the sink, which means there's either a leak somewhere, or someone is in the bathroom.

I take a cautious step toward the center of the living room, and the floor creaks under my foot. The sound is ridiculously loud in the quiet space, and a shiver runs down my spine.

"Hello?" I call out. "Is anybody here?"

CHAPTER 4
NOT QUITE WHAT I EXPECTED

Van

Everything about Pearl Lake is steeped in nostalgia—full of some of the best summer memories. I spent my youth here, staying at my grandmother's cottage on what she cheekily referred to as the right wrong side of the lake.

On my way through downtown, I smile as I pass the specialty candy shop with treats from England, homemade ice cream, and deluxe chocolates. In all the years I've been coming here, I've only been inside once. I was eight at the time and had never so much as cleaned my own room, let alone anything else. Grammy Bee had offered to pay me twenty dollars for helping her wash all the windows on the cottage. I'd been bored, and I couldn't say no to her, so I'd picked myself up off the front porch swing and got to work.

It had taken me almost the entire day. Plus, I was only eight, so reaching the top of the windows meant climbing up and down a ladder for hours. Regardless, as soon as she handed over the money, I jumped on my bike and pedaled to town—without a helmet, despite her constantly telling me how important it was that I protect my brain, since it couldn't be upgraded or replaced—and the first stop I made was that fancy candy store Grammy Bee refused to let me go in whenever we went to town.

I'd been so excited. I left my bike outside and rushed in, and I ended up spending almost everything I'd earned. I gorged on ice cream, chocolate, and soda. When I left the candy shop, I crossed the street, my paper bag of treats in hand, and stopped in the convenience store to pick up a copy of the city newspaper that Grammy Bee liked to read on the weekends.

I rushed down the aisle and came to an abrupt stop when I noticed the same glass bottles of soda and the same fancy candies, except instead of being in large glass jars with ornate tongs to handle them, they were stacked in plastic Tupperware, and salad tongs sat on top of each bin. Everything cost half as much.

I learned a valuable lesson that day: just because something looks prettier doesn't mean it's better.

When I left the convenience store, I crossed back over to the candy store without a paper because I was fifteen cents short. And I realized my bike was gone because I'd forgotten to lock it up. The hour-long walk home was another lesson. By the time I got back to Grammy Bee's, I was fuming, frustrated that the candy store jacked up their prices like that and that someone had stolen my bike.

Two days later, the bike showed up on the front porch. It was the first and only time I didn't lock it up, and the last time I ever went to that specialty candy shop.

I pull into Grammy Bee's driveway. *My driveway.* The thought is intrusive and unwelcome. I push it aside, determined not to let sadness override all the other emotions that come with being here. Grammy Bee wouldn't want me to fixate on her absence. She would want me to find the joy in being here again. Even without her.

The gravel pops and crunches under my tires as I pull up next to her ancient truck, still parked in the driveway. I shift into park and take in the sight before me. It's been six months since I've been here. And even when I came to Grammy's funeral, I avoided coming here specifically. I wasn't in the right place emotionally to deal with the cottage. I didn't want to face the loss more than necessary. I'm finally ready to properly say goodbye to her.

I smile as I take in the modest three-bedroom cottage. Old and run down, but so full of love and memories. I open the door and breathe in the fresh sweet air. A combination of pine, sunshine, and lake water. The gravel crunches beneath my running shoes—I know better than to wear anything other than casual footwear when I'm here, which, of course, is part of the allure. I shed city life like a stuffy suit and slide into the comfort of worn T-shirts and age-softened shorts.

The deck boards creak under my feet. They're in worse shape than I remember and definitely need to be fixed. Or replaced entirely. I slide the key into the lock and have to do the jiggle and turn thing a few times before it finally gives.

The Dillion dude who's been communicating with me via email about Grammy's place is supposed to come by every week and check on things, but based on how hard the lock is to turn, I'm not sure that's been happening. Why did he promise he'd take care of it if he had no intention of doing so? Why Grammy picked him as executor is beyond me; he seems a bit irresponsible. He couldn't even bother to attend the funeral.

I take a deep breath and brace myself for the visual onslaught I'm about to face. Grammy Bee loved her trinkets, and patterns, and wallpaper. I always loved that about Grammy Bee's cottage—the fact that nothing ever changed. Being here was reliable and predictable. Comfortable and homey. I needed that when I was a teenager, maybe more than I realized.

I push the door open with a creak and step inside, breathing in the familiar scents. Despite the place having been vacant for six months, it still smells almost exactly as I remember it. The air is stale, but the faint smell of Grammy Bee's homemade potpourri, a combination of cloves, cinnamon, and citrus, still hangs in the air. Nothing inside has changed in the past twenty-five years. It's like being stuck inside a time warp of floral patterns and teacup wallpaper.

I realize how much I need this. To be here. To grieve her properly and remind myself why this place is so special and needs my attention.

My phone buzzes in my pocket, breaking the spell. I sigh, annoyed by the interruption. I've taken the week off so I can come here and deal with the cottage and finally put the will into probate. Something I should have done months ago. I fish my phone out of my pocket, intending to send the call to voice mail, but pause when *Dad* flashes across the screen.

There are few people in the world whose calls I don't avoid. My father, while admittedly not the best at the job of parenting, is still my father and the only parent I have left, so I generally don't ignore his calls. I answer and put the phone on speaker. "Hey, Dad, what's up?"

"Donovan, hello, are you still in Chicago?"

Something in his tone unsettles me. "No, I'm already in Pearl Lake. Remember, I'm here to settle the estate?"

"Yes. Of course I remember. We have an issue."

"An issue?" I cross over to the kitchen and turn on the tap. The water sputters for a few seconds before the pump kicks on. "What kind of issue?"

He clears his throat. "With Adelaide's Love."

My mother, Adelaide, died when I was eight years old during surgery to have her tubes tied—and a tummy tuck and a breast lift to restore her body after three pregnancies, per my father's suggestion—but she had a rare and unexpected reaction to the anesthesia and died of a heart attack. One morning she was there kissing me goodbye, telling me she'd see me after school, and the next, she was gone. The loss threw our family into a state of upheaval.

But when I was in my late teens, I asked if we could create a memorial foundation for Mom, and my dad, of course, said yes. Don't let that fool you, though. I'm pretty sure my dad agreed to it for an opportunity to rub elbows with the Chicago elite and paint the picture of a devoted husband who wanted his wife's legacy to live on. Besides attending galas and events in the name of the foundation, I don't think my father has ever made it much of a priority. But my mother always liked working with children, so I helped create the foundation to provide scholarships to disadvantaged children for their education.

I turn the faucet off and stop moving. "What about it?"

"There's money missing."

I sincerely hope my dad isn't starting to lose his faculties. My grandfather was sound of mind all the way until the end. "I transferred funds last week for the sports scholarship. Right after the board meeting." For the past ten years I've sat on the board of directors, along with my father and siblings, and it has grown into a decent-size fund. While my family's role is more in name only, I'm actively involved in the management of the fund.

"That's not the money I'm referring to. If you've been having financial troubles, you should have come to me, Van. We could have found a better way to deal with it. Gotten you a loan."

"I'm sorry, what are you talking about?" I don't have financial issues. I never want to be in the position my father is—always spending money he doesn't have. It's gone before it even has a chance to hit his bank account.

"Three million dollars is missing from your mother's foundation."

"That's not possible. The check was for five hundred thousand." I run a hand through my hair, panic starting to take hold. "This has to be some kind of mistake."

"I'm afraid it's not. The board called a meeting this morning after reviewing the books. Millions are missing, and everything is pointing at you, son."

I drop onto the ancient, faded floral sofa. "This doesn't make sense. Why would I steal from my own mother's memorial foundation?"

"Are you telling me you didn't take it?"

"How can you even ask that? Of course I didn't take it!" My voice rises, right along with my incredulity.

"I'm sorry, Van, but your signature is on all the documents, and you're one of the few people with access to the accounts."

"Well, I didn't steal three fucking million dollars from my own mother's memorial fund!"

"Okay. I trust that you're being honest." I can hear my dad's pen tapping on the desk.

"Should I come back to Chicago?"

"No, no. I think it's probably better you stay put for now. I'm going to do what I can, but you don't want to be in Chicago if the media gets wind of this."

"Shit. Do you think that's likely to happen?"

"I'd like to say no, but I can't be sure, and I'd rather you be out of the line of fire for now. We'll get to the bottom of this. I promise."

My phone buzzes with another call. This time it's my boss. "Can I call you back, Dad? That's my work calling."

"Of course. I'll call my lawyer."

I end the call with him and answer the one from my boss, dread settling in my stomach, especially with him calling me on a Saturday. I'm right to be worried. Because word has gotten out that I've apparently stolen three million dollars. And now, in addition to being accused of theft, I'm also no longer employed, since all the accounts I was working on have asked I be removed from their projects.

They give me a two-month severance package.

I toss my phone on the cushion beside me and press the heels of my hands against my eyes. "What the fuck is happening, Grammy Bee?"

The wind chimes on the front porch tinkle loudly.

"Sorry 'bout my language, but this is kinda messed up," I mutter.

My phone rings for the third time in the past hour. I reluctantly glance at the screen. It's my sister, Teagan. Mood-wise, I'm not in the best form, but I'm guessing that she's probably heard the news, and now she's going to be on the receiving end of the backlash. "Hey, Teag."

"Have you talked to Dad?"

"Yeah. Just a few minutes ago."

"I know it wasn't you. I don't care what proof they think they have. There's no way you'd steal from Mom's foundation."

Her conviction makes me feel the tiniest bit better. But then I remember I'm also freshly unemployed, to go along with my new status of thief. "Dad is going to get his lawyer to look into it."

"I know. I just talked to him. Is there anything I can do to help? Do you want me to come up to Pearl Lake? I could do that. If you need me to."

I adore my sister. She's my favorite sibling and one of the kindest, most giving people I know. But I don't know if her coming up here on the heels of this scandal would be best. "I appreciate it, but I don't honestly know what I need right now. Other than to find out what happened. There has to be some kind of mistake with the paperwork or signatures or something." I need more details. Like how $3 million goes missing without any red flags being raised in the process.

"I'm sure that's what it is, Donny. We'll get to the bottom of it." I cringe at the horrible nickname she can't seem to give up, and then a buzz comes through the line. "Crap. That's Troy. I bet he's seen the freaking media coverage on this and wants to know what's going on."

Troy is my sister's boyfriend. I'm not his biggest fan, but my sister loves him, so I tolerate him. "Wait. What media coverage?"

"Uh . . . it's really nothing. You know how they like to blow everything out of proportion."

"This has already made the news?" I find the remote for the TV and turn it on. Grammy Bee didn't like to spend money on unnecessary things, but she did invest in cable and high-speed internet because she loved being able to FaceTime with me.

"Just the local stations."

I've never been the subject of any kind of drama. Until now. Luckily I don't find anything on the TV here and turn the TV off again. "Shit, Teag. This is bad."

"It'll be okay." The reassurance sounds empty.

"I'm not sure about that. I just got fired before you called."

"No. How? Why?"

I'm assuming the questions are mostly rhetorical. "Apparently my former employer doesn't love it when people are accused of stealing millions from charity."

"I'm so sorry, Donny. We'll figure it out. Whoever did this won't get away with it."

I sincerely appreciate her vote of confidence. Especially since my father immediately believed it was true. She and I have always been close, she being only two years younger than me. We're like minded, so we've always confided in one another.

"Three million dollars doesn't grow legs and walk away," she continues. "We will track that money down, and we'll get your name cleared and your job back." I tune back in as my sister finishes her we're-going-to-fix-this spiel.

"Fingers crossed." Even if I do get my job back, which I know is a long shot, I just want to know what happened to the money and how my name ended up being the one attached to the fact that it went missing in the first place.

"I promise we'll get to the bottom of it."

I know she's running out of positive things to say, and frankly, hearing them makes me want to slam my head into a wall. "Thanks, Teag. I need to process, but we'll talk soon, okay?"

"I'll call you tomorrow?"

"Sure. Tomorrow works." I end the call and blow out a breath.

What started as a great day has swiftly done a swirly down the toilet. Up until a few minutes ago, I had a fantastic job working at a prestigious company as an architectural engineer. I worked my ass off to get that job, and I had to deal with my dad's moderate disapproval over the fact that I was his only child who decided not to come work with him, my brother, and my sister at Smith Financial, where my father is the CFO.

Teagan gets it. Losing our mom when we were young was hard on her, and she feels an extraordinary responsibility to be there for our dad and Bradley. And he, in turn, has showered her with gifts and a pampered lifestyle she's become used to, even if she doesn't necessarily want it. It's a tough place for her to be in. She doesn't want to say no, or make him feel like his gifts are unappreciated, but she's become the child my dad puts the most energy into. Probably because she is the spitting image of our mother. It's sort of a toxic relationship, one that's cost my dad thousands in therapy, and still she's under his thumb.

I'm not knocking him. He's a good guy, and he basically raised us on his own after our mother passed away. Well, actually, it was nannies who raised us, since he buried himself in work to avoid being a single father. But he did the best he could, I guess.

My dad blamed himself and became a workaholic, Teagan developed abandonment issues, and the youngest of us, Bradley, who was only four when it happened, lived a carefree life playing video games all the way through until the end of high school, and he put in just enough effort to get the grades he needed for college. Despite Mom's death messing us all up, we came out the other side okay. I think.

Until now.

What was supposed to be a one-week vacation is now a permanent job hiatus. And with these accusations flying, it seems like finding a new job is going to present a real challenge.

I survey the cottage, drinking in the sight of mismatched furniture and Grammy Bee's love of eclectic trinkets. At least I can stay here while I'm avoiding the media scrutiny in Chicago.

I grab my duffel and bring it to the spare bedroom I slept in when I spent time here in the summer as a teenager. I need to get my head

around what I'm facing. And a shower. And probably a bottle of bour-
bon. I make my way to the bathroom and hope like hell the hot water
is still working.

A text from Bradley comes through right before I get in the shower:
I hear you just got three million richer. Share the wealth bro.

Of course my brother is making a joke about this. It's just like him
to not take anything seriously. Twenty minutes later I'm still standing
under the pounding spray of water. It's a great distraction from the shitstorm that has suddenly become my life. Fast and hard, the water pelts
my back like a freaking jet stream. A few years back, when I was working on a project in college, I tested out some new plumbing options.
Grammy Bee's water pressure was terrible, as sometimes happens when
the pump bringing the water up from the lake isn't strong enough.
Seems like maybe I overcompensated. I add it to my to-do list, which,
based on what I've seen so far, is going to take the entire summer to get
through. On the upside, it looks like I'll have nothing but time to take
care of all the home improvements.

I'm in the middle of rinsing off when I swear I hear someone's
voice. A female someone.

I step out from under the spray and listen. And there it is again.
Faint, but there—a voice that belongs to a woman. It would be like
Grammy Bee to start haunting my ass while I'm in the middle of a
shower, on what's turning out to be one of the worst days of my life.
Considering how morose I am, I should think about dying my hair
black and putting on some of Grammy Bee's old Cure albums.

After a few seconds of silence, I decide I'm probably hearing things,
and it's more likely that this place has a raccoon problem, not an issue
with undead visitors. Still, I'm sufficiently creeped out, so I turn off the
shower and grab a towel. I scrub it over my face and grimace as soon as
the dampness hits the fabric, bringing out a mild funk. The last thing I
want is to dry myself off with a towel that smells like it sat in the washing machine too long, so my only option is to drip dry.

I make a mental note to see how ancient the washing machine is and whether it needs to be replaced. I have a feeling that list is going to be just as long as the to-do list.

I open the bathroom door and step into the hall. I have to cross the living room to get to the spare bedroom—no way am I sleeping in my deceased grandmother's bed—and I manage to make it halfway across the living room before a banshee-level scream scares the crap out of me.

It's not the undead coming to haunt me, though. It's a woman. An attractive one. Her sandy-blonde hair falls in chaotic spirals to her shoulders. Her ocean-green eyes are wide, lashes coated with mascara, full lips parted in shock. She's wearing a buttery yellow shirt that almost matches her hair and skinny jeans that highlight her curvy hips and athletic legs. She's also wearing very impractical heels my sister would probably approve of. My gaze springs back to her still-shocked face. There's something familiar about her, but I can't put my finger on it.

"Who the hell are you, and how did you get in here?" I shout at the woman standing between me and the bedroom, where my clothes are. I'm not in the mood for guests or being nice, apparently, based on my volume and my tone.

Her wide-eyed gaze dips down and then springs back up, her cheeks flushing red. "Who the hell are you, and why are you naked?" she yells back.

She doesn't bother to turn around. Instead she stands there, eyes bouncing between my face and my nakedness. As if I need to be objectified after the hellish day I've had.

"Seriously? Are you checking out my junk?"

"It's right there! How am I not supposed to check it out?" She's still yelling and turning even redder. At least her face has the decency to show her embarrassment. That still doesn't explain who she is or what she's doing here.

I drop a hand to shield my stupid penis, who has decided, regardless of the fact that this woman has broken into my grandmother's cottage, that we still find her attractive and would like to give her the one-eyed salute. Maybe it's an anger hard-on. "You could turn around!"

"You could put some clothes on!"

"I can't! You're blocking my way to the bedroom!" I bellow.

"Oh. Sorry." She steps aside, obviously flustered, and *finally* raises her hand in front of her face.

I stalk past her and notice the gap between her fingers. "Are you still checking me out?"

"You still haven't told me who you are! For all I know you're some perv who likes to break into deceased women's cottages and jerk off in their showers."

I make a gagging sound and point aggressively at her. "I'm Bee's grandson, and you'd better not move while I'm putting clothes on, or I'm calling the police."

"What if I am the police?" she calls after me.

I'm tempted to yell something about showing me her badge, but based on the heels she's wearing, I'm going to go out on a limb and say she *isn't* the police. Besides, if she was, the first thing she would have done was show me her badge. For a moment I consider that I could end up going to jail for stealing money I didn't take. This day keeps going from bad to worse.

I grab the first pair of shorts I can find—screw the boxers—and jab my feet through the legs. I do up the button and nab a shirt, pulling it over my head as I walk down the hall. I'm still wet, so everything sticks to my skin, but I'm not leaving a random stranger in my grandmother's living room unattended any longer than necessary. I should have ushered her out the door and made her wait on the porch, but I didn't want to get that close to her while I was free-balling it and risk getting kicked in the nuts.

When I return to the living room, she's not standing in the middle of it anymore. Instead she's over by the credenza, rolling one of my grandmother's knickknacks between her fingers.

"Hey, that's not yours to touch. Put it down," I bark.

She nearly drops it because I startled her, but she manages to recover and sets it down carefully. When she turns to me, her arms are crossed and her eyes are narrowed. Despite her ire, she's still frustratingly attractive. "You said you were Bee's grandson. Which one are you?"

I raise a hand in the air, because seriously, who does this woman think she is? Also, I'm done with people being assholes today. "I'm not answering any of your questions until you answer mine. Who are you, and how did you get in here?"

"I'm Bee's neighbor, and I used a key." She dangles one from her ring finger. It's hooked onto a tiny needlepoint chain, which is definitely something Bee would've used to keep track of her keys.

"First of all, 'Bee's neighbor' is not a name. And secondly, that could be any key. Maybe you picked the lock. Maybe it should be me threatening to call the cops on you, since you're the one breaking into my grandmother's house." Hell, she could be the reason I'm in so much trouble. The only reason I'm not calling the cops is because I already have enough going on without getting local law enforcement involved.

"Bee called me Lynnie. And you can call the cops if you want, but they're probably on break, since there are only three in the whole of Pearl Lake and they're friends of my family. I live over there." She thumbs over her shoulder. "I've known Bee my whole life. Knew her," she says, correcting herself, and then looks away, rubbing at her lips with her thumb. "So which grandson are you?"

Well, that explains why she's so familiar. I used to see her all the time, but usually from a distance, through the barrier of trees that separates her property from my grandmother's. She worked at the food truck one summer. They served the worst hot dogs. "I'm Van."

"Van?"

"Donovan," I say in frustration. My grandmother only shortened my name when she was talking to family.

Her eyes flare, and this time not because I'm flashing her. "Donovan? Firestone?"

"Yeah. That's me."

"Oh." She blinks a few times, and her expression goes stony. Or stonier than it already was, anyway. "We've been emailing." She motions between us.

"Huh?" Today has been a cluster, and I'm about ready to throw in the towel.

Her lip curls up in a half sneer. "About Bee's estate. We've been emailing back and forth for months."

I give my head a shake and drag my gaze away from her mouth. "Nope. I've been emailing with some dude named Dillion."

"Not some dude—me. I'm Dillion. *Dillion* Stitch." She crosses her arms, eyes narrowed in distrust.

"I thought you said your name was Lynnie." I rub my temple; my brain hurts from the crap I've been through over the past couple of hours, and this sure isn't helping.

"No. I said Bee called me Lynnie. My actual name is Dillion." She pokes at her cheek with her tongue, gaze flitting from my mouth to my eyes and back again.

I rub my lip self-consciously. "Do you have any other names you go by that I should know about?"

"Nope, that covers it."

"Why did Bee call you Lynnie?" I don't know why I'm entertaining this. For all I know she's lying about who she is. I hate how paranoid I suddenly am.

"Because Bee thought Dillion was a boy's name, so she dropped the first half. I don't know why she added the *i-e* to the end, though. I never asked, and she never offered." She blows out a breath and looks around the cabin, eyes suddenly soft. "Not that that matters. Anyway, I'm guessing you're here to put the will into probate. You must be here to have the place appraised so you can sell it to developers or whatever.

42

Good luck on getting the lot divided, by the way. Parceling off the land will never happen. Besides, the zoning laws on this side are different, so whatever plan you're probably hatching isn't going to work. You might get a fair price for the land, but I'm not sure whoever buys it is gonna get much love from their neighbors."

"Right. Okay." I have no idea what she's talking about, or why she's so damn hostile. "I can't sell right now anyway, so chill out." As of this moment, this is the only place I have to go while I'm figuring out what my next steps will be. And I love this place, so I have no plans to sell—not that it's any of her business.

She frowns, her eyes narrowing. "But you'll sell eventually."

"What's it to you if I do?" I've had it with people today.

"You might be able to sell, but you'll never get them to agree to subdivide the lot."

"Good to know." And I'm about done with this conversation.

"I'm keeping an eye on you." She points her index and middle fingers at her own eyes and then jabs them in my direction. "Both of them, actually."

And with that she storms out.

The screen door hits the side of the cottage and bangs shut but then bounces open again. I watch as she nearly loses her footing on a loose board. "You should have that fixed before someone breaks an ankle!" she shouts as she stalks across the gravel driveway.

"Maybe you should consider wearing different shoes!" I call after her. "Or you could stay off my property from now on!"

She bats at the trees as she stomps her way through the bushes. There's another small cottage-style house beyond the brush, but that isn't where she goes. Instead she heads for the rusted trailer almost completely hidden by the trees. A few seconds later a door slams shut.

So much for a peaceful vacation in Pearl Lake.

CHAPTER 5
FAMILY BIZ

Dillion

I've been working for the family business, a.k.a. Footprint Renovations and Home Maintenance, all weekend, and now it's Monday. In that time, I've discovered how lackadaisical they've been about the bookkeeping and contract management. I have my work cut out for me, but I can already see a bunch of ways they can be more organized, reduce costs, and save me time. Starting with their filing system, which seems to be several piles stacked around the office and on top of the cabinets instead of in them.

I'm currently sitting cross-legged on the floor with a stack of file folders in front of me, trying to arrange them in some kind of logical order. What I really want to do is take them down to South Beach and start a bonfire. Especially the file I found citing a dispute between Footprint and a north side client who called some of the charges into question. It looks like it's been resolved, but it's something that shouldn't have happened at all.

"You all right, Darlin'?"

"Totally fine." I flip the folder open and sift through the contents. The file is fourteen years old. They only need to be kept for seven years, so I move the folder to the shred stack. It's substantial at this point.

A coffee appears in front of my face, my dad's thick, scar-riddled, and callused fingers wrapped around it.

"Oh, bless you and the coffee gods. I needed this more than you can know." I cradle it between my hands and take a tentative sip, humming contentedly. "This is from Boones, isn't it? Did you get apple fritters too?" I finally lift my gaze to find my dad smiling down at me, a greasy paper bag dangling from his other hand.

I try to snatch the bag, but he lifts it out of reach. "You can only have one if you take a break."

"Do I look like I have time for a break?" I motion to the mountain of file folders.

"You'll be more effective if you stop for ten minutes and eat something. You didn't come in for breakfast this morning, and unless you're grocery shopping on the sly, the only thing in the trailer fridge is beer."

I ate half a bag of stale salt-and-vinegar chips this morning, and that was hours ago. We start early, and my neighbor apparently likes to stay up late working on construction projects and listening to music. He also likes to burn crap in Bee's firepit. The worst part is that the firepit is close to my trailer, so I not only get to listen to his music and his hammering, but everything I own now smells like campfire. The charred aroma is embedded in my hair, so I've given up on wearing it down and instead keep it in a ponytail. Even still, every once in a while I get a solid whiff, and it's highly unpleasant.

My dad is still standing in front of me, waiting. So I give in, partly because he has a point and also because there is nothing more delicious than one of Boones's apple fritters. I step over the maze of stacked files and follow him into the break room, where my uncle John and one of their employees, Aaron Saunders, are seated around the small table, both cupping take-out coffees. Aaron and my brother were friends in high school, but Aaron disappeared for a few years after graduation. No one knows where he went or why he came back, but when he returned to Pearl Lake, he immediately started working for Footprint.

"Hey, guys, how's it going?" I cross over to the cupboards and grab plates and napkins for the fritters. Normally the guys shove their filthy mitts into the bag and get sugar flakes and crumbs all over the table, which no one bothers to clean up. In the three days since I've been here, I've begun the process of encouraging basic table manners. So far, I'm not having much success.

"Good, good. How's file Jenga?" Aaron asks.

I don't have to turn around to see his smirk. Yesterday I was in a mood over the number of ancient, misfiled documents. It's a pain in my ass to go through everything, but once I'm done, they'll have a much more streamlined, organized system.

"It's a work in progress." I pass out plates and napkins and snatch the bag from my dad before he can pass it around to the guys. I use a pair of tongs to distribute the fritters before I dump the rest on a communal plate and take a seat.

Conversation ceases, replaced by the sound of chewing and humming. I take a bite of my own fritter, teeth sinking into the sweet, light dough, past the apple center. These aren't like normal fritters from regular doughnut shops, where they cut the apples into chunks. These are made with an entire ring of apple, dipped in lemon juice and cinnamon sugar and then again in fresh batter, fried in batches, and then coated in a sweet icing sugar glaze or another round of lemon and cinnamon sugar. They're sweet, decadent, and delicious. I polish off the first one and reach for a second, aware they won't last long. This one I savor.

"How's the McMansion reno going?" I ask between bites.

"You know how it is over there. The owners always hover," Uncle John grumbles.

"At least they're keeping us busy," my dad says. I found out that they lost a couple of big contracts after Billy's accident. There were rumors that he showed up to work high and drunk on more than one occasion, and people were worried about the liability. I don't know if it's true or not, but I have to hope that the gossip dies so that the business doesn't take a hit. "And this one isn't making it any easier to get things done." Dad nods to Aaron.

Back in high school, Aaron played on the school football team. He was a sophomore when I was a senior, but that didn't stop the girls from trailing him, starry eyed and desperate for his attention. I doubt much has changed. He's grown up, his soft boyish features sharpening into a rugged jawline and a full-lipped smile. Not to mention that he's filled out, thanks to his athletic history and his current job.

"Mowing lawns shirtless these days?"

Aaron shrugs and grins. "Might as well work on my tan while I'm grooming lawns."

I roll my eyes at the thinly veiled innuendo my dad and uncle miss. I have no doubt that Aaron is grooming more than the lawns on the other side of the lake. With his chiseled features, ridiculous body, and the tattoos he's added over the years, he's every rich girl's idea of a bad boy they want to tame.

"I hope you're following safety protocol while you're mowing all those lawns."

"Don't worry, I always protect what matters." He knocks on the side of his head, but we both know which one he's actually referring to. "And I love that you're still looking out for me, Dee. It's just like old times."

I snicker and shake my head. Aaron was notorious for asking me to grab him a handful of condoms every time I went to the birth control clinic to have my prescription filled back in high school. The last thing I wanted was to end up a teen mom. No judgment, but there were enough of those around here.

Aaron used to hang out with Billy, since they were in the same grade. Aside from providing free prophylactics, on plenty of occasions I picked them up from some beach party or other, drunk and barely coherent. "I'm actually more worried about the liability for these guys than I am you." I motion between my dad and Uncle John, who remain oblivious as they chuckle.

The conversation shifts to the project they're currently working on. Most of the time the projects for the richies are things like garages, boathouses, and pool sheds—yes, they have pools, even though there's a gorgeous, pristine lake they can swim in. But this new contract is a first, and also, from what I'm gathering, it's a headache.

"I need them to make a decision on the flooring. It's not like it's life or death," Dad says.

"Did you at least persuade her not to go with the brazilian cherry? That stuff burns through saw blades like nobody's business." Aaron stuffs another fritter in his mouth.

"Are you billing for all the extra time? Mileage and whatever other incidentals there might be? Does she realize that her not making choices also means she's delaying the project?" I ask.

"I got it all marked down," Uncle John replies. Which I take to mean he hasn't actually billed for those things.

I lick the icing off my finger. "Look, these people have money to burn. They aren't going to balk at being charged for whatever runs you're making to the hardware store, but at least let them know that the more they delay the decision, the longer the job is going to take, and rush deliveries add charges. And I doubt Harry's stocks brazilian cherry, so you have to be ordering it from Chicago or something, and there's bound to be additional delivery charges on that, or at the very least mileage if you have to pick it up."

My uncle nods, as if he agrees with me, but I know he has an excuse for being hesitant to do what I'm suggesting. "They're spending a lot of money. And it's not like she's difficult. She's forever making us meals, and coffee, and they're nice people. She agonizes over every decision, and her husband is so wrapped around her finger he won't press her on anything. All he says is, 'Whatever Lainey wants, she gets,' which is fine and all, but man, it makes it hard to finish a job." I can tell that since he likes these clients, he doesn't want to cause conflict.

"Do you want me to come in and talk to her about flooring choices so you don't have to deal with it?"

"You'd do that?" Uncle John glances at my dad and then back at me.

"Well, yeah, of course. That's about fifty percent of what I did when I was working in Chicago. I dealt with the client questions so the people who did the actual work could manage that aspect." Project management is basically the same, no matter what field it's in.

"Well, hell yes, please, then. I need to be able to get moving on this, or we'll be even more behind, and every single decision requires a freaking FaceShield call."

"Do you mean FaceTime?"

Uncle John throws up his hands. "How'm I supposed to know? They have those expensive tablet things that are bigger than my head, and they walk around and talk on them like it's freaking normal. All I have is this." He waves his phone around in the air. Based on the size of it, I'd have to guess it's fairly old and likely doesn't have many of the apps and updates it needs to function properly.

I make a mental note to check their phone and data plans. Sometimes the internet can be slow and sketchy out here. It's not like Chicago, where there are satellites everywhere and everyone is plugged in all the time. This is farther off the beaten path, and that means some days service goes out. It's better now than it used to be back when I lived in town, but whenever I visited for holidays, I made sure I brought a pocket Wi-Fi device so I could send emails without them taking twenty minutes to load.

My parents even have a landline, because in the winter you can lose power for a few days at a time, and then the only way to call anyone is if you have a rotary dial phone.

"When's the next time you're discussing finishes with her?"

"We have to swing by this afternoon," Dad says.

"Why don't I come with? I need to stop in town and grab some office supplies anyway."

"Sure, that'd be great."

"Perfect. I've already looked over the project specs, so if you can fill me in on the budget and what all she still needs to choose design-wise, I can go in with a plan of attack."

Two hours and a very practical conversation later, Lainey Bowman makes a decision on what flooring and cabinetry will work best with the existing design and will preserve the rustic quality of the room. She signs off on the materials and the cost, and I manage to do it all electronically, without even one piece of paper to file.

On the way out, I stop to talk to my dad, who's already back to work on the pool-house project. "Want me to check Harry's to see if they can order this stuff in, or go directly to your contacts in Chicago?"

My dad taps the side of his hard hat and sighs. "I don't think Harry's going to have any of this stuff, except maybe the paint, but you can give it a shot? I'd at least try to give him the business, but he's usually only got the basic stock, not the real high-end stuff these folks are looking for."

"Okay, I'll pop in on the way through town."

"Great. Thanks, Darlin'. You're a real godsend." He gives my shoulder a squeeze and goes back to measuring two-by-fours.

I hop into the "good" pickup truck, the one that's used more for advertising than it is for hauling building supplies. Unlike the "work" trucks, the interior is clean, there are no coffee cups or wrappers littering the floor, and it smells like fresh pine with a hint of sawdust.

I pull out of the driveway and pass more mansion-style homes with long driveways, all either paved with formed concrete or interlocking stone. The garages are generally bigger than most of the houses on the south side of the lake. And every year another McMansion pops up on the north side, changing the landscape and edging the neighborhood out to the east and the west. The marina and downtown area stop them from swallowing up the townies completely.

It's not that I don't appreciate the money they bring in. Tourism is the reason our community stays afloat during the winter months, but I can't pretend it didn't burn my ass when those rich summer kids strung along my townie friends. Or how easy it was to fall into the trap of wanting something you could never have. Even I wasn't immune. I only made the mistake once, and it was only one impulsive kiss, but I've never forgotten it—not the feel, the smell, or the bitter taste it left in my mouth when someone reminded me where my place was, which was nowhere near those rich kids.

When I was young, I believed that life was easier when you had money. And after moving to Chicago, I learned all about the grass on the other side being greener, and how wide the divide was between me and those who had more than average. Even in college there were cliques. They wore brand names and drove around in sweet cars I'd have to work a lifetime to afford. No matter where I was, or where I worked, there would always be a hierarchy that I wasn't sure I'd ever be able to get close to the top of. Back then, it was easier for people with everything to have more, and harder for those of us at the bottom to secure a place a few rungs up the ladder without being kicked back down. Being back here is a reminder of that.

I turn onto the main road and head into town. The first stop is Harry's, on the off chance that he has everything I need, including the office supplies.

Harry greets me with crinkled eyes and a wide smile. "Well, if it isn't wee Dillion Stitch. I heard you was back in town!"

Of course he has. That news must've spread like wildfire. It feels like a bitter pill I have to swallow every time I run into someone new. When I left, I was sure I'd never have to come back for more than a holiday visit. I force a smile, because it isn't Harry's fault I feel the way I do. "Sure am. How are things with you? Looks like it's business as usual around here."

He hoists up his pants by the suspenders and rocks back on his heels. "Doing better than ever, actually. Hired on some new summer help to keep up with things. Plus, my son got himself engaged to sweet little Miss Claire Bell. You remember her, don't you?"

"Of course, I saw Claire the other day. Congratulations, that's such exciting news."

"Sure is. The missus is hoping they're not gonna wait too long to start giving her grandbabies to look after. Anyway, Claire's planning to help out around here, but she's been busy with online classes and working at Tom's Diner. Her sister works at the rental shop by the beach, but I'm sure you already know that. You and Allie were thick as thieves back when you were kids."

"That we were." I nod my agreement.

"Have you run into her since you've been back in town?"

"Not yet, but soon, I'm sure." I don't know how excited Allie will be, actually. In the years since I moved to Chicago, I allowed my friendships to languish, too busy with work and my new life to make time for them. At first there were phone calls and text messages, but over the years they got fewer and farther between until they were mostly happy-birthday GIFs or holiday wishes. And whenever I came back to town, I'd spend a few days with my family and Bee and leave again. Mostly it's been work and sleep and not much else since I've been back in Pearl Lake.

I give Harry the list of things I need and am pleasantly surprised when he can fill almost everything on order. As expected, he can't provide the flooring option, but he puts in a call to a distributor in Chicago and gets us his wholesale discount. I feel good about the fact that we get to support local, and we're able to get a better deal on the flooring by taking advantage of Harry's contacts.

"I heard Tommy's working here now too. Is he around?"

"Sure is. He's out back. If ya want, you can head back and talk to him directly about some of the supplies, see if we have what you need on hand or whether we'll have to place an order. Or I can do it if you're in a rush."

"I can do it; thanks again, Harry. And I'm glad things are going so well."

He tips his hat, gives me a wink, and then opens the door, ushering me into the lumberyard behind the store. I breathe in the fresh scent of cut wood. The sharp smell of cedar makes me smile. The scent lingers long after the construction phase is over, warm and sweet and comforting.

I spot Tommy at the back of the lot. He's impossible to miss. His large, bulky frame has filled out and then some since I last saw him. Where his dad is tall and lean with a small paunch, Tommy is broad and thick, like he was built for swinging an ax. He was always a nice kid who got into a little trouble back in the day, but he never meant any harm.

I tuck my thumbs in my pockets and head for him. I'm less than fifteen feet away when I realize he's talking to someone else. As I get closer, I realize it's Bee's grandson. Van.

Before I can do an about-face and tell Harry I'll call the order in, Tommy's gaze shifts my way and his face lights up like a winning slot machine. "Holy shit! Darlin' Stitch! Claire told me you was back in town." He makes a face and addresses Van. "Sorry 'bout my language."

Van shrugs and mutters something I don't hear, but he looks my way, eyes falling from my head to my feet. Today I'm dressed in jean shorts and a company T-shirt that's about three sizes too big because all they have in stock are large, extra large, and double XL. It's twisted up and tucked into one side of my waistband to keep it out of the way. I'm also wearing an old pair of work boots from back when I was a teenager and into floral-print Doc Martens.

"Sorry, I don't want to interrupt. I can come back later." I glance at Van suspiciously.

"Nah, it's cool. I'm just about to grab a few things for Van here. Did ya know he's Bee's grandson?"

I force a stiff smile. "Yup. We met a couple of days ago."

"Well, that's great. You've got some real fine neighbors, Van. Darlin's dad runs Footprint Renos, so if you're needin' any help, I'm sure they'd be happy to oblige. I'll be right back."

Before Van or I can stop him, Tommy's off, leaving us on our own. An awkward silence follows. One in which the memory of exactly what I walked in on the other day returns in ridiculous detail. Today Van is dressed in a ratty T-shirt with a college logo on it, a pair of black shorts, flip-flops, sunglasses, and an old ball cap. My eyes skip from his feet, pausing briefly at the waist because the stupid memory of him naked refuses to go away, before moving all the way to the brim of his hat. It's from the same college in Chicago I went to.

I cross my arms. "What are you doing here?"

He mirrors the movement. "What are *you* doing here?"

"I asked you first." What the heck is wrong with me? I'm acting like an angry PMSing teenager.

His lips thin into a line. "I asked you second."

Heat creeps up my neck and settles in my cheeks. One of us has to be an adult. "Ordering building supplies for my dad since, like Tommy said, he owns the construction company in town." The *duh* is implied in my tone. I should probably dial back my bitch a notch or two, but I don't trust this guy as far as I can throw him, which isn't very far, since he's a big dude. I don't like that he pretended he didn't know what I was talking about when I mentioned him calling and asking all kinds of questions about the property.

I have to tip my head back to meet his eyes, which is frustrating. I make a go-ahead motion. "So?"

"So?" He lifts one shoulder and lets it fall.

I can't see his eyes because his sunglasses are the mirrored, reflective type. All I can see is my own red, flustered face. "Why are you here?"

His lip twitches. He has nice lips, full, soft looking. They part and his tongue drags slowly across the bottom one before he responds. "Why do you care?"

I make an annoyed sound in the back of my throat. I don't see how this guy could possibly be the grandson Bee loved so dearly. He's an antagonistic jerk. A total McMansion-level asshole. "Do you have so much damn money to throw around that you can use up all the resources in this town on projects that don't even matter?"

His brow furrows. "What?"

"You know what. Never mind. I'm done talking to you." I spin on my heel, irked by how blasé and oblivious he's being, and head back to the store. I'll call in the order later.

"It was great talking to you again, Darlin'!" he shouts after me. "Glad to see your choice of footwear today allows for safer temper-tantrum stomping!"

It takes everything in me not to flip him the bird. I give his city-dwelling ass two weeks before he gives up on whatever project he thinks he's going to tackle and has to call my dad's company in to help him fix it.

CHAPTER 6

ANOTHER BLAST FROM THE PAST

Dillion

I give myself five minutes to calm the heck down. Bee's grandson riles me right up. It's frustrating. So is the fact that he's disgustingly attractive. It's only a matter of time before some poor townie woman goes gaga over his pretty smile and his delicious body. At least I'm secure in the knowledge that it isn't going to be me.

My next stop is the office supply/printing store. I have no clue how they stay open. I'm assuming most people in town have no idea how to one click on Amazon. The moment I walk in, I automatically want to turn right back around. Running into Tommy is one thing, but standing behind the cash desk is Tawny Lefrink. Back in high school she was part of my girl gang. There were four of us in total—Sue, Tawny, Allie, and me. Sue was also more of what I would call a frenemy, not an actual friend. Half the time I think she wanted in the group so she could steal *my* friends. But Allie, Tawny, and I always hung out together. Until I left and they stayed.

Her eyes flare as they move over me. "Dee Dee? Holy crap! I heard you were back in town but thought it had to be a bunch of bullshit rumors." She comes out from behind the cash register and pulls me in for a tight hug.

The affection surprises me, so it takes me a few extra seconds to react in kind. Tawny's hair is the same color as her name, but not the reason her parents named her that. She has deep-blue eyes the color of sapphires, a smattering of freckles across the bridge of her nose, and a wide smile that pops a dimple in her left cheek. She's tall and willowy, to the point that everyone was always worried she had an eating disorder back in high school. She didn't. In fact, she could eat half the guys under the table. Not much has changed since high school. She's still tall and lean.

She steps back, hands still on my shoulders. "Wow. You look amazing. The city agrees with you, doesn't it?" There's a hint of something like longing in her voice.

"I liked it. Always lots of action."

Her eyes narrow. "Liked? As in past tense?"

"Still like. But I'm on a hiatus, you know, with Billy having that accident and all." It's not like everyone doesn't already know why I'm here—might as well address the elephant in the room. And out of all the people in Pearl Lake, Tawny definitely wasn't one to be judgmental.

Her expression softens. "How is Billy? Is he doing okay? When I heard about what happened, I sent a box of chocolate to the house. Those Big Turk things he always loved."

We both make a face and laugh. We always joked they tasted like soap covered in chocolate, and he must've developed a real taste for soap, since he'd had his mouth washed out with it so much as a kid.

"What'd you do, drive all the way to Canada to get those?" As far I know, that's the only place you can find them. We went to Niagara Falls on one of our rare family vacations, and Billy went a little wild in a candy store.

"Nope. Ordered them online."

"Wow. That's a heck of a lot more convenient. He couldn't get enough of those chocolate bars, or Thrills gum."

"Both so gross." I always thought Thrills gum, like Big Turk, also tasted a lot like soap.

She smiles and tips her head to the side. "So does that mean you're back for a while?"

"My dad needed some help with the books and managing his projects, and since that's my jam, I said yes. Helps that I was in the middle of trying to find a new apartment and a new job, so the timing worked." I don't include that I'm unsure of the kind of job I would've looked for had I stayed in Chicago. Having some time to figure things out isn't necessarily a bad thing.

"Oh, right. I didn't know that part. It's temporary, then?" She sounds disappointed.

"I'm probably going to be here for at least a few months." Until Billy is out of a cast and back on his feet, anyway.

"Wow. How do you feel about that? You can usually only handle a few days here before you're gone again." A hint of hurt threads through her tone, and once again, I'm reminded of how awful I am for ghosting everyone here.

"Eh, I'll survive. Lots to keep me busy, and there wasn't much left to miss in Chicago after my company disbanded."

She nods, as if she understands, but I'm not sure she can. "Well, if you wanna grab a drink with me and Allie, let me know."

"What about Sue?"

Tawny makes a face. "She's a hot mess these days."

"Wasn't she always?"

Tawny lifts one shoulder in a half shrug. "Worse than before. She got married a while back to Nelson Fry. You remember him, don't you?"

"I think so. Lived and breathed dirt biking?"

"That's the one."

"Wow, he doesn't seem like her type."

That earns me another shrug. "Everyone was her type at one point or another. Anyway, that lasted all of six months, because he's married to his dirt bike and can't handle more responsibility than knowing where his helmet is. And that's on a good day. So she went through a rough patch there. Then she started seeing someone new." Tawny looks away and bites at the skin around her nail.

"Someone local?"

She nods.

"Are you gonna tell me who?"

"Tuck."

"Tucker Patrick?" It's my turn for my eyebrows to rise.

She swallows audibly and nods again.

"Wow, that's . . . unexpected. Or maybe it shouldn't be?" This is a small town, and Tucker was always smooth with the ladies.

"You know she always kind of had a thing for him." Tawny bites the inside of her lip.

I nod, aware that Sue often wanted what I had. It was a weird, not entirely healthy friendship. I dated Tucker on and off for almost two years, and when I moved to Chicago for college, I ended things for good.

He said I'd come back for him. I told him he was wrong; that wouldn't happen. Ever.

And yet here I am. Back in the place where I made endless mistakes growing up. I put him in that category. He was the devil I knew. It was easier to let him do what he wanted, rather than make my life more difficult by taking issue with the crappy way he treated me. I was always planning on leaving Pearl Lake, him included, so I did what I had to do.

"Wait a second. I thought he moved to Lake Geneva and worked in real estate there."

"He was and he did. But he moved back a few years ago. Said he knew the area better. Between you and me, I think he got himself into some trouble out there. Not that he hasn't gotten himself into more trouble since he moved back."

"I guess he hasn't changed."

My phone buzzes with a message from my dad asking me to pick up a few missing supplies. Which means I have to head back to the freaking hardware store. Hopefully Van isn't still there. "My dad needs me to grab a few things, so I gotta run. Is your cell number still the same?"

"Yup, so is Allie's."

"I'll message you about that drink?"

"Allie and I usually get together on Wednesday nights for a drink, if you're interested. Half-price ladies' night at the bar and all."

"That sounds great, actually."

I leave feeling lighter, and like maybe being home isn't all bad.

The rest of the day is great, and I don't even balk when my dad forces me to join the family for a sit-down dinner, like we used to do when we were kids. I can't resist a good burger, and my mom's potato salad is the best. I bite my tongue when Billy takes a seat at the table, a fresh beer beside his plate.

"How's that job for the Bowmans going? You think you'll be done before I get this cast off?" Billy takes a giant bite of his burger. A pickle slides out and lands halfway on his place mat, and ketchup drips like fresh blood onto his plate.

My dad makes a noise. "We'd better not still be on that project, or we'll be more behind than we already are. I have a good feeling there will be more like it, though. The neighbors from two doors down stopped by to see the progress, and they were asking what our schedule was like for the fall. Pretty sure they'll be throwing out some stuff along the way, Marilyn, so if you have any big wants, let me know and I'll keep an eye out."

"We could always use a new TV," Billy says through a mouthful of burger.

"We got a new TV last year," Mom reminds him. "Have you taken your medication today?"

"Took it a couple hours ago." Billy washes down his burger with a gulp of beer.

"What kind of medication?" I ask, feeling like now is a good time to broach the subject.

"Oh, just stuff to help manage the pain and antibiotics because his stitches got infected."

"I don't think you're supposed to drink when you're taking antibiotics, or pain meds." I give a nod to the beer in his hand.

Billy rolls his eyes. "It's a light beer. It's not like I'm pounding a bottle of rye or anything."

My brother's attitude these days sucks, although I can't say he doesn't have a reason to be grumpy. I would be, too, if I was dealing with a broken ankle, a beat-up face, and pending drunk driving charges that could include a suspended license for the next six months, and that's if he gets the lesser charge.

"When's your court date?" I ask my brother.

"Geez! Can you get off my ass for two fucking seconds? I screwed up. I know that. I don't need you rubbing it in my goddamn face every time you see me." He pushes back his chair and tries to get up but loses his balance, knocking over his chair and landing on his ass.

My parents' chairs screech across the floor in tandem, and they both push out of their seats.

"I'm fine. I got it." He struggles to pull himself to his feet. His face is red, and he's huffing by the time he manages to right himself. He's tall and gangly and the spitting image of our grandfather when he was Billy's age. He plants one fist on the table, grabs his half-empty beer, and chugs the rest of the contents while glaring at me. He finishes his tantrum by slamming the empty can on the table. Then he grabs his crutches and wobbles his way through the living room to my old bedroom and slams the door.

Dad sighs, and Mom pokes at her potato salad with her fork.

"I wasn't trying to rub it in his face. It was a simple question. And he really shouldn't be drinking if he's taking painkillers and antibiotics." I leave out the part about how the drinking is the reason he's in this predicament in the first place, since that's a whole different beast to tackle.

"I know, honey. Remember that this is hard for him. He's always felt like the moon to your sun, so he's more sensitive than usual, especially with you coming home and helping out with the business while he's healing. I'll have a talk with him," my mom says, always standing up for her little boy.

I don't push it, in part because I'm tired and this conversation requires energy I don't have. Besides, Billy's room is down the hall, and the walls are thin in this place.

We finish up dinner, and I head back to the trailer, glad that I don't have to worry about running into my brother for the rest of the night. It's weird being in my late twenties and dealing with teenage-style sibling squabbles again.

The low tones of rock music come from next door, accompanied by the repetitive pounding of a hammer and the occasional obnoxious whirl of a skill saw. And of course, because the night wouldn't be complete without a campfire, he has one going, except he must be burning something wet because the plume of smoke is thick and acrid. I immediately zip up the interior lining on the big window in the dining area so the campfire crackling less than thirty feet away doesn't choke me out. It's meant to keep rain out and let fresh air in—when there isn't a stinky fire going next door.

I don't bother to shower. It's pointless with a campfire raging beside me. Instead I turn on my TV and flip the limited channels I have access to. My parents have basic cable with a sports package add-on, so finding something semientertaining that isn't a football game can be a challenge.

The TV drones in the background, mostly drowned out by the noise from next door, but I'm so engrossed in setting up a new online version of my dad's invoice form that I don't notice it for the most part.

Two hours later, I have several new streamlined forms that I'll introduce slowly, one at a time, so as not to overwhelm my old-school dad and uncle. I've also revised all their spreadsheets, categorized their expenses for the bookkeeping software, and created a spreadsheet for billable hours to use moving forward. My hope is that I'll be able to increase their bottom line, lower their expenses, and give them a better sense of exactly how much each project is going to cost with built-in incidentals—especially if they're looking at more projects on the other side of the lake.

It's well after ten by the time I finish getting ready for bed, and still I hear music and hammering next door. Not to mention a giant spotlight aimed in this direction. I still don't understand why he's trying to fix up Bee's place. It's not like an investor is going to keep Bee's cottage. Not when they can knock it down and build something better. All it will take is one McMansion on this side of the lake to drive up property taxes and make it harder for the locals to stay afloat.

I pull my pillow over my head and try to block it out, but I'm a light sleeper and this is honestly too much. Plus, now I'm spitting mad because all I want is Bee back and not Douche McJerk who has no respect for his neighbors. I toss my pillow aside and inchworm to the end of the bed, slide my feet into my flip-flops, grab my phone, and step out into the inky darkness.

It's a muggy night with the promise of rain in the coming days, which reminds me that I need to patch the bigger holes before that happens. We've had a few little showers, but not an actual summer storm that can pull shingles off roofs and raise the water level a couple of inches. I turn on the flashlight and trudge through the brush and past the campfire, which incidentally has been left unattended. It's down to a smolder, but Van has left out hot dog sticks and a bag of buns.

I keep going, toward Bee's front porch and the blinding spotlight. Standing in front of the cottage is Van. Shirtless. Sweaty and shirtless. The bright light shines directly on him, accenting the dips and ridges, the smooth planes of muscle.

Van is ripped. Probably because he spends a lot of time at the gym, staring at his own reflection in the mirror. He lifts his ball cap from his head and runs a hand through his deliciously sweaty dark hair before he flips his cap around and replaces it, backward this time.

I roll my eyes at myself. What the hell is wrong with me? *Deliciously sweaty.* "Hey!" I bark.

He startles and the hammer in his hand goes flying, but he was on the back swing, so it heads in my direction. I sidestep it, and it manages to miss me by about six inches. He spins around, eyes wide as they land on me. "What the fuck?"

"Do you realize what time it is?"

"Do you realize that you scared the living shit out of me and I could've hurt you, or myself?" He motions to the hammer lying on the ground next to me.

"Wouldn't that have been a pity," I snap.

"What the hell is your damn problem?"

"You." I point a finger at him. "You are the problem. It's after ten. There's a bylaw in place around here that stipulates all construction takes place between the hours of seven a.m. and nine p.m. from June to August, and you're violating that. And for what? It's not like whatever you're doing is going to matter when your damn plan is to parcel out the property!" I'm yelling now, and heaving. And my nipples are peaking under the white tank I wore to bed. I hug myself to hide them.

"This is the second time you've said that. What the hell are you talking about?"

"What do you mean, what am I talking about?" I flail for a second and then cross my arms again. "You called me about it. Bee wasn't gone a couple of weeks, and you were already asking about acreage and subdividing. It doesn't take a genius to know what your plans are!"

"I don't even know what you mean by subdividing, and I never called you."

"Yes, you did!" He's just so infuriating.

"No. I didn't. Believe me, I'd remember dealing with someone as hostile as you."

"I am not hostile."

"Really?" Van props a fist on his hip. His narrow hip.

I follow the movement, which leads my eyes to his waist, that enticing V of muscle dragging my gaze down farther. Of course, because my brain is a jerk, the image of him naked pops back into my brain.

As if he's reading my mind, his brow arches. "You're picturing me naked right now. Aren't you?"

"What? No!" My eyes snap back up to his.

"Yeah. You are." His lip curls, somewhere between a smirk and sneer, his tone needling. "You were staring at my crotch, probably thinking about the last time you visually molested my junk. Is that why you stopped by? To check me out again? This whole fake phone call thing is an excuse for you to come back over here and get a look at the goods again." He runs a hand down his chest.

"You're an egotistical asshole. I realize that this might be some kind of fun holiday for you, and that you're probably sleeping until noon every day, but some of us have to be up at the crack of dawn. Bylaw hours are seven a.m. to nine p.m. Next time you break them, expect to get a visit from the sheriff." I spin around and stomp over to the extension cord, find the place where it's joined to the lamp, and break the connection, submerging us in darkness. "Next time I won't be so nice about it."

"Hate to break it to you, but you weren't very nice about it this time," he calls after me.

It drives me crazy how easy it is for him to push my buttons.

A few seconds later I hear an oof and a clatter, which means he's tripped over something in the dark. I smile to myself. Hopefully this time he'll get the message.

CHAPTER 7

WHY DO YOU HAVE TO BE
SO PRETTY?

Dillion

Two days after the hammer incident, my neighbor comes knocking on my door, very early in the morning. I know it's him because he tromps through the bushes like a moose, making a racket. He'd make a terrible sniper.

At first I assume he's finally stopping by to apologize.

I should know better.

I open the door, and his annoyingly attractive, very angry face appears, unfiltered by the screen. I get that fluttery feeling in my belly. The one that tells me I'm probably going to fantasize about him during my shower later. It's happened a couple of times since I moved back. Okay. More than a couple. But he really is stunning. Apparently, I'm a sucker for dark hair and eyes the color of maple syrup. And chiseled features and an athletic physique. It's why I ended up dating the quarterback in high school, and also how I ended up with Jason for two years in Chicago.

I have a type, and as much as I don't want to admit it to myself, this guy is 100 percent it. At least physically. Personality-wise, I've tried my best to stay away from the assholes since I left Pearl Lake. I haven't always been successful, but I've done better than Tucker.

Van waves a bunch of papers. "What the hell is this?"

I bat them out of my face and step forward so I'm blocking the way into my trailer.

He's a big guy. Giving him an opportunity to barrel his way into my personal space doesn't seem like a smart idea. Sort of like inviting a grizzly bear to lick honey off your face in a cave.

My move forces him to step back down, putting him a few inches below me. I grab the papers and scan them. It's a cable bill. For a grand. And a printout of this month's bill as well, which has already amassed a similar amount in charges. "It's an expensive cable bill."

I try to hand it back to him, but he shakes his head. "I've been here a week! How could I rack up a thousand dollars in charges?"

"Why are you asking me? It's not like I know what your TV habits are."

"It's all for on-demand porn! Hundreds and hundreds of dollars on porn! You don't even need to pay for that shit. You can watch it for free wherever and whenever."

He has a point, but the internet connection up here is basically crap. At least the package my family always had is. I have never been an internet-porn watcher, but I've tried streaming, and I can't even watch a music video or a news clip without it buffering at least once. I imagine with actual porn it's probably way worse. I flip through the pages, noting charge after charge for on-demand adult movies with bad titles like *Buffy the Penis Slayer* and *Let's Get Pucked*. They all seem to be toward the end of the month and have increased in frequency and volume over the past two weeks. I had no idea that a cable bill could be so detailed.

I drag my eyes back up from the endless list and meet his angry maple gaze. "I don't know what you want me to do with this. Unless you're looking for a referral for counseling or something because you're a sex addict."

"I'm not a sex addict! I haven't even had sex in, like . . . months!" He tries to flail but hits his hand on the trailer door.

"Well, that might explain all these charges."

"They're not my charges!"

I shrug. "They're not mine either. I've been here for less time than you! Besides, there's a video store in town. They have an adult section. You could rent a few and save yourself the money. Or, like you said, you could browse the free sites instead of paying all this money to watch the on-demand stuff. Now if you'll excuse me, I have to get ready for work." I toss the papers at him, and they scatter on the ground at his feet.

When he bends to pick them up, I close the door and lock it.

By the time I've gathered my shower supplies, he's gone. Thankfully.

I head to the house wearing my nightshirt so I can pick a non-campfire-scented outfit to wear to the office. It doesn't take me long to shower and get ready for work.

On my way through the kitchen, I pour myself a travel mug of coffee and nab one of my mom's famous homemade granola bars. She wraps them individually so they stay fresh. I toss the Saran into the garbage and notice the mountain of tissue sitting on top.

And then it dawns on me.

Those charges have been building for a while now.

And the recent uptick seems to correspond quite nicely with the amount of time my brother has been laid up with a broken ankle.

I set the coffee on the counter and head for Billy's bedroom. He doesn't answer when I knock, which isn't much of a surprise, since it's only six forty-five.

I open the door, cautiously, with one eye closed and the other one squinty, on the off chance he's sleeping naked or something.

Thankfully he's not. He's lying on the bed, mostly cover-free, wearing a pair of boxers. He's always been a wiry guy, but instead of filling out in his twenties, he stretched and got even leaner.

His mouth hangs open, the black eyes from the airbag deploying in his face during the accident now faded to green. He looks almost childlike while he's sleeping. For a moment I'm sad that this is where he's ended up and that I've had to come home, too, as a result. We weren't exactly close, but we didn't fight all the time. Except when he was getting up to no good and I was saving his ass. I couldn't help him this time, though.

I spot his laptop on the floor beside his bed. I pick it up and sit down on the chair in the corner of the room, piled high with laundry that, based on the smell, needs to be run through the washing machine. It's password protected, so I hit the number one four times and press enter. I roll my eyes when it lets me in. It's also his phone password.

I click on the internet icon and find it linked to Bee's Knees, which is the name I gave Bee's connection when I set it up years ago. Somehow my brother has managed to figure out the password and tap into her internet, which has always been better than ours. She wanted to be able to video chat with her favorite grandson, and she liked watching YouTube videos about figure skating and those shows where people dance and stuff.

Next I go to my brother's browsing history. As expected, I find multiple hits to the on-demand account associated with Bee's cable provider. Several a day, in fact. I guess Van had a right to be pissed, since it's my brother who's been racking up charges. I poke Billy's shoulder. He makes a disgruntled noise and bats my hand away.

I snap my fingers beside his ear. "Hey, wake up. I need to talk to you."

"Time is it?" He rubs at his eyes and cringes, probably having forgotten that they're still bruised.

"Time to stop hacking into Bee's cable so you can watch porn."

"Huh?" He blinks a bunch of times, panic flashing across his face.

I drop the laptop on his bed, his browsing history on display, and give him the middle finger. "Rule number one: always clear your history, dumbass." I hold up my pointer finger beside the middle one. "Rule number two: four ones is the most obvious password in the world, and it's your fault if people hack into your phone and steal information." I hold up my pinkie so I'm giving him the shocker sign. "And rule number three: don't use our neighbor's internet connection to watch freaking porn. It's a wonder you haven't rubbed your dick off with the amount of whacking you must be doing." The thought makes me shudder.

"Porn is the only good thing left in my life, and Mom and Dad canceled the good cable package. Besides, her internet connection is way better than ours."

That this is Billy's defense is not particularly surprising, but it is annoying. "You owe our neighbor a grand."

"What? No way. That's insane."

"So is the fact that you ordered enough dirty videos to rack up that kind of bill." I grab his laptop off the bed and head for the door.

"Hey! Where are you going? That's mine!"

"Not anymore it isn't. It's collateral until you cough up the money to pay Van's cable bill." I slam the door closed behind me and run into my dad on the way through the kitchen.

I can hear Billy swearing a blue streak from his bedroom.

"What's going on?" Dad takes a tentative sip of his coffee.

"Other than your son having a porn addiction, nothing much."

He sprays hot coffee on the counter. "What?"

"I'm taking care of it. We should get going. I have a conference call with a new lumber company outside of town at eight. Harry suggested them."

"Right. Okay. That's good. Is that Billy's laptop?"

"Yup."

"Well, I guess that explains why he's screaming like you've lopped off a limb."

I shoot him a look.

He mumbles something about moody kids and follows me out to the truck. He doesn't balk when I take the driver's seat, happy to sit back, relax, and enjoy the bumpy ride to the office at the edge of downtown.

"Are you serious about Billy having a porn addiction? Is it something I need to talk to him about?" Dad rubs the back of his neck, his face flushed with discomfort.

The only time either of my parents mentioned sex when I was growing up was to tell me not to have it. I told them it was easy for them to say. They'd grown up together and got married at sixteen with the consent of their parents. Which is incomprehensible to me. At sixteen I was barely capable of keeping my room clean and handing my assignments in on time, let alone running a household. And sex is one of the very few activities that's free and entertaining when you're a teen living in a small town.

I went to the clinic in the next town over with Tawny and Allie, got myself a prescription for birth control pills, and made Tucker wear a condom anyway. Turns out that was a good idea, since he had a habit of hooking up with other girls on the side—usually while we were on a break, but not always.

"If you want to embarrass the hell out of him, sure. I get that he's bored, but there are a million other things he could be doing besides ordering dirty videos all day. I think the bigger problem is that he managed to hack into Bee's internet and cable because it's faster and racked up a thousand-dollar bill."

"A *thousand* bucks? Isn't internet porn free?" Dad's eyes look like they're about to pop out of his head.

I cock a brow. "Not when you're ordering specific movies on demand all the time."

"Geez." He runs his hand through his hair again and blows out a breath.

"So I confiscated his laptop until he coughs up the money. I'm assuming he must have something in the bank, since he lives with you guys and works a full-time job."

"You'd think. Boy doesn't seem to have your money sense. He'll do well for a while, socking it away, and then boom." He snaps his fingers. "He'll get an idea in his head that he wants something, and all of a sudden his savings disappear. That's how we ended up with the dirt bike, the ATVs, and the IROC-Z in the garage."

Billy has always been on the impulsive side. It's why he's ended up in trouble so much, but he's taken it to a whole new level of impulsivity lately.

"He has to have a grand, though, don't you think?"

"Usually his paychecks are gone by the time they hit his account." Dad shrugs, not because he's apathetic, but more that he's at a loss. "At least we did good with you, right?"

I give him a small smile. "Yeah, you did good with me." But it makes me sad that so many people have already written Billy off as a screwup, and I wonder if I've taken to the narrative, too, and whether we're making it impossible for him to feel like he can clean up his act.

When we get to the office, I head to my desk, fire up my computer, and get ready for my conference call while the guys load the trucks in preparation for the day. By nine thirty I've managed to work out a deal with a new local lumber supplier with tiered pricing that includes deeper discounts as we reach order thresholds. It's a great step forward.

Once I end the call, I hop in the truck and head to town so I can pick up a few things we need in the office, including dusting cloths and a lamp for my desk. The fluorescent lights are brutal and give me a headache. They were the reason that I hid behind a baseball cap in high school most of the time. That and I couldn't be bothered to style my hair most days. Now I just pull the curls up in a ponytail to keep them out of the way.

Uncle John asked me to stop by the real estate office this week, and I figure I might as well get it out of the way. We have a good relationship with them, because they're always letting us know when renovation projects are coming up on the market, and they send a lot of referrals our way. Anything on the north side of the lake is generally going to undergo a substantial renovation, and being the only construction outfit in town makes it easier to snatch up local business opportunities.

I'm crossing my fingers that I don't run into Tucker, since I'm now aware he's working for Pearl Lake Realty. I do all my running around and picking up of things before I stop at their office. Luck seems to be on my side, and Tucker is nowhere to be seen. I make small talk for a few minutes but do my best to get out of there as quickly as I can. My last stop is Boones so I can pick up lunch for the guys and, of course, apple fritters.

I've reached my truck when a very familiar male voice calls out, "Darlin'? Is 'at you?"

I deflate like a popped inner tube. Looks like my luck has run out. I plaster on a smile and turn around.

Tucker jams a hand into his black dress pants as he saunters down the sidewalk toward me wearing his signature smirk. He's wearing a light-blue golf shirt, and despite the fact that it's in the mideighties, he has a sweater tied around his neck like he fell out of a bad nineties movie. He's completed the look with tan penny loafers, with pennies.

"Babe, look at you." His gaze roves over me in a way that makes me want to immediately jump in the shower. He whistles. "Wow. The city done you good, huh?" He makes that twirl motion with his finger, as if he expects me to do a spin.

I'm wearing jeans, flats, and a company T-shirt, still two sizes too big because the ones I ordered for me aren't in yet. There's nothing sexy about my outfit, and there is no way I would ever do a spin for Tucker.

Even if he paid me a million dollars. Okay, maybe for a million. But I'd want payment up front.

"Hey, Tucker."

"That's it? After all these years, all you're gonna say is 'Hey, Tucker'? How about a hug?" He opens his arms wide.

"I'm not a hugger, and my hands are full." I hold up one of the take-out bags and use the other as a convenient shield.

"Uh-huh." He leans against the truck, right over the lock. "I heard you were back in town. Finally realized what you were missing?" He winks.

"Still as smarmy as ever, I see." I can't believe I wasted two years dating this jerk.

He throws his head back and laughs, but when his gaze returns to mine, it's colder. "You were always trying to be better than you were, Darlin', and now look where you are. Back where you said you never wanted to be. You and I both know you'll be under me eventually, even though you pretend it's not what you want."

I'd say I can't believe what I'm hearing, but this is Tucker, and it seems as though he's gotten worse over the years, not better. "First of all, my being here has nothing to do with you at all. In fact, you're basically the reason I don't want to be here. Also, sexual harassment much, Tucker? Who says that kind of shit? And aren't you with Sue?"

"It's not harassment if it's the truth. And Sue and I are on a break."

"A break? Is that still your way of justifying being unfaithful? You really are a piece of work, you know that? Clearly the only thing about you that's changed is where your hairline starts."

He runs a self-conscious hand through his hair. It's not as if he's balding, but he used to be so paranoid about it back in high school. His older brother already had a receding hairline by the time he was in his sophomore year of college, so Tucker has always been sensitive about it. Especially since he has a widow's peak. "There's nothing wrong with my hair."

I roll my eyes. "Well, this has been . . . disturbing. I have to get back to the office." I glance to the left as a familiar black sports car parallel parks directly across the street from us. Awesome, as if this morning hasn't already been an epic suckfest. The last thing I need is another run-in with my neighbor, in a public place.

It's bad enough that I'm out here talking to Tucker where everyone can see. At least three locals have passed on the other side of the street, and there will undoubtedly be gossip. It wouldn't be a small town if there wasn't.

"Come on, Darlin', don't be like that." He reaches out to touch an errant curl that fell from my ponytail, but I lean back to avoid contact.

The car door closes on the other side of the street. I fight not to look, but my stupid head swivels, wanting the hit of eye candy as a reward for not kicking Tucker in the junk. Van's wearing a threadbare T-shirt with the name of a band I used to listen to in high school written across his chest in faded letters. His jeans have holes in them. Not the expensive, strategic ones, but the kind that have been worn so many times, with so much love, that they've started to disintegrate. He almost looks like a local.

His gaze meets mine briefly before it shifts to Tucker, who's leaning against the side of my truck, making it impossible for me to leave.

"Who's that guy?" Tucker asks.

"Huh?" I reluctantly drag my attention back to Tucker.

"That guy." He tips his chin toward Van. "How do you know him?"

I'm about to tell Tucker it's none of his business, and that I don't actually know him at all. Although I have seen his penis, and it's far superior to Tucker's, at least from what I remember in high school. But my neighbor heads directly for me, a look I can't quite decipher on his face.

"Hey, Dillion, aren't you a ray of sunshine on this gorgeous morning. Let me give you a hand with those, beautiful."

He swoops in and grabs one of the bags right out of my hand. I'm so stunned, and frankly confused, that I don't even have the opportunity to fight him on it. Now I don't have a buffer between me and Tucker. At least until Van turns to Tucker and flashes him a megawatt smile. "Hey, man, so sorry to interrupt, but do you mind opening the door for Dillion? These bags are mighty heavy."

Tucker's brow furrows, as if he's trying to figure out the dynamic. I know I am as well. "Uh, yeah, sure. You shoulda said something, Darlin'."

I still don't know what's going on. But I manage to unlock the door, which Van swings open. He sets one bag on the center console and takes the other from me so he can do the same. "What are you doing?" I ask through clenched teeth.

He drops his head, mouth right next to my ear. "Saving your surly ass from this douche; what does it look like?" His warm breath hits my neck and sends a shiver down my spine.

He moves back a step and winks, except it's more playful than it is anything else. Which doesn't make sense, considering every single one of our interactions so far have been tense and mostly unpleasant.

I guess it wouldn't take a genius to sense the tension between Tucker and me, especially with the way I've been using takeout as a shield and Tucker being his skeezy self, preventing me from getting in my truck. But I can take care of myself, and I don't need anyone, especially Van, to save me. Besides, it still doesn't answer the question of *why* he'd willingly intervene.

Van wipes his hands on his shorts and grabs the edge of the door before spinning around to face a confused Tucker. "My apologies, I should introduce myself. I'm Van, Dillion's neighbor. And you are?"

"Tucker Patrick." He holds out his hand somewhat reluctantly. "Did you say you're Darlin's neighbor?"

Van gives him a wide smile. "That's right. I live right next door to this ray of sunshine." He winks at me again.

Tucker's eyebrows pull together. It doesn't take much. He almost has a unibrow to begin with. "Next door?"

"Van is Bee's grandson. He's staying at her place right now, which is technically now his place."

Tucker's eyes light up like he won the lottery. "Oh yeah? You looking to sell? I'm in real estate, and I can get you great money for that place."

I roll my eyes. Again. I remember Tucker hated when I would do that, so I add in an extra one to make up for lost opportunities. "Could you be any less chill? He can't sell right now. It's not even on the right side of the lake." My phone buzzes in my purse. I rummage around until I find the device, happy for the distraction. I have no idea what's going on right now, and I'm super confused by Van and his behavior. I'm even happier when it's a message from Aaron asking when lunch is arriving because Uncle John is getting hangry.

"I gotta deliver lunch."

Van steps aside and offers me his hand. I look at it, not sure what he expects me to do. Eventually I slip my hand in his palm, assuming he means to shake it, which is weird, but then so is this entire situation.

The second his hand wraps around mine, I feel like I've been shot through with electricity. And he doesn't release my hand. He just keeps holding it. I look from our clasped hands to his face. He's smirking again, and those warm maple eyes are locked on mine. He tips his head toward the truck. "Up you go, gorgeous."

"Laying it on a little thick, aren't you?" I mutter.

"Absolutely."

At this point, Tucker looks annoyed more than anything else. And I'm completely discombobulated. I climb into the truck, to end this weirdness and get the heck away from these two.

Once I'm in the driver's seat, Van releases my hand. He hits the automatic window button, and the window whirs quietly as it descends.

Once it's all the way down, he closes the door and tugs on the seat belt. "Don't forget to buckle up."

"Right. Thanks." I pull the belt across my chest, still trying to figure out his angle.

He continues to stand there, grinning like he's in on some secret.

I grip the steering wheel and blurt, "I talked to my brother. He's the reason for your ridiculous bill. I'll leave a check for you. Sorry 'bout that."

"Will you break in again to do that?" His grin widens.

I can feel my face heating up at the memory of Van dripping wet and naked, standing in the middle of his living room. "I didn't break in the first time. I used a key. And to answer your question, no, I'll slip it under your door."

"That's considerate of you."

"That's me. Miss Considerate."

He chuckles and steps away from the truck, tucking his hands into his pockets. "Have a good afternoon, Dillion. I'm sure I'll see you later."

"I should only be so lucky."

I shift the truck into gear and pull away from the curb, leaving Tucker and Van standing on the sidewalk. For the first time, I'm grateful that I ran into him.

Confused, but still grateful.

CHAPTER 8

SPITFIRE

Van

Dillion's tires squeal as she pulls away from the curb. I smile as her truck disappears up the hill. I'm not sure if it's me she wants to escape this time or the assclown standing beside me.

"So you're Darlin's neighbor, huh?" His smile is one I'm familiar with—stiff, practiced, and lacking authenticity.

I'm also on the fence about Dillion's apparent nickname, or maybe it's the way everyone pronounces her name here. I'm not sure if *Lynnie* suits her, but *Darlin'* makes me think of fifties-style housewives, which she definitely is not.

"Yup. I'm her next-door neighbor." I give him the same smile back.

He nods, gaze sliding over my shoulder to my car and then back to me. "You from the city?"

"Chicago, yes." I've noticed that everyone in town says "the city" instead of "Chicago," as if Chicago is the only city that exists.

"How long you planning on sticking around before you sell?" He rocks back on his heels. His whole persona screams *trying too hard.*

"Dunno that I'm gonna sell." Or that I want to, especially with my prickly neighbor, whose buttons I enjoy pushing entirely too much, and the fact that this is the only place I can be right now. Going back to Chicago isn't an option. Not until we can figure out what happened to the missing money. I considered draining my dwindling savings to pay back at least a tiny part of it, which my father and brother seemed on board with, at least until my dad's lawyer pointed out that it would only serve to solidify the appearance of my guilt.

Tucker pulls his wallet from his pocket and slides a business card out while flashing a wad of hundred-dollar bills. "Well, if you decide you want to, give me a call. I've got lots of buyers looking to get into the market. And don't listen to Darlin'—it's not about what side of the lake you're on. She just doesn't want a new build going up beside the shithole her family calls a house."

"How do you know Dillion, again?" No one offered the information in the first place, but I'm banking on him wanting to tell me.

"We go way back." He smirks.

"How far back?" I press.

"Dated in high school. Popped her cherry and taught her everything she knows. Girl's got a mouth on her, if you know what I mean." He follows that comment with a wink.

"Wow. That's not the kind of information I was looking for." This guy is a jackass extraordinaire. It's hard to believe that the woman who reams me out for hammering past nine o'clock at night would put up with this guy and his shit. Although I'm guessing his shit is why he's an ex.

"I give her three weeks before she's on her back for me. Or her hands and knees." This time he waggles his brows.

"Is that right?" I glance at his hands and see he's not wearing a ring.

"She couldn't stay away from me then; can't imagine much has changed. You can take the girl out of the trailer, but you can't take the trailer out of the girl."

That's it. I can't stand this jackass. "Could you be any more disrespectful? I don't know you, but I'm going to go out on a limb and say that there's probably slim to no chance that she's interested in doing anything but kicking you in the nuts." I say it loud enough that a couple walking down the street give me a disgusted look.

Tucker's expression shifts to something like embarrassment. "What the hell, bro?"

I motion between us. "We're not bros. The last thing you should be doing is trash-talking your ex to someone you just met. It sure as hell isn't a way to get my business."

He opens his mouth to respond, but I flick his business card back at him. It hits him in the chest before it falls to the sidewalk.

"You don't even know me, and have no business discussing Dillion's skill sets with anyone, let alone a stranger. And if I do decide to sell, it won't be you getting the commission." I walk away, thankful the street is empty of cars and I can make the somewhat dramatic exit I want.

I get back in my car and drive away without my lunch from the diner, all in the name of sticking up for a woman who hates my guts and doesn't even know I stood up for her or witnessed my awesome exit. But I've learned a few things about Dillion today—her ex is a jerk, she doesn't put up with crap, she doesn't like being rescued, and she's honest.

I make a stop at the grocery store on the way home and pick up sandwich meat from the deli counter and a loaf of fresh bread. The good thing about small-town living is that almost everything is owned by locals, and that also means most of the food is fresh and locally sourced. The bread only stays fresh for a few days, but it's freaking amazing.

When I get back to Grammy's place—I'm still struggling to call it mine—I drop the groceries on the counter, then go back to close the front door.

I find an envelope on the floor with my name scrawled in neat writing on the front. I carefully tear it open and find a check for a grand inside and a note from Dillion asking me to let her know what this month's porn charges are so she can cover those too. I feel mildly bad that I'm going to accept her check. Unfortunately, being unemployed means I have reason to be concerned about the cost of the cable bill.

I rub the space between my eyes and sigh. I have no idea how I'm going to clear my name, or find out what happened to that money. The foundation was supposed to make a hefty donation in the next few months, and if that falls through, the literacy program might not be able to run at all. I hate all this sitting and waiting for something to happen. Especially since now no one will tell me anything, and I don't have access to any of the foundation's financial records, having been removed from the board.

I'm not particularly hungry anymore, but I make myself two turkey-and-cheese sandwiches with the horrible fake cheese my parents would never buy when I was a kid that I secretly loved.

Grammy Bee always had it in the house because it made the best grilled cheese sandwiches. And she bought the Velveeta kind, in block form, which she said was better than the individually wrapped slices.

After lunch I step out onto the new front porch that has yet to be stained and head to the garage. I'm saving the staining for the evening, since it's quiet and won't get me yelled at by my neighbor. Although, knowing her, I'm sure she'll find something to yell at me for. I smile just thinking about her. I don't know what my fascination with her is, other than her being a welcome distraction from my life.

Over the past few days, I've managed to make some headway on cleaning out the garage, which is saying something, since it was practically stuffed full of Grammy's treasures and Grampy's old tools. It's a big space, and I'd like it to have a function other than being a hoarder's dream.

I've looked into some of the building bylaws, and it's pretty tough to get permits for new structures, so I'm thinking my best bet is to turn it into a second living space, once I've cleaned out all the junk. With some modifications, it should be big enough for a one-bedroom loft above the garage space, which it was something Grammy Bee used to talk about but never had the chance to do.

It's also an excuse not to tackle the actual cottage, which is daunting. Grammy Bee's house is the only place I've ever been sentimental about. It's filled with great memories from my childhood, and I'm not ready to sift through those yet.

I spend the afternoon dragging stuff into the driveway and separating it into piles. There are three: toss, keep, and sell. The toss pile is the biggest, which isn't a surprise. The garage is basically full of all the things no one wanted in the house anymore but couldn't be bothered to take to the dump. Or maybe Grammy Bee thought it would be useful to someone. Regardless, it makes for a lot of full black bags.

I've started tossing the bags into the bed of Grammy's ancient truck—which I'm stunned still runs, considering it's from the sixties and is rusted out in places—when I get a call from my buddy. We went to college together and have stayed close ever since. I've talked to him a couple of times since I arrived in Pearl Lake. He's aware of the dumpster dive my life has done.

"Hey, Frankie, how's it going?" I put him on speakerphone and heft another bag into the truck.

"Good, good. How's the backwoods treating you? You doing okay, man?" The clickety-clack of his keyboard comes through the phone.

I glance to the right, where Dillion's trailer is barely visible beyond the trees. Is my life a mess? Sure. But at least I'm not in Chicago in the direct line of fire. According to my dad, the media is all over the story, so staying here is better than being there. "As well as can be expected."

"That's fair, all things considered. Getting day drunk would be completely within reason."

I laugh, although I'm not sure he's joking. "Reliving my college days, while fun, wouldn't be particularly good for my brain cells." I'm also not sure I can afford to pick up a bad habit at the moment.

"Everything okay with you?" I toss another bag into the back of the truck, and it lands with a metallic thunk.

"Yeah. Just wanted to check in on you. You busy with something? Did I catch you at a bad time?"

"Not a bad time. Trying to keep myself occupied, you know? I'm cleaning out the garage, getting rid of stuff that should have been tossed a couple of decades ago."

"Productive is always a good thing." There's a brief pause in the typing. "Don't want to let the small-town work ethic rub off on you, otherwise you might get stuck at the bottom of the ladder. Gets tough to climb your way back up."

"I don't know that the work ethic around here is all that low."

"You know what I mean. Small-town life equates to small aspirations. You were on your way to the top. You can get back there."

"Is this a good news call, then?" Frankie is a well-known recruiter in Chicago, always looking for the newest hot commodity and then placing them in high-performing companies. He's excellent at what he does and was the one who hooked me up with my previous employer. I've only been out of a job for a short time, but I'm already getting antsy about not having a steady income. I want to get the ball rolling and start applying for new jobs, but with this scandal hanging over my head, I'm not so sure it's going to be easy to convince anyone to hire me.

Frankie sighs, and I take that as a bad sign. "I'm going to be real straight with you, Van. The situation is fresh, and the media is just getting started, from what I can see. No one wants to touch you right now. It'd help if you could clear you name. People need some distance, time for a new scandal to brew, before they can forget about this one."

I bristle at his tone. I hate that I'm in this position, and that my character and my integrity have been called into question, especially by my friends. "You believe me when I tell you I didn't take the money, right?"

"Yeah, man, of course. I mean, it doesn't make sense for you to go stealing the money from the foundation you helped set up. Unless you've developed some kind of gambling problem."

"I don't have a gambling problem."

"That was a joke. You won't even chip in for lottery tickets, like you're going to blow your money on slots. I think you need to look at the bright side."

"You mean the fact that I'm not in prison for stealing money from my mom's own foundation and I don't have some bearded, tattooed cellmate who wants to make me his pet? That kind of bright side?" I'm grateful that my dad hired a lawyer to help me manage this entire situation. Jail time for something I didn't do would be a real kick in the teeth.

"Well, yeah, kind of. I'm just saying, it could be worse, Van. Didn't you say that they're not taking you to court, or pressing charges?"

Not yet, anyway, and hopefully not at all. "Yeah, I'm just accused of stealing money I didn't take. I lost my job, and now I'm being told I should stay where I am because of the media garbage." And who knows how long that's going to go on for. It's like my life was hijacked. In one day everything that was stable is now up in the air.

"You're a genius at what you do, Van. You have classic taste in architecture, with a modern, contemporary outlook. But the jobs you work on are for big clients, and we're talking a lot of money. It's an asset and a liability, you know? You're too fucking smart for your own good, and that means people don't know if they should trust you enough to put so much money into what you're suggesting. They're worried you'll be able to pull one over on them too."

"I didn't pull one over on anyone, though. And I don't see how my job and what happened with the foundation are even connected. I'm good with numbers, but I'm not that good. According to what my dad told me, someone has been skimming money for the past five years without getting caught. I honestly wouldn't even know how to do that, even if I wanted to." The money has been going missing for years: small amounts that individually would never be missed, but over time they added up to millions in lost donations.

"At least you can escape it all. Take a break from the crazy for a while. Let your family deal with the fallout," Frankie suggests.

"What's going on with my family?" My dad has checked in a few times to make sure I'm okay and update me on the legal side of things. Teagan and I have talked every day, but she's been trying to keep things positive. Bradley was on one of the calls with my dad, but mostly he texts with jokes or GIFs and tells me to "look on the bright side."

I can hear Frankie drumming on his desk. "It's not good, Van."

"How not good is it?"

He blows out a breath. "They're looking into your dad now too. You know how rumors are."

"My dad? Why?"

"Because he's on the board of directors for the foundation, and you're related. I'm sure it's just protocol when something like this happens."

"Right. Yeah, of course. I would've thought he'd mention that, though." I talked to him yesterday, and he seemed calm, reassuring me that everything was going to be okay. It was the most supportive he's been in years.

"He probably doesn't want to stress you out more than you already are. And it's probably all for nothing."

"Maybe I need to come back to Chicago and deal with this."

I can hear the creak of his office chair, which means he's probably swiveling, something he does often. "You're better off staying where you are. I know it's not ideal, but let your dad and his lawyers manage this. Look at this as an opportunity to reinvent yourself. You weren't in love with your job. Relax for a few months, figure out what you want to do next."

"A few months? I was thinking more like a few weeks." But considering how long I've been here already and how little progress I've made, Frankie's timeline seems more reasonable, although less desirable.

"It all depends on how long it takes for this thing to sort itself out. Take up whittling or something."

"Whittling?"

"I don't know. Build something cool. Go fishing. Just give it time. Me and Chip will come for a visit in a couple of weeks. Sound good?"

"Yeah, that'd be great. You think Monica will let Chip come, though?"

Chip is one of our mutual friends. We went to college together and have stayed tight since graduation. His girlfriend, Monica, is high maintenance. Nice enough, but she has Chip wrapped around her finger.

"I'll get him to start working on her now. I'll rent one of those party RVs. It'll be awesome."

"Sure, sounds good." And it does. If I can't be in Chicago right now, at least my friends can come visit me here.

A ping comes from the other end of the line. "I have to go," Frankie says. "Got a hot date tonight."

"Oh yeah? With who? Anyone I know?"

"Nah, just some girl I met at a club last weekend. I'll fill you in when I come visit. Stay chill, my man." He ends the call, and I tip my head up, staring at the nearly cloudless blue sky, sun shining down on me like it has no idea my life is a mess.

I don't like that I'm here, in Pearl Lake, and that my dad is now under investigation. Or that he didn't bother to tell me when I spoke with him. It makes me paranoid. Like people are keeping things from me, and I no longer know who I can trust.

CHAPTER 9
EVERYWHERE I GO, THERE YOU ARE

Van

I don't have time to wallow in self-pity, unfortunately, or obliterate brain cells with alcohol, neither of which would be particularly productive. The alarm on my phone reminds me that I have an appointment with Bernie, the lawyer who dealt with my grandmother's will.

I should've done this months ago, but I wasn't in the headspace to manage it. There's some irony in the fact that the moment I arrived to finally deal with things here, my life in Chicago turned upside down. I'd rationalized that as much as I loved Grammy Bee, she wasn't leaving behind much. Just the cottage and a lot of junk to sort through. I've always loved the place, but cleaning it up wasn't a job I had the time to take on. Now all I have is time.

I hop in the truck, the springs in the seat squealing in protest (although almost everything in this truck protests), and make a stop at the dump—again—before I drive into town. The law office is on the edge of downtown in a small outbuilding on the same piece of property as Bernie's house. It's actually the office for the only town lawyer, an accountant, the city planner, and an art therapist. I'm not sure what the therapist has to do with law and accounting, but there it is.

When I get there, my favorite surly neighbor happens to be coming out of the building. She's with a guy on crutches. He's tall and thin, with the same sandy-blond hair, his a shorter mop of curls. If I had to guess, I'd say he's her younger brother. I never saw much of him when I stayed with Grammy Bee, but then again, I didn't see much of Dillion either.

I pull into the spot beside her truck, purposely crowding the driver's side door. I'm about ten minutes early for my appointment, so instead of heading inside, I cut the engine and wait.

She frowns when she sees the truck, and her eyes turn to slits when she spots the narrow gap I've left between our vehicles. The side mirrors are almost touching. Her tongue pokes at the almost-closed gap between her front teeth, and she knocks on the hood of my truck.

I wave.

"What the heck?" She motions toward the space between our vehicles.

I pretend I can't hear her and tap my ear. Her brother continues around to the passenger side, not even sparing her a glance.

"You can hear me just fine, asshole!" she shouts.

I can't help it. I grin. Man, she's fun to piss off, and it seems to be something I excel at. Annoying her is a bright spot in my otherwise lackluster day.

Her nostrils flare, and she pushes her side mirror in so she can get between the trucks without having to do the limbo. Her face appears in the passenger-side window, eyes on fire. She makes the roll-down-the-window motion with her hand.

I slide across the bench seat and roll it down a couple of inches. She arches a brow, so I roll it down a few more, until it's below her eye level. She's not short, but she's not particularly tall either, so it's about halfway down. "I got the check, thanks for that."

"Awesome. Do you think you could move your truck over, oh, say, about a foot?"

I ignore the question. "Did you just come from the lawyer's office?"

Her elbows jut out, which makes me believe that she's propped her fists on her hips. "That's actually none of your business."

"Or maybe you were visiting the art therapist, talking about your anger issues and such." I tip my head, waiting for her reaction.

"I don't have anger issues!"

"Then why are you yelling at me?"

"What is your deal? I don't get you. This morning you were all 'gorgeous this' and 'beautiful that' and doing whatever the heck you were doing downtown, and now you're boxing my damn truck in. Why are you such a confusing asshole?"

"Why do you hate me so much?"

"Because you want to subdivide Bee's lot. Or sell. Or build a freaking McMansion on it!"

"I'm not subdividing Bee's lot. Or selling. I already told you that."

"Why should I believe you?"

"Why shouldn't you? And this morning your expression said everything, so I figured I'd save that guy from getting punched in the nuts—although I'm kind of regretting that I didn't do it myself, since he seems to think you're interested in getting on your back for him. Or your knees."

"Excuse me?"

"Those were his words, not mine."

Her lip curls. "Tucker is a delusional jackass. I would do neither of those things, even if he was the last man on earth."

At least I was right about that.

The horn blares in Dillion's truck, and she fires the bird at the window behind her. "Just a second, Billy!" She blows out a breath. "Think you'd mind giving me some room to get into my truck?"

I roll the window down the rest of the way and poke my head out. I'm so close to her I can smell her shampoo. Her breath breaks across my cheek. It smells like cherry candy.

I meet her somewhat annoyed gaze. "Guess I'm kinda close, huh?"

"Kinda? There's no way you could get out of the passenger side without hitting my truck!"

"I could probably manage."

She rolls her eyes. "Yeah, right."

I'm having way too much fun with her, so I make a move to open the door.

"What're you doing? You're going to crush me!"

"Well, move out of the way and I won't."

"You're impossible!"

"And you're like one of those little windup toys, bouncing around all pissed off."

"I am not!" She tries to cross her arms, but there isn't enough room between her and the truck.

I grin, and she frowns, brows furrowing. "Oh my God. Are you doing this on purpose? Was this intentional?" She motions to the lack of space between our vehicles, mouth agape.

My smile widens. "Why would I do that?"

She snaps her mouth shut and points a finger at me. "You're infuriating."

"I know. And you're fun to rile up." I waggle my brows at her.

"I can't even." She turns around between the trucks, though it isn't easy.

"You're welcome for saving you from Tucker the Fucker."

"I didn't need saving." She opens her door and shimmies into the driver's seat.

"Kinda seemed like you did."

She slams the door closed and turns the engine over. The window whirs down as she puts the truck in gear. "I can hold my own with Tucker."

"You're still welcome. Maybe I'll see you later tonight. I'm planning to take a shower around eight thirty, in case you wanted to schedule your home invasion accordingly!" I shout as she drives away.

Her hand appears, the middle finger aimed at me, as she pulls out of the parking lot and back onto the road.

I don't bother rolling the window up or locking the truck. No one is going to try to steal this hunk of junk.

I'm in a much better mood as I head into the lawyer's office. I'm a couple of minutes late, thanks to my conversation with Dillion, but no one seems to care if you're on time around here. Appointment times appear to be a suggestion more than anything.

Bernie is an older man who looks to be in his late sixties, possibly early seventies. He's missing most of his hair, wears bifocals, and has huge eyebrows that remind me of caterpillars. His desk is organized chaos, stacks of manila folders arranged around it. A twelve-inch space is carved out in the middle, almost like a door or a window, so I can see him. It would annoy the crap out of me to work like that.

He plunks himself down in his faded leather chair. The arms are so worn that the leather has split and the foam padding peeks through. "I think I remember you from when you used to come visit Bee in the summers. Or was that your brother?"

"My brother never really came—maybe only for a few weeks when we were younger." He would have spent the entire summer lounging by the pool at our house in Chicago if that had been an option, but it wasn't. Bradley has always been driven by the almighty dollar, and he couldn't stand the clutter at Grammy Bee's, or her eccentricities. He also isn't a fan of bugs. Or manual labor. There was a lot of both when we visited. Grammy Bee never let me sit on my ass and do nothing all summer.

"Ah, yes. Now I remember. You stayed the whole summer up until college. Right?"

"That's right."

"Well, I hope you've changed your mind and decided not to sell the property. When you're able, anyway. Besides, getting town approval on subdividing isn't likely to happen."

I frown. I have to wonder if Dillion said something to him. "I'm not planning to sell, or subdivide. Can I ask where you heard that?"

His bushy brows pull together. "Um, from you? We spoke on the phone once, right after Bee's death."

"No, we didn't." Is there something in the water in this town?

Bernie looks confused but pushes on. "Sometimes people get forgetful after someone passes away. It's not uncommon. You asked me how much land there was and what the value was. You also wanted to know whether you could parcel off the land to sell, or if it would be worth more to put a single-family dwelling up."

"I would definitely remember that conversation. Which we didn't have. And I'm not planning to sell." I could never do that to Grammy.

He folds his hands on his desk and smiles patiently. "Hmm. Well, is it possible someone else might have called on your behalf? Maybe your family lawyer?"

"Maybe?" It's possible my dad's lawyer called. Another thought I don't like. Especially with everything else that's going on right now.

"Ah, well, it's good to hear you're staying. Let's review everything, shall we?"

We go through the details of the will, which are straightforward. My sister and brother both received checks for $50,000 each, the value of one-third of the standing cottage. At least at the time the will was written. Things have changed in the past couple of decades, with all the renovated mansion-style cottages on the other side of the lake. Regardless, I've inherited everything else, which consists of the property and all its contents. A small amount is left in the bank, but most of it was cleared out by the checks to my brother and sister. By the end of the meeting, I've signed everything I need to get it all transferred into my name.

On my way back through town, I decide to stop at the bar. I miss socializing and friends. So far the only people I've spoken much to are cashiers and Dillion. Although Frankie and Chip have both reached out, it's not the same as hitting the bar or the golf course. I'm not even particularly good at golf. I just play because my friends do.

I scan the bar, take one of the empty seats near the end of the row, and order a glass of their best whiskey—which is pretty cheap shit. It tastes like lighter fluid and smells about the same.

Two women who are most definitely locals take the seats to the right of me. I know they're local because they're fresh faced and natural looking, not overpolished like most of the women in Chicago. Like they've already added the Snapchat filter so they're always social media–post ready. These ladies look low maintenance.

Also, they order beer.

Usually the women at the bars Frankie and I used to frequent would drink martinis or wine.

I raise my glass. "Evening, ladies."

They arch their eyebrows in sync and look around the bar. It's full of townies. "You should probably head next door if you're looking for a good time, buddy," the one closest to me says.

"My good time is right here." I tap my glass.

The two women start talking to each other, mostly ignoring me but giving me the occasional side-eye. The TV above the bar is set to a dirt bike competition, so I focus on that while I eavesdrop.

"Tommy said he took the mailbox right out, and you know that was a steel post anchored in, like, six feet of concrete," Woman One says.

"Do you think that's why Darlin' came back? Because of the accident?" Woman Two asks.

"Who knows? But Sue is fair well losin' her damn mind over it, thinking she's gonna try 'n' steal her man."

Woman Two rolls her eyes. "That man can't keep his pants zipped to save his life. I heard Sue's only staying with him because of the baby, and she doesn't want to have to move back in with her parents or get government assistance."

"Excuse me." My mouth works before my brain does.

Both women turn to look at me.

"I don't mean to eavesdrop, but would you two happen to know a woman named Dillion?"

Woman One's eyes narrow. "What's it to ya?"

"I'm her neighbor."

That gets me some more raised eyebrows. "You have a place on the south side?"

"My grammy did. Grandma, I mean. Bee Firestone."

"You're Bee Firestone's grandson?" Woman One seems to be the talker of the two. This gets me another head-to-waist visual inspection.

"Yeah. She gave me the cottage. So I'm living there now. Next door to Dillion. Who everyone apparently calls Darlin' for whatever reason. There isn't even an *r* in Dillion, so I don't get how that even happens."

Woman Two laughs, big and loud.

"Why is that funny?"

They look at each other. "Because Dillion is nobody's darling."

"And that's funny?"

"Look, I wouldn't expect you to understand. Dillion was always determined to get her ass out of here, and she did. Worked hard to do it too," Woman One says, slightly defensively.

"When you come from a place like this, you can try to fly all you want, but your roots always bring you back," Woman Two says.

They clink their glasses and take another drink.

"Right. Of course." But I don't really get what they mean, because I've never lived here. Sure, I'm happy to be back, in part because it reminds me of good times and Grammy Bee, but also because it means escaping Chicago and all the crap that's currently going down as a result of the missing money.

I don't know what it's like to come from a small town. I only know what it's like to visit one. But I guess I'm learning, because here I am, sitting in the local bar, not fitting in because I'm from the city, when really, the only place I've ever felt comfortable is where I am right now. Not the bar, but Grammy Bee's.

I keep sipping my drink, listening to the two women whisper-gossip about everyone in town. Apparently Tucker the Fucker has earned that title. It's amazing how much everyone is up in everyone else's business.

"Oh hell." Woman One nudges Woman Two. "Speak of the devil."

I follow their gaze across the bar. Leaning against the wall near the pool tables is Dillion's brother.

"Has he lost weight? He looks thinner, doesn't he?" Woman Two observes.

"Mmm. He was always lean, like a runner, but I don't know—he's not looking good these days."

"Too bad, really. He's a good-looking guy, but a real mess."

"Didn't Sadie McAlister go out with him for a while?"

"That's right. I heard he got her pregnant, but she miscarried."

"He's had a rough go of things, eh? Makes you wonder if some of his sister's shine is eventually going to rub off on him one of these days. Lord knows he could use it."

They sigh and sip their beers.

I sit there for a while, listening as their conversation veers away from Dillion's brother. I can't imagine how hard it must be, living in a place where everyone knows about the mistakes you've made. It would make it impossible to live things down, or hide who you are. I watch

Billy pound beer after beer. It's not my place to intervene, especially since he doesn't even know me.

A guy with a full-sleeved tattoo takes the seat beside mine—it's the only empty one left—and the bartender nods to him. "The usual, Aaron?"

"You got it." He pulls his wallet out of his back pocket, sets it on the bar in front of him, and then turns to give me a nod. "You're new around here, yeah?"

"That obvious, huh?"

He cracks a smile. "Everyone knows everyone. You're familiar but not known, if you know what I mean." He holds out his hand. "Aaron Saunders. I'm a local."

"Van Firestone. I'm staying at Bee Firestone's place."

His grin widens. "You're the grandson. The one she left the cottage to."

If I was in Chicago, this conversation would be unnerving, but I'm finally figuring out small-town life. People knowing things about you is not weird here. "Uh, yup. That's me."

"You're driving my friend Dillion up the wall these days."

"You're friends with Dillion?" I want to ask what kind of friend, but I bite back the question.

"I work with her, for her dad's construction company." He flips open his wallet and pulls out a ten-dollar bill. "She seems to think you're working on Bee's place for no reason, since you plan to sell. Or build or whatever. Gotta say, not much rattles Dee, but you sure seem to."

"A lot of people think I'm planning to do a lot of things with Bee's place, none of them accurate." I kind of like the fact that I get under her skin enough that she's talked to this guy about me.

The bartender returns with Aaron's drink. At first I think it's a Guinness with an excessive amount of head. But I realize it's ice cream floating in a glass of root beer. Aaron tips his head in the direction of Dillion's brother. "Can you do me a favor and pour me a pint of the near-beer stuff for Billy? I don't think he needs to drink any more, judging from the state of him."

"You got it. I was getting ready to cut him off, but the poor guy has had it rough. Don't want to bruise the ego if I don't have to."

"Thanks." The bartender takes the money and returns a minute later with a pint that Aaron delivers to Billy. He sits with him for a few minutes but then gets called to the nearby pool tables.

Aaron motions me over, and I join him and his buddies for a round of pool that turns into several hours.

Eventually, the lights come up, signaling it's time to go home, which is when I notice that Billy is slumped over in his chair on the other side of the bar.

Aaron gives his shoulder a shake, trying to rouse him. Billy is slurring and mostly incoherent. I slide off my stool and head their way. "You want some help?"

Aaron runs a hand through his hair. "All I have is my bike, and he's not with it enough to catch a ride on the back. I don't want to call Dee this time of night."

"I live right next door. I'll take him home."

"You're sure about that? It'd be a real big favor; might even put you on Dee's good side, which is always a nice place to be."

I laugh. "I kinda like her bad side."

"I'm sure you do. She's all fire, that one."

It takes Aaron and me both to get Billy out of the bar and into the truck. He might be a lean dude, but he sure is heavy. He's mostly passed out the entire ride home, head lolling back and forth, bumping off the passenger window every time we hit a pothole, which is often.

I pull into my neighbor's driveway just after twelve thirty. The house is dark, which isn't a surprise, considering it's the middle of the week.

I poke Billy's shoulder. "Hey, man, you're home."

He rouses and blinks a few times. "Huh?"

I point to the house. "You're home. Time to sleep off the beer in your bed."

"Oh. Yeah, right. Time's it?" He slurs the words and fumbles with his seat belt.

"After midnight. Need a hand?"

"I got it," he mutters, but he continues to struggle to hit the release button.

I don't think he's going to have much luck getting out of the truck and into the house without assistance, so I unbuckle my own seat belt and hop out. I grab his crutches from the bed and round the passenger side. By the time I open the door, he's managed the epic feat of unbuckling his seat belt.

I'm in the middle of trying to figure out how I'm going to get his drunk ass out of the truck and to the front door without throwing him over my shoulder when I hear the sound of a screen door slamming shut.

"What the heck is going on out here?" Dillion's hand is raised in front of her face to shield her eyes from the glare of my headlights, which are pointed directly at her trailer.

Her hair is a chaotic blonde halo. She's wearing a pair of barely there sleep shorts and a tank that, thanks to the headlights, is basically see through. Her nipples are peaked against the white fabric, and my stupid eyeballs home right in on them.

And because I'm fixated on her and her outfit, I'm not paying attention to Billy, who's decided he doesn't need my help getting out of the truck. He knocks into me with an oof, and I barely manage to stay upright while Billy sprawls across the driveway.

"Oh my God! Is that Billy? What did you do to him?" Dillion's flip-flops slap angrily against the gravel drive.

"I didn't do anything to him." I prop the crutches against the side of the truck and crouch so I can help him up. He's sloppy and heavy, and I'm starting to regret driving him home.

"Billy, are you drunk?"

"I had a few beers, chill out, Dil," Billy mumble-slurs. "Chill, dill. That rhymes." He barks out a laugh and then proceeds to vomit, barely missing my feet.

"You got my brother drunk? What is wrong with you?"

I pin her with a look. Her attitude is getting tiring. It might have been fun to poke at her and get a rise, but I can only take so many accusations. I have enough of those to deal with without her stupid ones. "You have an awful way of saying thank you. I didn't get him drunk. I found him like this and wanted to save you and your family the trouble of coming to pick him up at the bar."

Her hands drop from her hips, and her anger deflates like a popped balloon. "Oh. I didn't even know he'd gone out."

"Apparently he did. You're welcome for making sure he got home safely." I round the front of the truck and hop back in, ignoring Dillion when she calls my name. I don't have the patience left not to be the jerk she assumes me to be tonight.

CHAPTER 10
NOT WINNING ANY POINTS HERE

Van

I don't see Dillion for the rest of the week, but she does leave me a twelve-pack of beer and a thank-you note for bringing Billy home from the bar. I'm still irritated with her, but I appreciate the beer delivery.

I spend time emptying out the rest of the garage so I can get started converting it into a livable space based on the preliminary building plans I sketched out. It's something I'm actually excited about and keeps my mind off what's happening in Chicago.

Normally I develop structural plans and leave the building to someone else. But since I'm out of a job and every call I've made so far has come to a dead end on the employment front, contracting out the work would be a frivolous expense I can't afford. Which means I'm going to do the work myself.

On Friday morning I get a call from Frankie to let me know that they're coming to Pearl Lake and to make sure I'm well stocked on the booze front. He seems pretty damn excited about the party bus he rented, and I'm grateful that I don't have to get the spare bedrooms ready for him and Chip. Especially since one of them would have to sleep in my grandmother's bed. I've avoided going in there, apart from a couple of times since I arrived. It's not that I think it's haunted or whatever, but I'm not ready to face packing away her things. Her bedroom remains a shrine to her and my grandfather and all the years they spent together here.

While this place is full of memories, it's also full of crap, and spiders, and an overwhelming amount of patterned wallpaper. It's nothing like the pristine condo in the city that I left behind.

As much as I miss my job and the bustle of Chicago, there's something to be said for the peacefulness of living here. Of not falling into the trap of feeling like I need the newest car or the nicest clothes, or the compulsion to keep climbing the social and financial ladders so I can be the best and have the most. Looking back, I don't even know why I cared about all that. I haven't even driven my BMW since getting here, preferring Bee's truck instead.

It bugs me that I give a shit about what my friends will think of this place. That they might feel sorry for me because I lost my six-figure-a-year salary. My dad has always been the kind of guy who thrives on appearances. Part of it was to mask the damage losing our mother did to him, a way to look like he had it together when he was falling apart. Buying things was a Band-Aid for the partner he lost.

At six in the evening Frankie pulls down my driveway in the most ridiculously ostentatious RV I've ever seen. It's a garish metallic purple with the words **PARTY BUS** scrawled across the side in gold letters. It looks like something a band would drive across the country.

He nearly clips the truck, which might be old and not in the best shape, but it was one of my grandfather's and Grammy Bee's favorite possessions. She taught me how to drive in that truck when I was fourteen years old, so it holds a lot of memories. The kind that aren't replaceable.

Frankie parks the RV in front of the garage, turns off the engine, and climbs out. "The party has arrived! I hope your liver is ready for a workout this weekend!" He pulls me in for a hug and a backslap. "I'm sorry, dude—Chip's balls are in her pocket."

"Huh?"

Chip appears, his face screwed up in a grimace as he turns around and holds out his hand, answering my question without saying a word. Monica, his girlfriend, apparently decided to crash the party.

I arch a brow at Frankie. "What happened to the boys' weekend?"

"It was the only way he was allowed to come," he mutters.

She adjusts the brim of her oversize hat and attempts to strut across the driveway. It's gravel and dirt, though, so her heels keep sinking, making her strut a challenge. "Wow." She pushes her sunglasses up her nose. "This place is—"

"Rustic and awesome," Chip supplies, and I'm unsure if he did it purposefully to cut off anything rude she might say or if he genuinely feels that way.

"I was going to say *condemnable*, but I suppose *rustic* works." She air-kisses my cheeks. "I'm so sorry you're stuck here, Van. I can't imagine how awful it must be for you."

"I'm surviving." Monica is a socialite and very used to five-star everything. The party bus is her idea of roughing it. "Did you steal this thing from an eighties hair band?" I motion to the RV.

"Isn't it awesome?" Frankie pats the side of it.

"It's something, that's for sure."

The guys are totally into the whole "camping" situation. Honestly, the RV is probably as big as my cottage and is outfitted with two bedrooms, a full kitchen, and a deluxe bathroom. It means they don't have to come inside the cottage, which is good, since the only thing I've done in there is sleep and burn grilled cheese sandwiches.

At first it seems like things are going to be okay. At least until we sit by the campfire. Monica keeps making people switch chairs with her, depending on what direction the wind is blowing. She also can't understand why she's being eaten alive, and the drunker she gets, the louder she becomes.

"Ah! Why won't these things leave me alone?" Monica slaps the side of her neck for what has to be the millionth time this evening.

"Because you're delicious, babe." Chip nuzzles through her mass of hair to bite her neck.

"Chip!" She swats him, but she's giggling. Loudly.

I glance over my shoulder. It's late, but it's a Friday, so I'm hoping the noise isn't a problem for my surly neighbor.

"Dude, I might be crashing in the cottage tonight if these two keep it up," Frankie mutters.

"Just keep drinking, and I'm sure it'll be fine."

Frankie makes a noise in the back of his throat but chugs the rest of his rum and Coke.

This whole drunk-affection gigglefest is Chip and Monica's version of foreplay. Often the giggles turn into irritation when Chip gets too sauced, and they end up fighting. Which then turns into angry-loud makeup sex. We know this to be the case because we've dealt with it before. Not the actual act, but the soundtrack is impossible to tune out, because Monica has never been known for her quietness.

The giggle turns into another shriek, and Monica's back to slapping her legs.

I did offer her bug spray, which she said no to because she didn't want to put those kinds of chemicals on her skin.

Her volume increases with each martini she consumes, despite my requests to keep it down.

So I should not be surprised when my neighbor appears at the edge of the trees and scares the living crap out of Monica. Her chair tips over, and she loses her hold on her martini glass. Thankfully it's made of plastic.

"Ahh! What the hell! I'm covered in vodka and olive juice and dirt! Chip! Help me up! There are bugs everywhere!" She grabs on to Chip's arm and tries to scramble to her feet. I should mention that she's wearing white jean shorts. At a campfire. In the woods.

Dillion, on the other hand, has clearly come from bed. Her hair, which is usually pulled up in a ponytail, is down, the curls framing her face and making her look like an angry angel. She's wearing a pair of flip-flops, gray shorts that show off her toned legs, and a thin, worn tank that reads BEDHEAD IS MY NATURAL LOOK across her chest. As usual, it's white, which means the glow of the fire highlights her pert nipples and the fact that she's definitely not wearing a bra, just like the last time she chewed me out, for keeping her awake with my hammering.

Her eyebrows pop at the spectacle that is Monica, and she quickly shifts her attention to me. She props a fist on her hip. It seems to be her go-to move. "I get that it's Friday night, and you're reliving your frat party days or whatever, but you're literally twenty feet away from my bedroom. It's two freaking a.m., and unlike the rest of you, I have to work in the morning. Do you think you can wrap this up for the night or at least tone it down and cut the rave music?" She motions to the portable speaker, which is blasting Monica's favorite club playlist.

Monica, who has completely lost her filter, scoffs and wipes away fake tears. "Aww. Does your shift at the gas station start early on the weekend?"

Oh shit.

Dillion's lip curls, and she slowly turns away from me so she can angry glare at Monica. "Ex-freaking-cuse me?"

Monica's lip turns up in a sneer, and I glance at Chip, who tugs on her arm and mutters, "Babe." But she doesn't heed the warning.

She waves Dillion off and slurs, "Tell the trailer trash to stop being such a party pooper."

"Whoa, whoa, that's not cool, Monica." I push out of my chair and take a step toward Dillion, who looks mighty unimpressed, and for good reason. I look to Chip and Frankie to help me out here, but they don't seem to know what to do. We're used to Monica's antics, but I don't think we've ever heard her be so offensive to someone else.

There might not be much to Dillion's frame, but she seems like she has the ability to get scrappy, and while Monica is forever at the gym burning calories, I don't think she'd stand a chance against my neighbor. As much as Monica might deserve to get her ass handed to her for those comments, the lawsuit that could come out of that would not be in Dillion's favor. It will also create more tension between us rather than less, and since I'm living next to her for the foreseeable future, I'd like to avoid pissing her off because my friend's girlfriend is a jerk.

"Well, it's true, isn't it? She lives in that trailer, doesn't she?" Monica flings a drunken hand in Dillion's direction.

"Wow, stereotype much?" Dillion gives me another unimpressed look. "You've got some classy friends, Van."

I move to stand in front of Dillion, in part to act as a barrier between her and Monica, so she doesn't end up clawing her eyes out. "I'm so sorry. She's had way too many martinis and doesn't even know what she's saying. I didn't realize how late it was, or that we were being that loud. We'll take it inside."

"Great. Thanks." Her tone is flat.

The last time I saw her, I was the one irritated with her, but after the garbage Monica just spewed, it's my turn to apologize. "I'm really sorry, Dillion."

"Sure you are."

She turns to head back to her place, and Monica mutters something under her breath that I don't catch, but I'm pretty sure *stupid bitch* was in there.

Chip hisses her name, and Dillion spins around. "*I'm* stupid? You're the idiot who's been sitting out here moaning about being eaten alive. You're wearing enough perfume to give someone an asthma attack. I can smell it from here. Do everyone a favor and use the bug spray so we aren't subjected to your noise pollution." And with that she whirls around and stomps back through the trees, flip-flops slapping angrily at the ground.

I sort of want to follow her so I can apologize some more and also so I don't have to deal with Monica, who is now ranting about how bug spray causes cancer and her skin is too sensitive.

Chip takes her back to the RV, but even behind closed doors we can hear the bickering.

"I'm sorry, man. We didn't mean to get you in shit with your neighbor," Frankie says. "I can't believe Monica said that. She's always been annoying, but never cruel. Next time we'll leave her at home. Who knows? Maybe this will finally put Chip over the edge and he'll break up with her."

"We can hope."

They end up leaving first thing in the morning, mostly because Monica is mortified and hungover. Normally I'd let something like this roll off me, but in this case I don't like that one of the people in my close-friend group could treat someone they don't even know with so little respect. So I can't say I'm all that heartbroken about the fact that they don't stick around. I don't need more problems than I already have. Especially not with my neighbor.

CHAPTER 11
BEACH PARTY

Dillion

"You think you can give me a ride to the beach tonight?" Billy asks no one in particular as he shovels another mouthful of hash brown casserole into his mouth. His face is about three inches from his plate. He reminds me of a cartoon character with his mouth wide open and a conveyor belt dumping food down the hatch.

"I can drive you," I offer.

Billy frowns. "You hate the beach parties."

He's right. I generally avoided them when I was a teenager, and the few times I did go, I ended up regretting it. There was the time Tucker had initiated one of our many breaks and ended up hooking up with one of the summer girls from the other side of the lake right in front of me. I'd retaliated by kissing some random dude in a game of truth or dare.

Was it stupid? Yup. Did I regret it? Yes and no. I made my point, and Tucker, being the idiot he was, immediately called an end to our break. Not because he'd seen the error of his ways, but because he couldn't stand the thought of me with anyone else.

To this day I wonder about that boy. Did I ever pass him on the street in town without realizing it? Had I imagined the energy that had zinged through my veins and lit me up from the inside? That kiss had sparked a fire in me, one that had been stoked and snuffed almost as quickly.

Or maybe I'd been drunk, and it wasn't as magical as I remembered it to be. I don't even know his name. Or even what he looked like from the nose down, since he'd been wearing a ball cap, and all I could make out was his mouth. Beach parties on this side of the lake are always a drunk fest, lots of hookups and general stupidity, which I'm still not a fan of—see what happened last night with Van and his friends for details. That whole fiasco reminded me of those parties back when I was a teenage girl, looking for a way out. And I have a particularly sore spot over Van's friend's shitty comment. I hate that I've once again become the small-town stereotype I've tried to escape my entire life.

I'm willing to set aside my disdain for beach parties, however, because as much as I dislike them, I also don't like the idea of Billy being there with no one to watch out for him apart from his drunk and disorderly friends, who have already proven they can't be trusted to take care of him. That much was clear when Van brought him back from the bar, drunker than a frat boy on frosh week. Last night was the first time I'd seen Van since then, and I still felt bad for assuming he'd had a hand in Billy being drunk, despite his shitty friends.

Even Tawny suggested I come, and I haven't had a chance to get together with her and Allie yet, so this seems like as good an opportunity as any to make that happen.

I shrug. "If I'm not having fun, I won't stay."

An hour later I'm dressed in a pair of jeans and a T-shirt. I bring a zip-up hoodie, just in case. It's closing in on eight, and the sun is heading toward the horizon, kissing the tops of trees far off in the distance. Sometimes the breeze coming off the water can cool things down in the evening this early in the summer. It isn't until mid-July that we get the truly hot and humid nights. Besides, it's black fly season, and I don't want to get eaten alive.

I even put on makeup, not because I think I need to impress anyone, but if I'm going to see all the people I went to high school with, I don't want to look like a hag. I check my hair one last time, add some scent-free product to keep the curls from frizzing, and grab my purse, tossing a bottle of water in there so I can stay hydrated.

Billy's already waiting for me on the porch, six-pack of beer at his feet, an open one in his hand. I'm almost certain he's done with his antibiotics, since the infection has cleared up. I refrain from asking, though, not wanting to push his buttons. He's in his midtwenties, and a lot of the guys I used to hang out with when I was his age could pound a twelve-pack without batting an eyelash.

He drains the rest of his beer, tosses the can in the recycling bin, and pushes out of the chair. He hops once, regains his balance, and reaches for his crutches propped against the screen next to his chair.

"You forgetting something?" I point to the six-pack.

He looks down. "Shit. Yeah." He tries to bend over to pick it up with his crutches still tucked under his arms, which proves fruitless.

"I got it." I nab them and head for Billy's truck—the one he didn't plow into a mailbox—with him crutching after me. This one he restored back in high school. It's a 1980s Ford F-150 that's in decent shape. A few dings in the fender and the tailgate, but otherwise it looks great and drives smoothly.

I drop the six-pack in the bed and get in, not bothering to ask if Billy needs help, since I'm aware he'll most definitely not want mine.

"You gonna lecture me about drinking responsibly tonight?" he asks when we're on the road, heading toward the beach.

"I wasn't planning on it, since this is a beach party and I kind of figured the point is being irresponsible."

He makes a noise in the back of his throat.

"Spit it out, Billy, say what you want to say."

"I don't need you to keep an eye on me. I'll be fine with my friends."

I sigh. I don't want to fight with Billy. Ever since I've been home, that's all we do, but his friends are part of the problem. He was with them the night he got that DUI, and they didn't stop him from getting behind the wheel. Although I don't have the full story, only the version my dad has given me. "These same friends who left you at the bar the other night?"

"Dean's sister was picking him up, and I wanted to finish my beer."

"Right." That's why he was having a nap in one of the booths. I heard from Aaron that all the guys he'd come with had bailed, and no one aside from him and Van had done anything about it. I don't bother to get into it with him, though, because I don't want to set him off. "I'm not going to keep an eye on you. Tawny and Allie invited me."

"Oh."

"Yeah. Oh. Look, I'm not trying to be overprotective, or a buzzkill; I just want you to be safe. You could've been hurt far worse than you are. You're my only brother. You can't fault me for wanting to keep you around."

"If you care so much, why haven't you been home for more than a couple of days at a time since you went away for college?" There's bite in his tone, but under that I can hear the hurt.

I tap the steering wheel, considering this. My leaving town had nothing to do with getting away from my family. It was the whole living in a small town, everyone knowing everything about me, all the relationship drama that people couldn't help but get involved in; that was the reason I wanted out. "I don't have a good answer for that, Billy. I'm here now, though, so maybe we can have a do-over? I'll try to be more like a sister and less like another overbearing parent, and you can try to be less surly?"

He runs his hands down his thighs. "Yeah, I'll work on being less of an asshole. Being cooped up all day in the house kinda sucks. And honestly, it kind of freaked me out having you back home. Dad's always been so proud of you, going to college, moving to the city, getting a degree and a great job. Always talking about you to his friends with so much pride. And then there's me."

Billy started working for my dad right out of high school. In fact, he was already working for him in the summers as soon as he was old enough, and after school and on weekends during the busy season. They've always been tight, so hearing my brother talk about himself as though he's less because he didn't go to college isn't something I expect. "You and dad are so close, though. You've been working together forever."

He shrugs. "It made sense to work for Dad. I'm good at following orders and working with my hands, but only if the end result is money in my pocket. You're good at everything. I've always been the trouble, and you've always been the golden child. It's just how it is."

"I got up to just as much mischief as you did. I just didn't get caught."

"Because you're smart enough not to. I'm obviously not."

It never occurred to me that Billy didn't go the college route because he wasn't capable. He had decent grades, not awesome, but then he spent as much time skipping classes as he did going to them. And I always assumed he did this because he was bored and preferred the hands-on stuff to the paperwork. "I'm good with a textbook, and you're good at all the things I'm not. Boys are always more impulsive than girls and more prone to finding trouble. Remember that time you and Tommy rigged up a zip line with a bike? That was insanity, and none of us tried to stop you either."

Billy laughs at the memory. "Tommy wasn't allowed out with us for a while after that."

"Well, he did break his collarbone. And honestly, it probably would have worked if someone who didn't weigh two hundred and fifty pounds had gone first."

"I purposely drew the short straw so it wouldn't be me."

"See? That's smart. Let someone else be the guinea pig so you're not the one breaking bones." I grin at my brother, who's smiling back at me.

This is better. More like how it used to be when we were younger. When things were less complicated and there weren't responsibilities to get in the way. I used to pick him up all the time after he'd been out with his friends, smoking weed they'd grown in the forest or drinking beers they'd stolen from someone's older brother. I covered for him all the time, but when I went to college, I couldn't do that anymore.

It was like taking the leash off a dog without teaching him not to run away. At least that's how it seems. I'd been so focused on getting out and away from Tucker and everything else in Pearl Lake that I hadn't considered how it affected Billy. Or how he might feel like he was part of the reason I'd left in the first place.

The beach parking lot is full by the time we get there. I drop Billy off at the path and drive a block west before parking the truck in an old brush- and weed-filled turnaround. There's an overgrown path that forks off at the edge of the small clearing. The right side will take me to the beach, while the other one twists and turns and forks again, eventually leading to a tiny abandoned hunting cabin I found when I was a teenager and then used as my thinking spot. I never told anyone about it, mostly because I didn't want the guys to ransack it.

I check my reflection in the rearview mirror and consider putting on some lip gloss, but I decide that would be a step too far in the "I care" direction. I shoulder my purse and check my messages, relieved to find one from Tawny letting me know that she and Allie are already at the beach, near the old docks.

I swallow down my nerves, worried about seeing Allie for the first time. Tawny has always been an easy-to-forgive kind of person, but I'm not sure Allie is going to let me off so easy. I shake off the apprehension and head down the path, the weeds soon giving way to soft sand.

There are two main beaches on Pearl Lake: one on the McMansion side, which is maintained by the town, and the townie beach, where all the parties are held. It's set on the southwest side of the lake, but the town doesn't have the funds to maintain it, so it's grassier and lined with old falling-apart docks. Mostly it's the townies who hang out here, but sometimes the kids from the other side will catch wind that a party's going on and will show up. When I was young, that often resulted in a lot of random hookups, broken hearts, and broken noses.

I pop out of the bushes at the far end of the beach. It's already dotted with people drinking out of red Solo cups. I haven't been here in years, and the beach has degraded in that time. It's sad, really, because with a little effort, some money, and community help, it could be a gorgeous place for families to picnic, not just a place for people to hang out and drink at night.

I glance up at the sky and see dark clouds rolling in. I didn't think it was supposed to rain tonight, but the weather here can change on a dime, and it's prime thunderstorm season. Besides, we could use the rain. I scan the beach, full of so many familiar faces. Almost all the people I went to high school with are here, older now, some already married with kids. I was one of the few people who left. I think Aaron was one of the only other people, and Tucker briefly, but look at us, all back again.

A pit opens in my stomach, those stupid nerves making me edgy. I have so many memories of this place, some good—most of them, actually—but a few bad ones seem to overshadow those, and they're all related to Tucker. Looking back, I realize he was such a waste of time, but if I'd broken up with him for good, I might have ended up with someone who would have made me want to stay here, and I needed a reason to leave. Tucker was a necessary evil.

A huge bonfire has been set in the middle of the beach, with half a birch tree laid across it. Sparks spit in the air, beautiful and dangerous. A large group of people has congregated there, so I avoid it and stay close to the shore.

It takes me a good half hour to find Tawny and Allie, mostly because I only make it about five feet before I'm stopped by people I know. Some fish for information about Billy, most are surprised to see me back, but I feel . . . welcomed. Almost comfortable with how everyone seems to greet me, as if I'd gone on an extended vacation and eventually decided to come home.

I finally make it over to Tawny, who as promised is by the old docks.

"I thought you got here half an hour ago?" Tawny says, handing me an insulated coffee mug.

"What's this?" I sniff the contents.

"Vodka and cran, light on the cran."

I take a sip and fight a cough. "You're not kidding. Where's Allie?"

"She's breaking the seal."

"Already? She'll be peeing every half hour."

Tawny lifts one shoulder in a shrug. "That's what I said, but you know what she's like. Tommy mentioned having to pee, and that was it: she couldn't hold it anymore."

I shake my head on a laugh. "Nothing ever changes, does it?"

"Not really. Except for the receding hairlines, beer bellies, and stretch marks, as far as I can tell."

The sun is disappearing, only a sliver of it visible through the thick layers of low-hanging clouds. "Looks like a storm might be rolling in."

"Yeah. The weather forecast is looking grim tonight, which is why we figured it was a good idea to come early. Besides, you know how it is. The underagers always show up around eleven, and then things get shut down because they're too loud and create a ruckus."

"We used to be those underagers," I point out.

She clinks her insulated mug against mine. "Weren't those the good old days?"

"They were. Except on those occasions when Tucker couldn't keep his dick out of whatever girl caught his eye that night."

Tawny makes a face. "Not much has changed there."

"Not much has changed about what?" Allie appears from out of nowhere and scares the crap out of both of us. She's stunning, all long

115

legs and dark hair, full lips, and a smile that lights up any room. But she's not smiling now. "Wow, you showed. Gotta say, I half expected you to stand us up like you've been doing for the past decade." Allie arches an eyebrow, and her pursed lips disappear behind her thermal mug as she takes a sip of her drink.

"Allie, come on." Tawny has always been the peacekeeper of the group. Maybe to a fault.

"It's okay." I hold up a hand. "Allie's right. I've been a crappy friend, and there isn't an excuse that's good enough to explain why I've dodged everyone I know for the past decade."

"Why dodge us at all, though? I don't get it. We were all so tight for so long, and then, poof." She snaps her fingers. "You were just . . . gone." Underneath the anger is hurt.

And I realize that hurt is one of the reasons I ghosted people for so long. I knew Tawny would let it go, but Allie has always been confrontational. Not one to back down from a fight, she lays it all out, and I never gave her a chance to do that, because then I would've had to come to terms with the fact that I was a bad friend.

"I was afraid of this," I admit, motioning between us.

"What is this, exactly?" Allie's eyes shift away, focusing on some point in the distance.

"Knowing that I hurt you both when I left and didn't come back. I wanted to start over, but I did miss you both so much."

"So why ghost us, then? That doesn't make sense."

"Not to you, but to me it did. I was afraid if I held on to the people who made this place bearable, then I'd never be able to stay away. I didn't want to get sucked back in. I didn't want to end up stuck here."

Allie huffs. "Is it really so bad here?"

"No. Yes. To eighteen-year-old me, it was. I needed to leave. And I felt like the only way to do that was to cut ties to this place. But looking back, I know it was wrong. And here I am, back in Pearl Lake."

"I thought it was something we'd done, or that you were embarrassed because we're too country and you became all citified."

"Oh my God, no, Allie. I missed the hell out of you two. It was everything else I was trying to get away from that was the problem. I'm sorry if I made you think it was you."

She pulls me in for a hug. "You're forgiven. As long as you don't ghost us for another decade again."

"I won't. I promise."

She releases me and steps back. This time her smile is real. "It's good to have you home, Dee. We missed having you around; the Terror Trifecta isn't as effective with just the two of us."

"It's really good to be here." And I genuinely mean it. The good outweighs the bad.

CHAPTER 12
CONNECTED DOTS

Dillion

The three of us sit on one of the big rocks near the water—they're as uncomfortable as I remember—observing the party from the sidelines, just like old times. Half hall monitor, half voyeur. I scan the beach, looking for my brother. I find him close to the campfire, laughing boisterously with a group of guys.

"How bad are the bathrooms?" Tawny asks.

"Bad." Allie grimaces. "I used the bushes. It blows my mind how gross girls can be when they're trying to hover pee. And they ran out of toilet paper already, so these will have to do." Allie pulls out a wad of napkins pilfered from the diner and passes us each a small handful, which we tuck into our purses.

"Fair warning: I saw Tucker hanging out by the keg on my way back over here."

"Is Sue with him?" Tawny asks.

Allie arches a brow. "What do you think?"

"She's probably stuck at home with the baby, while he goes out, gets wasted, and hits on whoever."

I make a disgusted sound. "Baby? I didn't know they had a baby." It makes what he said about me ending up under him that much worse.

Allie looks to Tawny. "How old is the baby now? Maybe a couple of months?"

"Good grief. What a dog. He hasn't changed, has he?"

"Nope. Just a heads-up that word got back to Sue that you were talking with him downtown, and that new guy who's living at Bee's showed up and they got into it."

"Of course." I roll my eyes. "I can't say I miss the small-town gossip. And Van didn't get into it with Tucker." At least not while I was there.

"Maybe they did after you left? Anyway, apparently Sue lost her shit over it, and Tucker had to sleep in his car that night," Tawny says with a sigh.

"Wow. Tucker's made a real mess of things, hasn't he?"

"I sort of feel bad for Sue. I mean, I know she always had her eye on him, even when the two of you were together and solid, but he's way worse now than he was when he was with you." Allie gives me a sympathetic look.

"I put up with more than I should have, and it sounds like she does too."

"At least you smartened up and got the heck out of Dodge when you had the chance. Made a clean break and all that," Tawny offers.

"As much as it sucked when you left, I'm glad it's not you in Sue's position. No one should be that miserable," Allie adds.

"Well, let's be real, she's probably not hanging out with the baby on her own." Tawny glances around before she leans in closer and drops her voice. "I heard she's been taking her car to the garage the next town over lately—Carter's Car Repairs. You remember that place, right? Run by old man Carter?"

Allie and I both nod and mm-hmm.

"Well, apparently his son took over. Used to be the star quarterback for our rival high school team. All golden hair and blue eyes and a seriously pretty face. You remember him, right? Sterling Carter?"

"He was the only reason I bothered with the pep rallies, since our team sucked the big one," Allie mutters.

"Right?" Tawny looks over her shoulder before she continues. "Well, there was a rumor floating around a few days ago that a tow truck was parked down the street from Sue's house that just happened to belong to the Carters. Now, I'm not saying it's true, but Sue and Sterling had a thing back in high school, and then when you left, she broke it off with him and tried to get with Tucker. They hooked up, but nothing came of it. Until two summers ago. They met up at one of these parties, hooked up again, and starting dating on and off. Nothing serious at first, but she kept pushing for more, and he finally asked her to move in with him. Then she got pregnant, had the baby, and now they're both miserable."

"I still don't get why she'd want to be with him in the first place, especially when she knew he'd been cheating on me." Other than the fact that she always seemed to want what I had.

"Who knows? Maybe she thought she could do what no one else could and make him be faithful to her? He was pretty broken up about it when you left, and she basically threw herself at him. I used to think maybe the cheating was because he knew you were leaving, you know? Maybe trying to prove to himself that he didn't need you. But it just seems to be how he is. It's pretty sad." Allie takes a sip of her drink and makes a face while she sloshes it around, maybe to mix it up some more.

"His parents had a shitty relationship, too, so poor modeling and all that," Tawny says. "I read an article about that. How our parents' relationships frame our own. Makes sense that what you see is what you emulate."

"Yeah, doesn't excuse the serial cheating, though. And we all have the ability to break the cycle if we want to. Anyway, I feel bad for Sue, but I'm glad he's not my problem anymore." I hold up my glass. "To putting the past behind us." We all clink our tumblers together, tip our heads back, and make a face on the swallow.

"Is it me, or is this getting stronger the more we drink?" I ask.

"I don't think it's mixed very well."

Simultaneously, we shake our glasses, the ice clinking against the stainless steel sides, and chuckle.

"It really is good to be back, though."

I kick at a pebble on the ground. It skips a few feet, heading toward a group of guys I used to go to high school with, one of whom is Aaron Saunders. That's not a surprise; he always loved a good beach party. It pings off another bigger rock and bounces up, hitting a guy with his back to us in the calf.

I cringe as he turns around and adjusts the brim of his hat. Most of the guy's face is in shadow, apart from his chin and mouth. A flash of memory from a decade ago pops like a bubble, gone before I can catch it. He flips his hat around so it's facing backward, and I realize it's Van. Hanging with the locals.

Tawny gives a low whistle. "Who the heck is that delicious hunk of yummy man?"

"That's Bee's grandson. He's my neighbor."

"Holy hotcakes on the griddle, he's ridiculously gorgeous."

"He is that. He's got some asshole friends, though. And he can be an asshole at times too." I say that through gritted teeth while smiling and waving at him.

He tips his head to the side, a slow half smile forming on his lips. His eyes roam over me in a leisurely sweep. He doesn't so much as glance at Tawny or Allie. He tips his chin up in acknowledgment and then turns back to his group.

"Ooooh, looks like someone has a thing for his neighbor." Allie elbows me in the side.

I roll my eyes. "He doesn't have a thing for me. We can barely have a conversation without arguing." And he seems to enjoy pushing my buttons.

"Then why is he headed this way?"

"Huh?" I glance back in his direction to find that he is most certainly headed toward us.

"Crap," I mutter. I resist the urge to touch my hair or do any of the typical things women do when a ridiculously attractive man is approaching. It annoys me to no end that I react like this to Van. I don't even really know him, and what I do know, I'm still on the fence about, especially after last night.

"Howdy, neighbor, I didn't expect to see you here tonight." He tucks a thumb in his pocket and smiles, gaze still firmly fixed on me.

"It's a local party and I'm a local; not sure why I wouldn't be here." Clearly I'm dishing out my surly tonight.

Allie coughs into her elbow, and Tawny sucks her teeth, probably trying not to laugh.

Van's smile turns into a smirk. "You planning to police the noise and music choices?"

I don't return the smile. "There don't seem to be any screaming banshees around, calling people trailer trash, so it looks like I'm off duty tonight."

He sobers. "I'm sorry about that. Monica was way out of line."

"Nothing I haven't heard before." Which is true. It's not the first time that term has been directed at me. Although usually I'm not practically in my own backyard, nor is that negative slur coming from my neighbor. It frustrates me that a place that used to be a haven of fond memories is turning into something else.

"That doesn't make it better. She was horrified this morning, and hungover. Spent most of last night puking."

"Is that why she isn't gracing us with her presence tonight?"

"They took off early this morning. She wanted to go over and apologize, but it was early, and she was a hot mess. Besides, Monica is probably the shittiest apologizer in the history of the universe, so I figured it was better if she left the apologizing to me."

I shake my head and fight a chuckle. "If you invite her back and she insults me again, I'll probably toss her in the lake."

"I have zero plans to invite her back. But I would pay money to see that." He rocks back on his heels and glances to the right of me, where Allie and Tawny are raptly watching this interaction. "Oh, how rude of me." He holds out his hand to Tawny first. "I'm Van, Dillion's neighbor."

"I'm Tawny and this is Allie." She motions to her with her cup. "We've been friends with Dee ever since we could put two words together."

"That's a long time and some real devotion to the art of communication and friendship." He nods a couple of times. "Anyway, I thought I'd come say hi. And apologize."

"I think we're probably even with apologies at this point."

"Does this mean we're calling a truce?"

"As long as you're not hammering away on something before seven tomorrow morning and your friends aren't calling me names, I think we're good. And I won't accuse you of getting my brother wasted."

He holds out his hand, and I slip mine into his. The air around us suddenly feels charged, like the shock of a lightning bolt cutting through the sky.

Shouts and laughter draw my attention away from my suddenly charismatic attractive neighbor, and I release his hand, a shiver rushing down my spine despite the heat. I frown as I take in the scene unfolding next to the campfire. "Oh, for the love of Pete." The end of my brother's crutch is smoking. He stabs the bottom in the sand and stumbles forward, perilously close to the edge of the fire.

"Billy!" I call his name, but he either can't hear me over the shouts and laughter or he's ignoring me. "Hold this." I pass Tawny my drink and stalk across the beach toward my brother. He loses his balance but thankfully ends up on his ass in the sand, howling with laughter.

People move out of the way as I approach and come to a halt right beside him lying in a heap on the beach. I sincerely hope there are sand fleas crawling around in his boxers. "What're you doing?"

"Having fun! What are *you* doing?" He points the slightly charred end of his crutch at me, and I lift my arm, using it as a shield to keep the crutch from smacking me in the face.

"Dude. You're going to burn someone doing that, and if it's me I will one hundred percent be taking my old bedroom back and I'll be punching you in the nuts."

"You need to loosen up, Dee. You're more high strung than a guitar." He bursts into overly loud laughter.

I roll my eyes and point to Tommy Westover, who's standing off to the side with his thumbs jammed in his pockets, fighting a grin. "It's on you to keep him out of trouble tonight."

He shrugs. "I'll do my best."

When I get back to Tawny and Allie, Van is no longer with them and his friend group has moved on.

"Like hell he doesn't have the hots for you. He couldn't take his eyes off of you, and you were the same."

"I recognize he's nice to look at, that's all."

Tawny gives me a look. "Seriously? He lives right next door to you. How are you not taking advantage of that situation?"

"I don't even like him."

"You don't have to like him to ride him."

"What if he's a terrible lay and I'm stuck living next door to him until he finally decides to sell?"

Allie arches a brow. "The more important question is, what if he's *not?*"

CHAPTER 13
THE HUNTING CABIN

Dillion

An hour later I have to break the seal. Allie was not wrong about the state of the bathrooms, so I follow her lead and prop myself up against a tree. This is about the only time I wish I had a penis instead of a vagina.

I'm on my way back to Tawny and Allie when a flash of lightning brightens the beach and the sky opens up. It's like that here sometimes. One minute it's calm and balmy, the next you're in the middle of a torrential downpour.

In under a minute the campfire, which was raging, becomes embers, a plume swirling up to caress the sky with smoky fingers, leaving the beach murky and dark. The other side of the lake is dotted with lights, some brightening the fronts of the massive homes, their windows irisless eyes.

People run in every direction, seeking refuge from the deluge coming from the sky. I can't see more than a few feet in front of me. Which is how I wind up running right into a huge, hard body.

I topple backward, landing in the sand with a thud. I grunt when the body I ran into lands on top of me, almost knocking the wind out of me. Aside from the heavy weight, I'm blanketed by warmth and protected from the pouring rain.

"Shit. Sorry. I'm sorry. I didn't see you there. Are you okay?" Warm, humid breath that smells faintly of mint washes over my face, and the low, gruff tone sends a shiver down my spine that has nothing to do with the fact that I'm lying on the cold ground, or that I'm soaking wet.

"Van?"

"Dillion?" He pushes up onto his forearms, body still hovering over me, legs bracketing mine.

Of course he has to be the one I run into in the middle of a freaking storm, especially when not that long ago I was discussing whether he'd be good in bed and what the pros and cons were to finding something like that out. I still maintain that the cons would outweigh the pros.

"Yeah, it's me."

"I can't see more than a couple of feet in front of me." He scrambles to his knees and holds out a hand.

"Me either." I accept his offer of assistance. My hair is plastered to my head, and I'm seriously hoping I used the waterproof mascara, or I'm going to look like a cracked-out football player soon. I glance around the beach, but it's impossible to see anything apart from Van, who's directly in front of me. "I should find my brother."

"I think everyone's gone?" It's framed as a question. "I don't know my way around here, so I'm not sure how to get back to the parking lot," he admits.

"It probably won't last long. Come on. I know a place we can wait it out." I grab his hand as a crack of lightning lights up the beach, helping guide me toward the break in the trees.

"Is it a good idea to be running through the forest during a thunderstorm?" Van yells, fingers gripping mine tightly.

"We're not going far, and it's better than being on the beach," I shout back.

I take him down the trail that runs from the beach to the abandoned hunting cabin. It's closer than my truck. The brush has grown in since the last time I used it, disuse causing the weeds to sprout up and the trees to bend in.

The rain isn't as heavy under the canopy, so it's easier to navigate the narrow path. Van stumbles a couple of times on tree roots, so I fish around in my jeans for my phone and turn on the flashlight.

The cabin comes into view as another rumble of thunder makes the ground vibrate. I move the planter over a few inches and cross my fingers that the key hasn't disappeared in the years since I've last been here. I heave a sigh of relief when my fingers close around the cold metal.

I hold the flashlight to the door and slide the key in the lock. It wouldn't be hard to actually break down the door, but then it would mean that this place would be open to the rodents and animals living outside. Not that there probably aren't rodents living in here already, but I don't want to make it any easier for them than it has to be.

I have to jiggle the key a few times, but I finally get it to turn. I also have to bang the door with my shoulder to get it to open. I stumble a step or two, and Van follows me in, shutting the door behind him and sealing us off from the rain.

The tiny cabin creaks with the howling wind, but it's warmer and drier in here than it is out there.

"What the hell is this place?" Van turns on the flashlight on his phone and moves it around the room, his expression a mix of curiosity, confusion, and trepidation.

"It's an old hunting cabin."

The place doesn't have much in the way of space or furniture. There's an old rusted-out bunk bed with waterproof mattresses covering the bunks and rolled-up sleeping bags set on top. Everything is roughed in; there's no drywall, just boards and wooden studs. In the corner is a small table and two chairs. An old Coke crate is turned upside down to function as a kind of counter, holding a small washbasin.

"It hasn't changed since the last time I was here."

"This looks like the set of a slasher movie. Did you toss the bodies of poor unsuspecting vacationers in the lake when you were done with them?"

I roll my eyes. "The only thing that's died in here are probably some mice, and a lot of flies." At least judging from the extensive network of cobwebs lining the ceiling, almost like insulation. "I used to come here when I was a teenager and wanted to escape the world. I'd bring sleeping bags—not so I could sleep here, but the mattresses are foam covered in plastic and not very comfortable."

"What did you do when you were here? Is this, like, a teenager love shack? Did you bring your boyfriend here?"

I snort. "No. I came here alone. I was the only one who knew about it. And I used to read or write in a journal. Very typical teenage-girl things."

"Huh." He tucks his hands in his pockets. "Are there lights in this place?"

I chuckle. "No, Van. No lights. This is as rustic as it gets out here. Makes my trailer look like a luxury resort, huh?" There's bite in my words, mostly because I'm still miffed that his friend called me trailer trash.

"Your trailer is retro."

I give him a look that he probably can't see thanks to the lack of lighting in here. "There's duct tape holding some of the windows together."

"Have you seen Bee's cottage? When I first got here, I almost fell through the deck."

"I guess that explains the hammering at ten at night."

"I figured I should fix it before someone got a board in the face."

We listen to the rain batter the roof. Drops fall from the ceiling onto the top of the bunk bed, which explains the water pooling there. It's musty and dank, but at least it's mostly dry.

I pull out a chair and run a finger across the seat. It's covered in a thick layer of dust, but I'm already wearing sand from the beach and this outfit is destined for the wash, so I drop into it anyway.

He pulls out the other chair and makes a face but sits down. "What's the deal with that Tucker guy? The one in real estate. You two a thing?"

I laugh. "I'd rather drink shots of vinegar than be in a thing with him. He's my high school ex."

Van props his elbows on the table and folds his hands together so he can rest his chin on them. "So he's local?"

"Yeah. As local as they get."

He nods. "I think I might remember him from when I used to visit in the summers. Maybe I saw him around town? Or at the beach parties. Like this one."

"It's likely. He went to a lot of them."

He tips his head to the side. "With you?"

"Not usually."

"Hmm."

"Hmm, what?" The way he's looking at me is unnerving.

"I find that interesting, is all. So there's no chance you're getting back together with him?"

"Why would you ask me that?"

"Just curious, I guess. He was once your type."

"Well, he's not anymore." I can't tell if he's trying to push my buttons or what right now.

He nods once and looks away, eyes skimming over the cabin before they land on me. "That's good. You deserve better than that jackass."

"You don't even know me."

"I don't have to know you to know it's the truth. Besides, Grammy Bee always had nice things to say about you, and I trust her judgment."

I smile at that. "She couldn't stand Tucker. She probably asked me a million times what the heck I was doing with him."

"What were you doing with him?"

I shrug. "Passing time, I guess. Everyone knows everyone around here, so he would've been hard to avoid. I shouldn't have kept taking him back, but my friends were dating his friends at the time, and it was easier to turn a blind eye than to make a thing out of it."

Van makes a face. "Weren't there other options?"

"You mean like other guys I could have dated? Sure. But I never planned to come back here, and dating someone who I'd actually get attached to didn't seem like a good idea, so I dated Tucker."

"That seems . . ."

"Shallow?" I supply.

"*Calculated* was more the word I was looking for."

I nod my agreement. "It was calculated. If I'd dated a nice guy who treated me well, then I might have been less inclined to move to Chicago. Around here people tend to settle down early. Half of the girls I went to high school with had promise rings before they were even legally allowed to vote."

"And you didn't want to be tied down?"

"Not to this place."

"And yet you're back. So what changed?"

"My brother was in a car accident, and my dad needed help running the construction company." I leave out the part about the DUI, my company going under, my ex-boyfriend moving back home, and my needing to find a new apartment. "What about you? Why are you staying at Bee's place?"

"Well, it's technically my place now." I give him a look, so he continues with a sigh. "I'm in between jobs, and I needed a break from the city."

I lean back in the chair. "It sounds like there's a story attached to that."

"There is, but it doesn't paint me in the best light, and I don't want to give you another reason to dislike me."

"Well, now I really want to know what brings you to the wrong side of the lake."

Van laughs, but there isn't any humor in it. "It's not the wrong side; it's the best side." He takes his hat off and runs his hands through the damp strands. "I used to be on the board of directors for a foundation in honor of my mother."

"She passed when you were very young." I remember, vaguely, a period of time in which Bee wore all black and talked about her daughter. The summer that followed I didn't see much of her, but I remember her grandchildren being there and my mom telling me they needed family time.

"She did. It was supposed to be a day surgery, but she had a rare reaction to the anesthesia, and we lost her."

"I'm so sorry. That must have been so hard. Bee loved her very much."

"She did, and I think she blamed my dad for her death. I think he blamed himself too."

"That must have been so difficult for all of you. I can't imagine losing my mother at such a young age. How old were you?"

"I was pretty young. Eight. Old enough to understand that she was gone and not coming back, but my dad just sort of shut down. All he did was work. Nannies basically raised us, and he bought us whatever we wanted. He lost himself when he lost her. And I started spending the summers with Grammy Bee. So did my brother and sister at first, but we had a nanny that Teagan was particularly close with, and she didn't like being away from Dad for that long, so she stopped coming, and Bradley stayed home with her."

"Which left only you to visit Bee."

"Yup. Anyway, when I was eighteen I asked my dad if we could create a foundation in memory of my mom, and of course he said yes. I sat on the board right from the beginning. It was a way for us to connect. And it was good. But the day I arrived here was the same day I found out there was an audit and several million dollars have gone missing from the foundation."

"Holy crap! That's awful. What happened to it? Were they able to recover it?"

"They think I took it."

"But why would you do that with the foundation you started?"

Van shrugs. "It doesn't make sense to me, either, but all the bread crumbs lead back to me."

"But how?" I might only know Van based on our infrequent, often annoyance-based interactions, but I do know that Bee spoke very highly of him. And generally Bee was right about people. I honestly couldn't conceive of him doing something like that, or telling me about it if he had.

"I have no idea. That's what we're trying to find out. And we had this big donation going to this amazing literacy program, and now it's all on hold. I wanted to replace as much of the missing funds as I could, but my lawyer wants me to wait it out so I don't look guilty. I hate that this is dragging my mother's name through the mud. And stalling our projects as a result. All because of someone's greed."

It would be horrible to be accused of something I didn't do with no way to prove I didn't do it. "Can't you find out who did this? It can't be that easy to steal millions, can it?"

"About as easy as it is to frame someone, apparently. I've tried to figure out who it was, but whoever did it has been good at not leaving a trail or even a digital fingerprint behind. The real cherry on top of the shit sundae is that I lost my job over this. And honestly, I can't blame them for wanting to get rid of me. I'd do the same. As it is, my entire family is back in Chicago dealing with the fallout, and I'm here, waiting until we can come up with some evidence to prove it wasn't me."

"Wow. I can't even imagine how you must feel. I'm so sorry I've been such a jerk to you." It's amazing how much perspective one conversation can provide. Bee didn't talk much about her daughter, probably because the loss was so hard for her, but she always had good things to say about Van.

"Can you believe that all that happened right before I found you in my living room?" His smile is wry.

I slap a palm over my mouth. "No."

"I'd literally just arrived at Bee's to finally manage the cottage. I'd been planning to use some vacation time. I knew cleaning her place out was going to be a lot of work, so I took a week off, and boom, the second I walked in the door, I had that bomb dropped on me."

I put a hand on his arm. "I was so horrible when you first arrived. I've been awful."

"You've been the highlight of this exile, so far." His smile turns soft. "Look, I don't blame you. You don't know me, and I know you and Bee were close. Besides, I didn't do myself any favors with the late-night remodeling and the drunk and disorderly friends." Van tips his head down, and the brim of his hat casts a shadow over his face. Another flash of déjà vu.

I shake my head, trying to erase the memory. It was probably the last beach party I went to before I left for college, and tonight is full of memories.

"Anyway, enough of my sob story. Talking about this makes me sound like an emo teenager. I have a place to live, and once we figure out exactly what happened, I'll be able to clear my name, and I'll be employable again. I gotta say, despite the less-than-ideal reasons for me being here, this is a nice break from the city grind. The pace isn't as hectic. It's more relaxed. It's a good reminder that there's more to life than fancy cars and expensive clothes."

"There's something about Chicago, or any city, I imagine, isn't there? You're surrounded by people whose entire existence is about having more; it's hard not to get caught up in it."

"Are you speaking from experience?"

It's my turn to shrug. "I spent my entire life wanting to escape the small-town stereotype. I don't think it helps that one side of this lake is all about excess and the other is very much the opposite. It turned into one of those grass-is-greener-on-the-other-side scenarios. I wanted to have more, to be better, to get out of here and really *live*."

Van props his chin on his fist. "And did you?"

"In some ways, yes. I went to college in Chicago. Got a job, had an apartment, and made good money, but the thing about living in a major city is that it's expensive, and you have to work the hours to support the lifestyle."

"Or live on lines of credit," Van deadpans.

"The only thing worse than having nothing is having less than nothing because it's all borrowed money. So yeah, I lived that city life, and I loved it while I was in it. And then I came back here to help out my family and get my feet back under me before the city ate all my savings."

"Which you weren't all that happy about. The being-back-here part, I mean."

"Not really, no."

"Because of Tucker the Fucker?"

I laugh. "I used to call him that all the time after I moved away. And yeah, that's part of it. Although I don't think I realized how big a part that played until recently. Sometimes one person can muddy all your memories with a layer of discontent, and Tucker was that for me." Between the confrontation with Allie and opening up to Van, saying this all out loud seems to be making it clearer. I have been avoiding the bad memories, and facing my past. Ones I was responsible for creating with my complacency. But in doing that I lost out on years of friendship.

"And now, how do you feel about working for your dad's construction company?"

I tug on a wet ringlet. "At first I wasn't all that excited, but now I kind of love it. The woman they had doing the paperwork before she left to have a baby had the worst filing system ever, and as much as it's been a pain, now that I've organized it, things are running smoothly. It's rewarding to foster relationships with local companies that help keep the community going, you know? As much as I wanted to get out of this small town, I still cared about the people. We're all here supporting each other, just trying to make a living."

Van nods knowingly. "I get why Bee loves you. Loved you," he corrects, that smile turning wistful for a second. "She talked about you all the time. Sometimes I was a little jealous of your relationship with her."

"Jealous? Why?"

"Because you were so close to her. You had access to her all the time growing up, and I didn't. It's interesting how determined you were to escape the place I considered my haven. The weeks I spent up here in the summers were something I looked forward to every year. That never changed for me, not even as I got older."

"Well, it was sort of a vacation for you, wasn't it?"

"Yeah, but it was also more than that. Here, people seem to have each other's backs, at least for the most part. There's a community here that doesn't exist in the same way in the city. There's no anonymity."

"It's a blessing and a curse."

"I can see that. Everyone knows your business, but at the same time, the lack of posturing is a nice change. You are who you are. No one cares about what kind of car you drive or how much money you make. Except maybe Tucker the Fucker. Hell, it seems to be a badge of honor to drive a rusted-out, beat-up old pickup truck because it means you love it enough to keep fixing it."

"To be fair, I think Bee refused to give up the pickup truck because it was your grandfather's other lover. He spent as much time tinkering with that thing as he did sitting with Bee on the front porch. At least that's how it seemed when I was a kid."

"Whenever I visited, he spent most of his time in the garage," Van agrees.

We both smile, and Van tips his head, eyes dipping down.

"Does everyone around here mumble and add an *r* to your name and call you Darlin'?"

I chuckle. "Honestly, I think Billy is the one who started calling me that, and everyone else followed suit. Like he couldn't pronounce it properly, and then people started adding the *r*, and it stuck. Except Bee. She called me Lynnie, and sometimes people call me Dee because it's shorter, and we're lazy with our tongues."

"What do you like to be called?"

I shrug. "They're all fine. Apart from *trailer trash*, anyway."

Embarrassment makes him duck his head. "Monica is an asshole."

"She's the kind of person who made me hate the north side of the lake. All that entitlement and believing they're better because they were born with a silver spoon in their mouths. I wanted to prove to everyone who ever looked down on me that I could be just as successful. And I wanted to prove to this town that if you wanted to leave, you could." Between people like her and Tucker, I had motivation to get out. Spread my wings, and knock a few people off their pedestals on my way out.

"And now?"

"I'm starting to see this place differently." Having lived in the city, where anonymity is easy to come by, and then coming back here, to where everything and everyone is familiar, has changed things. And so has the guy sitting across from me. He's a link to Bee, and in many ways he embodies the nostalgia of my teens. And now that I'm getting to know him, I'm finding there's lots to like about him.

"Yeah, me too. At least when I'm around you." His eyes roam over my face, and this time I don't win the battle with my hand not to touch my hair.

I snicker. "You're a fan of surly neighbors?"

"Maybe it reminds me of Chicago. Everyone's surly there."

"That's a fact."

"Or maybe it's because you don't put up with shit."

"Oh, I put up with lots of shit."

"Not from me."

"You happen to catch me on particularly surly days, is all."

"I like your surly." His tongue peeks out and drags across his bottom lip. "Can I tell you something?" He tips his head down, the brim of his hat casting shadows over his face again.

"Sure." We've been open with each other tonight, and all that hostility I felt has dissipated, especially in the wake of his revelations.

He taps on the table, leaving fingerprints in the dust. "Remember the summer you worked at the french fry truck?"

"Yeah, it was my last summer in Pearl Lake."

"Mine too. I used to go to the food truck all the time and get fries and hot dogs, even though I'm not a fan of either."

"Who doesn't like fries? And why would you get them if you don't like them? For Bee?"

Van laughs. "No. I mean, sure, she liked them well enough, but I went just so I could talk to you. I kinda had a thing for you."

"A thing?"

"A crush, Dillion." His smile is wry.

"Oh. I had no idea." I lean back in my chair, which creaks ominously. "Why didn't you come over and say hi, when I lived right next door to Bee?"

He tips his head to the side. "Because I knew you had a boyfriend, and I was only there for the summer. I had a feeling if I acted on that crush, it would be hard to walk away come the end of August. I used to go to those beach parties hoping I'd run into you there."

"I hated those parties back then. It was always a bunch of summer kids trying to hook up with the locals." I rub my bottom lip, remembering the one time I went to a beach party while Tucker and I were on one of our breaks and ended up kissing a north side boy. "Did you ever make out with any of the local girls?"

"Only one. Did you ever make out with any of the guys from the other side of the lake?" he asks.

"Only one. And only because I got roped into a game of truth or dare that played out more like a game of spin the bottle. It ended almost as soon as it started, though, because some jerk made a trailer trash comment—"

"—and a fight broke out."

"How do you know that?" I can feel my face heating up. I'd hate to think that Van, who had been crushing on me back then, had witnessed that embarrassing moment.

"Because it was me."

"What was you?" My pulse speeds up at the memory. The way I hadn't been able to see that summer boy's face because the fire was burning low and he'd been wearing a ball cap.

"I was the one who kissed you. I didn't even know it was you," Van says quietly.

"Because I was wearing a sweatshirt—"

"—and the hood was up," he finishes for me.

I'd been hiding behind it, watching Tucker flirt with some girl from the other side of the lake. The bottle landed on me, and someone dared Van to kiss me. So he did.

I shake my head. "I thought about that kiss for the rest of the summer."

"Me too." He rubs his bottom lip, leaving behind a smudge of dirt. His left eyebrow arches. "Did you think good things?"

I breathe out a laugh. "Yeah. I thought good things. I wondered for the rest of the summer if it was you I'd run into, but you were too embarrassed that you'd gotten called out for macking on trailer trash."

"Stop saying that. It's pissing me off. If I'd known it was you, I would have been at your door every damn day for the rest of the summer."

"I still can't believe it was you," I say softly.

"Seems like fate is trying to tell us something, don't you think?" He slides his chair across the rough wood floor, closer to me.

"Maybe Bee is trying to send us messages from heaven."

"Maybe." He reaches out and drags my chair away from the makeshift table so we're knee to knee, his legs parting to bracket mine.

He props his forearms on his thighs; his knuckles barely graze my knee and send a shiver running down my spine. "Can I tell you something else?"

"Sure." It's more breath than word.

"You make me nervous." His voice is soft and low.

It's also not what I expected to hear. I tip my head, unsure where he's going with this.

He links our pinkies. "Do you want to know why?"

"Sure."

His fingertips glide along my palm, and a wave of goose bumps flashes over my skin. "Because I feel like you see me. Like it doesn't matter what I say or do. I'm transparent, and you're already under my skin."

"And why does that make you nervous?"

He runs his thumb over my knuckles and lifts my hand. "Because I want you to like what you see, the same way I like what I see in you." He drops his head until I can feel his breath break across the back of my hand. "Do you, Dillion?" The end of his nose brushes my knuckle. "Like what you see, that is."

Another shiver runs through me. "Tonight, I do." It's a breathy whisper.

He peeks up at me and grins. "And before tonight?"

"I was on the fence."

"What changed?"

"Tonight you showed me the real you."

His lips touch the back of my hand, and I exhale a shuddery breath.

"Okay?" he asks.

"Okay." I nod.

He lifts his head, eyes searching mine as he twirls an errant curl around his finger, then drags a single finger along the edge of my jaw.

"I'm sorry I haven't been very nice to you."

He nods in agreement. "It's part of your allure, just like mine is needling the shit out of you until I get a reaction."

"You're definitely good at that."

"Good enough that if I kissed you, you might kiss me back?"

"There's a reasonably good chance of that."

He leans in closer and tips his head to the right, so I angle mine and meet him halfway. Just before our lips connect, he tucks his thumb under my chin and mutters, "I'd better not fuck this up."

My chuckle turns into a sigh when his lips brush over mine, sending an electric jolt through me. We both still.

"Did you feel that?"

"It's probably just the storm." I wrap my hand around the back of his neck and pull his mouth back to mine to see whether I'm right. I also notice that the patter of rain has slowed significantly, and it's not nearly as forceful or violent as it was when we first stumbled in here.

I don't have much time to focus on those details because the moment Van's lips connect with mine again, a bolt of sizzling lust zings through me. Heat follows in a heady rush when his velvet-soft tongue sweeps out to meet mine. We both groan, and the hand around the back of his neck tightens, as if I'm trying to anchor him to me. At the same time his fingers slide along the edge of my jaw and tangle in my hair.

Van angles his head more, and I mirror him, opening wider, giving him access to explore, go deeper, give and take more.

I've been kissed plenty of times in my life—some of them have been amazing, while others have been lackluster—but this takes me right back to that kiss on the beach all those years ago. This is lust combustion. I don't know if it's pure, unfiltered chemistry or the fact that we've shared so much of ourselves tonight, but I find myself sinking into this kiss, desperate for it not to end.

Our twined hands part, mine finding his knee, and he mirrors the movement. He spreads his legs wider, and I slide to the edge of my chair, wanting to get closer. I haven't had this kind of contact in months. And what I did have with Jason was good—nice, like a pretty sunset, something to appreciate and enjoy—but this isn't the same.

When it's clear that my sitting on this chair is impeding our ability to get closer to each other, I snake my arm around his neck and rise, tapping on the outside of his left knee, hoping he understands what I'm asking without having to disconnect my mouth from his and use actual words.

Thankfully, he seems to be able to read my mind. He closes his knees and we change positions, his knees inside mine now, giving me the opportunity to use him as my chair. I sit on his thighs and slide forward until we're chest to chest.

It doesn't matter that we're both wearing jeans; I can still feel that prominent bulge, now nestled between my thighs. We make plaintive sounds into each other's mouths, the kiss gaining fervor. One hand stays tangled in my wet hair; the other arm circles my waist and pulls me tighter against him, bodies flush. I roll my hips and press closer, as if I'm trying to meld us into one.

All the while, I let my free hand explore, tracing the contour of muscle under his shirt. The hairs on his arm stand on end, and goose bumps flash over his skin. I edge back a little, the chair groaning with the shift in weight. Van's fingers flex on my hip, slipping lower, pressing into the soft fleshy part of my ass.

I find the hem of his shirt and ease a palm underneath, hoping he'll get the hint and do some exploring of his own. It doesn't take long for him to take the bait, and his warm palm slides up my back, pulling my shirt up, causing me to shiver as the cool air hits my skin.

I roll my hips again, and he jerks. And all of a sudden, a massive crack echoes through the cabin. For a moment I think it's the storm. At least until we both go crashing to the cabin floor, the chair a splintered, broken mass underneath us.

I push up on my arms, my wet hair hanging in my face and brushing Van's cheek as I meet his shocked gaze. I grimace when I notice the bead of blood welling on his top lip.

"You okay?" His voice is full of gravel, his erection still making itself known between my thighs.

"I'm fine." I swipe at the blood and hold my finger up. "I nicked you, though."

"Totally worth it." His tongue sweeps along the cut, and he curls his hand around the back of my neck, pulling me back in for another kiss. This one is as long and heated as the first, despite the fact that Van is lying on a filthy cabin floor with a broken chair underneath him.

Eventually I pull back, both of us breathing hard. "I think the rain has slowed enough that we could go back to your place. If you want." I bite my lip, aware that by putting this option on the table, I'm opening myself up to a whole host of potential problems. But the flip side is exploring the incredible chemistry we seem to have, and I'm not sure the downside outweighs the potential for some awesome sex with a really hot, surprisingly down-to-earth guy.

Van glances around the cabin. I can see the moment he comes to the same conclusion I have—that this place is disgusting. There's no way I want to have sex in this nasty old hunting cabin and risk the spider- and bug-bite mementos.

"Yeah. Yes. Absolutely. My place is way better than this."

CHAPTER 14
KISSES AND CHEMISTRY

Van

Dillion pushes to her feet and holds out her hand to help me up. We both stand there for a second, staring at the destroyed chair, before we turn to each other and glue our mouths back together.

Dillion is nothing and everything like I expected her to be.

She's a mix of bold and intense and soft and sexy.

And she sure as hell knows how to kiss, so I'm going to go ahead and guess that this chemistry we happen to share will be even more amazing once we get our clothes off.

After a few minutes of dancing tongues—or it could be longer than that; I lose track of time—she puts her hands on my shoulders and pulls back. We're both panting. She covers my mouth with her palm. "Let's put a pin in this until we get back to your place, yeah?"

"Yeah." The word is muffled by her hand.

She nabs her phone from the table and leads me back out into the forest. It's still raining, but it's slowed considerably. The path isn't wide enough for us to navigate side by side, so I follow behind, the light on her phone bobbing unsteadily with her hurried steps. We're almost jogging we're moving so quickly.

Eventually the path widens, and I fall into step beside her. We reach the turnaround where her truck is parked.

"Are you good to drive?" I ask. "I only had one beer, and that was a while ago."

She hesitates for a moment, teeth sinking into her bottom lip, before she passes me her keys. "I'm not sure what the vodka-cran ratio was, and one beer seems less potent than what I was drinking."

Dillion gives me directions back to the cottage. I park at her place, and she glances at the house, its windows darkened. We bypass the trailer and cut through the path between our lots, breaking into a run as the rain picks up again just before we reach the covered porch.

I fiddle with the lock, struggling to get it to open.

Dillion elbows me out of the way. "It's tricky sometimes, especially when it's damp." She gets it to turn, and we finally tumble into the cottage, blissfully warm and dry and so much cleaner than the hunting cabin, despite the amount of clutter. I still haven't tackled the inside, partly because I don't want to disrupt the memories, and also because it's a daunting task that feels like it will take an eternity. And I want to get the garage build underway. Cleaning it out has taken a lot longer than I expected.

Dillion glances around, eyes sliding across the open space, catching on trinkets, almost as though she's cataloging all the things inside, accounting for them like a checklist. It occurs to me that she's spent an incredible amount of time here. Far more than my few weeks a year plus holidays could ever account for.

A violent shiver rips through her, and she wraps her arms around herself, teeth chattering twice before her jaw flexes and she clamps them together.

"Hot shower?" I offer.

Her gaze swings to me, and she catches one side of her bottom lip between her teeth, the skin turning white briefly as it slides through on her nod.

"Alone or together?" I ask.

At the same time she says, "You're coming with me."

We both grin, and then we're heading for the bathroom. I turn on the shower, testing the water to make sure it's not scalding. I tried to adjust the pressure, but now it vacillates between jet stream and periodic trickle. We turn and step into each other's personal space. Our mouths connect, and this time it's not quite so frantic or intense. A slower build, the knowledge that we're moving toward more, the anticipation of pleasure causing us to take our time.

It's strange how we seem to know what the other is planning to do before we do it. Dillion and I both reach for the hem of each other's shirt at the same time, fingertips brushing over cool skin that pebbles in a wave. We break the kiss long enough to get our shirts over our heads, and then we're connected again, skin to skin, because Dillion isn't wearing a bra.

Her breasts are small but full and pert, her tight nipples brushing below my chest. She's a head shorter than me, forcing me to tip my chin down and her to tilt hers up. We kiss again, hands roaming over exposed flesh. I brush the underside of her breast, and she arches and moans, her hands gliding down my back. She cups my ass and gives it a firm squeeze before she follows the edge of my belt around to the buckle.

We break apart again, tugging, unbuttoning, unzipping each other and then removing our own pants, leaving me naked and Dillion in a pair of plain black panties. She hooks her thumbs into the waistband and drags them down her thighs, eyes locked on mine for a moment until gravity and curiosity pull them downward. Her tongue peeks out when her gaze reaches my erection, thick and straining toward her.

A slow grin forms, and she kicks her panties off and steps back into me. Her palms land on my chest, fingertips tickling my skin as they glide down and brush gently along the length of me. My erection kicks, and her smile widens, fingers wrapping around me.

I let my gaze drop as she strokes slowly, thumb sweeping over the ridge to the head and then back down again. "I think we're going to have a lot of fun tonight, Van."

I nod my agreement and pull the shower curtain back. We step in together, still touching, still exploring each other's bodies. We soap each other up, teasing and taunting, fingers dipping and skipping over sensitive parts as the bathroom fills with steam and we warm ourselves with body heat and sensual touches.

When the water starts to cool, I turn off the shower and we dry each other off, kissing paths along erogenous zones, seeing who can elicit the deepest groan or the loudest sigh. We're kissing our way across the living room, still naked, bumping into furniture along the way and laughing into each other's mouths, when I nearly trip backward over the coffee table. We finally make it to my bedroom.

I'm glad I took the time to make my bed this morning and put the laundry in a basket. It's a small space, just enough room for a bed and a dresser, but it doesn't need to be more.

I sit down on the mattress and pull her between my thighs. Her breasts are right in my face, begging for attention, so I latch onto her nipple. Dillion arches and slides her fingers into my hair on a low moan. The other hand drops to my thigh, fingertips ghosting higher until they graze my shaft.

When she makes a move to wrap her hand around me, I disengage from her nipple and lift my head enough so I can meet her slightly disgruntled, confused gaze. That bewilderment grows even more when I shake my head. At least until I say, "I'm already too jacked up; I don't need the extra attention right now."

Her eyes flare. "Oh."

"Yeah, oh." I flick her nipple with my tongue. "Don't make me regret telling you that."

She's about to reply when I latch on again and suck. Her fingers tighten in my hair, and her eyes roll up.

Everything about Dillion seems to be a contradiction. She's intense, harsh, and hard. She's soft, sweet, and saucy. And I have a feeling she's a bit of an adventure in the bedroom.

I wrap my hands around her waist and edge a knee between her thighs. "Open for me, please."

And she does. Immediately. Without question. I slide both knees between her legs and set her on my thighs, but far back, so her ass is resting on my knees.

"Hook your legs around mine," I tell her.

She gives me a questioning look but complies, probably wondering what the hell I'm doing. Even I'm wondering that. I don't know her that well, not really, but I *feel* like I do, as if I've known her my entire life.

Regardless, we're here and naked, and she's made it very clear she wants the same thing as I do—connection and orgasms.

I've missed this feeling. The one where I get to share power with someone else. To give and take. And know that when she comes, it will be because she trusts me enough to let go, even if we haven't spent that much time together without biting each other's heads off or pushing buttons just to get a reaction.

When her feet are hooked around the backs of my calves, I spread my legs, opening her wider. She jolts with the sudden movement, and her fingernails dig into the back of my neck until she steadies again.

I cover her knees with my palms. "Okay?"

She arches a brow. "I guess it depends on what you're planning to do now."

I slide my hands up the inside of her thighs, stopping when I reach the apex, and grin. "Make you feel good."

"Have at it, then." Her own smile is mischievous.

I brush along either side of her sex with my thumbs, but I keep my gaze locked on hers, at least until Dillion's eyes flutter closed. Then I look down, drinking in the sight of her spread wide open for me. I tease her until her toes dig into the backs of my calves and bring her to climax with my fingers, spurred on by her low murmurs of encouragement.

Her entire body goes still and rigid for a moment, a low groan bubbling up and spilling free as her hips jerk with her orgasm.

When she goes boneless, I slide back on the mattress, taking her with me as I stretch out along the comforter. Dillion straddles my hips and settles over my erection, hot and wet and right damn well there. Our mouths connect, and we swallow each other's desperate sounds. I slap blindly on the nightstand table, find the drawer, and pull it open.

Dillion breaks the kiss long enough to lean over and grab a condom. She sits back, tears it open, rolls it on, and rises up. Her gaze lifts to mine, and she sinks down. I grip her hips, the sensation too much and not enough.

She exhales a long, slow breath when her ass meets my thighs and rolls her hips, murmuring, "So good."

Her palms smooth up my chest and come to rest on my pecs. She leans in and sucks my bottom lip between hers, then whispers, "I want you on top of me."

I flip us over and settle in the cradle of her hips. Her legs wrap around my waist, feet hooking at the center of my back. And then I start to move, finding a slow rhythm that allows me to stay deep, at least at first. Soon the slow grind shifts, and with every *Yes* and *Please* and *Harder* and *Just like that, don't stop* I gain momentum, the bed creaking, headboard hitting the wall with each thrust. Something falls to the floor, a piece of art maybe, and for a moment Dillion cranes to look over my shoulder before she decides it doesn't matter and goes back to rolling her hips.

The orgasm sneaks up on me, rising up and crashing down like a tidal wave. I drop down, trying not to put my full weight on her, and nuzzle into her neck. We're both sweaty and panting and, judging from the feel of Dillion, basically boneless.

Eventually I push up on my arm so I can see her face. Her eyes are soft and glassy, cheeks flushed, curls spread out over my pillow in a sandy wave. She looks beautiful and like this is exactly where she belongs.

"Stay the night?"

CHAPTER 15
THE SECRETS OF BEE

Dillion

I must hesitate a beat too long before answering, because Van's deliciously gorgeous face goes from open to shuttered in a heartbeat. "Unless you don't want to." He starts to roll off me, and I stop him by squeezing my feet, hooked behind his back. He's still very much filling me up, and I feel residual aftershocks every so often, my muscles clenching below the waist, the orgasm slow to wane.

"I want to stay." I glance over his shoulder at the place where the picture was hanging, the single nailhead a pinprick. "But if more things fall off the walls in the middle of the night, I'm probably going back to my place."

His smile returns, and he barks out a laugh. "You think Bee is haunting us? That picture fell because I was plowing you into the mattress so hard the bed frame probably left dents in the drywall." He stretches out, hips pressing into mine as he skims the top of the headboard and shows me his white, powdery fingertips. "See?"

I fling my hand out in the opposite direction. "Yeah, but it fell off the wall on the *other* side of the room."

"You didn't seem too bothered by it when it happened."

"I was four hard thrusts away from an orgasm—a meteor could've been heading straight for us, and I maybe would have tried to roll us out of the way, but otherwise I was focused on the goal."

Van kisses the end of my nose and rolls off me. He's definitely an excellent lover. Attentive, demanding, entirely in control, and yet incredibly patient and unhurried.

I shiver at the loss of body heat, and Van slides off the bed. He tugs the sheets down on his side and pats the mattress, and I roll into his spot, sliding my legs under the quilt that was most definitely made by Bee.

"I'll be right back." He pulls it up to my chin and disappears down the hall.

I glance around the room, really taking in the space. I've been in Bee's place plenty of times over the years, but mostly in her kitchen or living room. A couple of times I changed light bulbs for her in her bedroom, but this room I've only seen in passing on the way to the bathroom.

I picture a teenage Van sleeping in here, the one who came to buy hot dogs at the food truck, back before life took us in different directions and then threw us both curveballs that forced our paths to cross again.

He returns a minute later, still totally naked but now holding two glasses of water. He sets one on the nightstand and hands the other one to me. I sit up, the quilt falling to my waist, and his gaze moves over me in a slow, heated sweep. I like the way he looks at me, as though he's hungry and I'm exactly what he needs.

After a few seconds he gives his head a quick shake and turns to the dresser. He finds a pair of boxer briefs and tugs them up his thighs, covering his glorious, sculpted butt. He also grabs a T-shirt. "Want this?"

"Sure. Thanks." I hold my hands up in a catcher's pose, and he tosses it to me.

It's a college T-shirt, the logo faded and the fabric soft from wear. I pull it over my head and inhale the scent of Van's laundry detergent mixed with the familiar smell of Bee's clove and citrus candles. He crosses over to the end of the bed, a furrow forming between his brows.

Bending, he picks up the picture that fell off the wall thanks to our aggressive sex. "What the heck," he mutters.

I set my mostly empty glass on the nightstand and lean forward so I can see what he sees.

The framed picture shows the lake, taken before all the monster cottages and homes went up. But that's not what has Van looking all confused. It's the confetti of twenty-dollar bills scattered across the floor, along with the ones clutched in his fist.

He waves the stack around. "Is this real?"

"It's likely, yeah." I consider all the things I know about Bee and her unconventional way of managing her finances.

The furrow in Van's brow deepens. "Why don't you look surprised?"

"Because it's pretty typical of Bee to hide money in places people aren't likely to look. Have you started cleaning out any of the rooms in the house?" A pang of worry hits me, because it would be awful if he's been throwing stuff out in here without realizing there might be treasure hiding inside.

"No. I've been focusing my efforts on the garage."

My shoulders come down from my ears. "Okay. Phew. That's good."

"I don't get it. Why is that good?"

"It's better if I show you."

"Show me what?"

I roll out of his bed and hold out my hand. "Come with me."

He laces his fingers with mine, still clutching the stack of money in his other hand.

We pad down the hall together, to the living room. I stop in front of the hutch, coated in a layer of dust that tells me it likely hasn't been touched since Bee passed. She dusted every day when I was a teenager.

I pick up an old canister. It's metal and dented, with a lid on it. Something from another era that held candies. I let go of Van's hand so I can open it and then peek inside. I lift the piece of paper and reveal a roll of bills, secured with an elastic band, and hold it out to Van.

His eyes flare as he takes it from me, tipping the can over and catching the roll in his palm. A one-dollar bill is wrapped around the outside, but I unfold the note on top and show him the number 5,001 scrawled in Bee's familiar writing.

"There's five grand in here? That can't be possible." Van tugs on the elastic securing the bills, and it breaks apart, pieces falling to the floor as he pulls the dollar bill free to reveal a hundred-dollar bill underneath. "Holy shit." He unfurls the rest of the roll, which matches the hundred. He looks around the cottage, maybe seeing it with very different eyes for the first time in his life. "How much money does she have hidden around the cottage? Is it just the cottage? Or the garage too?"

"Just the cottage. At least that I know of. And I don't know how much, but there's probably a lot."

"Holy fuckballs. Why would she do this? Why not keep it in the bank?"

For a moment I worry that I've made a mistake in telling him, but I realize I was going to have to eventually and probably should have long before now. I shrug. "She didn't always trust the bank, and she wanted to have cash on hand just in case."

"In case of what?"

"Another world war? An apocalypse? Her estate getting tied up with red tape? Take your pick of options, I guess. At first it was a few stashes here and there, but over time she kept adding to it, almost like a game? An Easter egg hunt, but with money instead of chocolate." I found out about it when I once helped Bee dust and dropped one of her many trinkets. A roll of bills had fallen out. She hadn't made a big deal of it. Just winked and said sometimes it was good to have a little cash hidden around the house, for emergencies.

I move to the wall of framed family photos and pick up one of her with Van when he was a kid, playing in the water down by the beach. I flip it over and push the pegs out of the way so I can remove the backing. Between it and the photo are two envelopes. One has a small stack of twenties, the other fifties. Each one includes a small slip of paper with the amount in each envelope.

"There could be tens of thousands of dollars in here. Maybe even hundreds," Van muses.

I nod my agreement. "It's certainly possible." And, based on how much we've found just by looking in three places, I'd hazard a guess that it's probable.

"You've known about this the entire time." It's not a question.

I nod. "I would have told you sooner, but I wasn't sure I could trust you at first. Or if you were even the right grandson. I should have said something right away, though."

"You could have taken money anytime you wanted," Van says softly.

"I would never do that." I take a step back. "Bee trusted me, and I would never take what wasn't mine."

Van holds up a hand. "That's not how I meant it. I'm not accusing you, Dillion. I'm just . . . I don't know. I'm kind of blown away." He runs a hand through his hair and grips it at the crown. "It's kind of a mindfuck for me. You know?"

I drop my arms and nod, the tension in my shoulders easing. "Bee did so much for me. She helped me with college. I earned scholarships to pay for tuition, and Bee helped me apply for a bunch of grants so I wouldn't end up with huge loans to pay back. She helped me with all of it." I bite the inside of my cheek and decide to tell him the entire truth, even the things I've never shared with my own family. "But it was more than that, Van. She sent me money every month to help with groceries and stuff. She never said it was her, but once I asked my dad about it, thinking it was him, and he had no idea. So of course I asked Bee, right? Because who else would it be?"

153

"Let me guess—she wouldn't admit it was her." A hint of a smile pulls up the corner of his mouth.

"Nope. Gave me her big old innocent doe eyes and told me she didn't know what I was talking about. She suggested that maybe there was a grant I applied for and didn't realize I'd been awarded it, but it had to be her because there wasn't anyone else who would do that for me." I hold up a finger. "Wait. That's not true. If my parents had the money, they would have given it to me, but it just wasn't there. So I kept track of every single deposit she made, and when I finished school and got a job, I tried to pay her back, but she refused to take the money. It was so frustrating, because I wanted to give her back what I owed, but every time I tried, she'd find a way to give it right back to me, so when she needed someone to help with her will, I stepped up. She asked me to be the executor."

"I wonder why she never asked me to do it." The question is laced with threads of hurt.

"I know the answer to that. She was worried your dad would step in and try to take over. She knew that he hadn't been smart with his finances after your mom passed. She'd even loaned him money a bunch of times to help with things, like your education." It's uncomfortable to tell him things like this. When I was young, I always felt like a bit of a voyeur when it came to Van and his family.

"I didn't realize that. I mean, I guess it makes sense. I came out of college loan-free, but I assumed my parents had set money aside for it."

"I think they had."

"But my dad spent it." Van drops his head and rubs the back of his neck.

I slip my arm around his waist and squeeze. "I'm sorry. This must be hard to hear."

"It's nothing I didn't already suspect. I just didn't realize it was this bad, or that my dad had been borrowing money from Grammy Bee."

"I don't know everything, Van, but I do know that Bee worried about what would happen to this place when she was gone, and she wanted you to have it because you valued it. So I went with her to Bernie's, and I promised I would make sure it was you who got the cottage and the property. Bee treated me like I was one of her own, and to me she was family, so there's no way I would ever touch what's hers. Or what *was* hers. It was never mine to take."

"You realize most people wouldn't even think twice about skimming, even a little."

"Oh, absolutely. But the thing is, when things got tight, I'd suddenly find money in my account that hadn't been there. It's like she knew before it even happened." I pick another framed photo off the wall, this time one of Bee with her husband.

Van steps in closer, his chest brushing my shoulder. "This was taken on Grampy's birthday. I think he turned sixty-five?"

"He passed away a couple of years later." I flip the picture over and slide the backing out to reveal yet another envelope. I hand it to Van before I slide the backing into place again.

Van peeks inside the envelope and shakes his head, but he's still smiling. "This was his favorite outfit that my grandmother wore. Didn't matter that it was ten years out of style; he freaking loved it when she wore it."

"Back in the day when shoulder pads were an in thing."

"She used to wear it every year on his birthday. I always tried to be here for that after he passed away, but it wasn't easy once I started working full time. Getting a day off in the middle of the week could be a pain in the ass, so sometimes I'd have to come here after work."

"And go back the same night so you could be at work the next morning."

Van's gaze shifts from the photo to me, his expression quizzical. "Yeah."

"She told me about that. I'd always call and have my mom bring her—"

"—an apple pie," Van finishes for me.

"From Boones," we say at the same time.

"I could've eaten the entire thing in one sitting if I'd been allowed to."

"But Bee liked to savor it, and you know how she was about sweets: loved them but hated them at the same time, because she didn't have a ton of restraint when it came to moderation."

"She'd portion the rest of the pieces out and put half of it in the freezer." Van chuckles. "Except it didn't work, and she'd end up digging them right back out the very next day."

"I really miss her," I whisper.

"Me too. More than I ever thought possible." Van's smile turns sad.

I wrap my arms around his waist, wishing that we didn't have matching Bee-shaped holes in our hearts. He returns the embrace, strong arms circling my shoulders. He drops his head, lips pressing against the side of my neck. "Why didn't I know you better when we were teenagers?"

"Because I was too busy with Tucker and trying to cut my roots so I could fly." I tip my head up. "We were young. We weren't supposed to know each other back then. And I just wanted something different than what I knew, so I went to the most opposite place I could."

And in doing so, I left everything that was comfortable behind and tried to build a new life, with new people who were more refined, shinier, and polished. Although now I'm starting to see that the shiny veneer is just that. Underneath the layers of polish are regular people, with the same problems as everyone else; they just have prettier masks to hide behind.

CHAPTER 16

BLEEDING HEART

Dillion

My alarm goes off at what would be a reasonable time the next morning if I hadn't stayed up until stupid o'clock. My dad and I have a meeting with a homeowner named something Kingston who's looking to renovate his kitchen this fall. He's one of the Bowmans' friends who also happens to be a former NHL hockey player. There seem to be more and more of those guys popping up on the lake.

I roll over and grab the device, silencing the alarm. Before I can slide out of bed, a strong arm wraps around my waist and pulls me back across the mattress.

"Where are you going this early?" Van's raspy voice sends a shiver down my spine. Last night, after I showed him where Bee had hidden pieces of her fortune, he took me back to bed, and we got naked again. It was even more intense than the first time and absolutely worth the very limited hours of sleep I clocked as a result.

"I have a meeting at nine thirty."

"On a Sunday?" I can practically feel his frown and the furrow in his brow against my neck.

"Unfortunately, yes." I shift so I can face him.

His dark hair is a tousled mess, he has sleep lines etched into his face, and his lips are gloriously puffy, probably from all the kissing. His dark eyes roam my face, hot and searching, and he brushes an errant curl away from my face. It springs right back into place. It must be a terrible rat's nest.

"Is it a long meeting?" His tongue peeks out, dragging across his top lip.

"I'm not sure." Sometimes they're short; sometimes they go on for hours. One thing the people on the other side of the lake seem to have is oodles of time. Decisions on things like paint colors and countertops can end up as long discussions on what colors and materials work best together. And when you're spending half a million on a renovation, I can understand why it's not a five-minute decision.

"Hmm." Van tips his head. "Would you like to have dinner with me tonight?"

"You mean here?"

"Or we can go somewhere. It's up to you."

"Like a date?" The words are out before I can consider them. And I immediately want to stuff them back in and swallow them down.

But a small smile pulls at the corners of his mouth until it makes his eyes crinkle with mirth. "Yes, like a date."

I don't know why I'm shocked. After all the revelations last night, I probably should have expected something like this from Van. "Um, sure, okay. Yes. But there aren't many restaurants in town, and if we go out together, people are going to talk."

"I'm okay with that if you are. I promise I'm not into excessive PDAs."

"What do you consider excessive?"

"Sharing a plate of pasta like Lady and the Tramp, under-the-table handies, quickies in public bathrooms—you know, excessive stuff." I'm not sure whether I should laugh until a huge smile breaks across his face and he chuckles. "Relax, Dillion. I won't try any of those things, especially not on a first date."

I push on his chest. "Oh my gosh, you're too much."

"Last night it seemed like you couldn't get enough."

I try to wiggle out of his arms, but he rolls us over so he's on top of me. "Six o'clock. No overt displays of affection. I won't even try to hold your hand. I'll leave two feet of space between us at all times. Unless we see Tucker the Fucker. Then all bets are off."

I roll my eyes.

"I'm taking that as a yes. I can't wait to not touch you in a public place later." He flops over beside me and tucks his hands behind his head, grinning like a loon.

"I bet you don't last more than twenty minutes before you put your hands on me."

"That sounds like a dare." He winks. "Careful, Dillion. I'm a fan of a challenge."

I leave Bee's cottage with a spring in my step and a smile on my face; despite the fact that I haven't slept much, nothing can get me down.

At least not until I step inside my trailer and find the place is a huge mess, thanks to last night's storm. I left the windows unzipped, and I was obviously too busy getting busy to remember to close them, so my sheets are soaked, and I'm betting so is my mattress. The floor has several puddles, and the paperwork I was going over on my table is scattered across the floor, the ink bleeding across the pages. I'm lucky my laptop is at work and not on the table where I usually leave it, since there's a very prominent leak there, based on the shallow pool that a few dead bugs and pine needles are floating in.

The rain has stopped, but the damage is already done, and there isn't anything I can do other than throw everything I can in the wash and put all the cushions out to dry in the sun for the day. I don't have time to tackle the rest of the mess, so I do what I can, then rush into the house and have a quick shower.

I'm grateful that most of my clothes are stored inside the house; otherwise, I'd probably be struggling to find a clean, dry outfit that doesn't smell like old wet trailer. My dad and I spend the next four hours at a huge, gorgeous five-thousand-square-foot "cottage" that has not one, but three kitchens: one on the main floor, one in the walk-out basement (which functions like a fully outfitted apartment), and a third outside.

It's amazing and lavish and probably one of the most beautiful homes I've ever been in. I've never had so much kitchen envy in my life. I've lived with secondhand, renovated kitchens or the kind you get when you live in a small apartment in the city—tiny, functional, and not very exciting. So helping someone else decide on the cabinets, counters, floors, and lighting for a kitchen that is literally my own personal version of heaven is both wonderful and painful.

Wonderful because we're building a whole new client base that will keep my dad busy through the entire winter; painful because my current kitchen status consists of a tiny sink, a hot plate, and two small cupboards.

One thing I did as soon as we started working on the Bowmans' place was to have signs made so we could stick them at the end of the driveway and another on the lakeside for all the nosy boaters. Since I took that step, we've had at least two calls a day from other interested lake dwellers. We've more than made up for the two lost clients resulting from Billy's accident.

With enough winter projects, my dad won't have to take on quite so many snowplowing contracts. Those contracts are lucrative but also dangerous, because the winter storms can be particularly fierce here, and a lot of car accidents happen as a result.

Limiting the snow removal to driveways and local businesses will mean my dad is safer, and we'll have less wear and tear on the company vehicles. It's a win all the way around.

My dad takes the wheel on the trip back home, and we stop at the diner to grab a bite to eat and pick up Mom, who sometimes works the Sunday-morning shift. She doesn't have to—the house is paid off, and my dad can easily afford to maintain their simple lifestyle on his salary alone—but she loves the socialness of it.

She tried to scale back her hours a few years ago, but she didn't like being idle, and she missed the conversation and the people. I also think she likes the opportunity to keep tabs on what's going on in town, and she doesn't want to get sucked back into the bookkeeping for my dad.

"Do you know what time Billy came home last night?" I ask as we pull off the smoothly paved road and back onto the pitted one that will take us through town.

Dad taps the steering wheel. "I figured he came home with you."

"I lost track of him when the storm rolled in." Worry and guilt make my throat and shoulders tight.

"Well, his door was closed this morning, and he left dirty shoe prints all over the kitchen floor, so he made it home fine either way." He gives me a small smile, the kind that holds strain.

"Do you know what's going on with him? I know he's always been a bit of an ongoing concern, but he's not a teenager anymore, and he's still kind of acting like one."

"You know boys are slow to mature."

I nod. "Sure, I get it, and he and I talked about how it's hard for him with me being back home, but I don't know . . . I worry that there's more going on. He has such huge ups and downs. Last night he was trying to do keg stands with a cast."

"He was just looking to impress his friends."

I should know better than to expect my dad to admit that there are more things wrong than he'd like there to be. It's not that he doesn't see it; it's more that he doesn't want to make Billy feel worse. Living in the shadow of a sibling isn't easy, and I'm sure finding the balance between celebrating one child's glowing accomplishments and another's less flashy ones is tricky.

"Probably," I agree.

I know he doesn't want Billy to feel like his path is any less valued than mine, and having me home, working with Dad, makes that so much more of a challenge. I let it be for now.

"Do we have any more news on the court date?" I took Billy to meet with Bernie not that long ago, but I haven't heard anything back yet, and I worry that if we don't obtain the information directly from the source, Billy might accidentally forget to say something and miss it.

"Not yet. Hopefully next month, though. It'd be great to get that over with so it's one less stress for your mom. I think we'd all like to move on."

Again, I bite my tongue. There's more to this than just getting it out of the way, but I don't want to make more waves than necessary right now.

It's early afternoon by the time we get back home, and I still have to tackle the mess that is my trailer. At least the sun is shining, and we're not expecting another storm, based on the current weather reports.

I spend the next couple of hours tidying up, but there's a musty smell in the trailer. I open the windows and haul everything out, fill a bucket with water, add bleach and soap, and get to work scrubbing down the surfaces. I also mark all the spots that leak and search my dad's garage for the supplies I need to patch things up.

The entire trailer probably needs replacing, but I can't see doing that now—not when I don't have plans to stay here past Thanksgiving. But even as I think it, I wonder if it's actually true, because as much as I love the city, I'm starting to find that I'm getting comfortable here, maybe more than I realized.

I'm in the middle of patching one of the bigger holes when my phone rings. The sound is muffled and probably coming from my purse. I drop what I'm doing, aware I haven't heard anything from anyone all day.

I find my phone before the call goes to voice mail. I've missed more than forty messages.

"Hello?"

"Why is it dinnertime and we still don't have an update on what happened last night?" Tawny barks.

"Unless you're still with Van the Man? Oh my gosh, you're breathing heavy. We totally interrupted, didn't we?" Allie asks, which means they're both on the call.

I check the time, worried I'm going to be late for my date, but it's only five. When I was growing up, Tawny's family always ate dinner at four thirty because her mom didn't like to eat after dark. "What? No. I wouldn't have answered the phone if I was having sex. And Van the Man is a terrible nickname."

"Not if he *is* the man." I can hear her brows waggling. "So? What the heck happened? The last message you sent was yesterday night at ten."

"We ended up taking cover and waiting out the storm."

"In the back seat of your truck?" Allie asks, voice vibrating with excitement.

"I would not have sex in my dad's truck!" I shout and then peek out the window to make sure no one's around to hear me. "I'm not in high school anymore. Back seat sexing is not in the cards. Besides, it's awkward as hell."

"So you waited out the storm. Then what?"

"We went back to his place."

"For heaven's sake, Dee, will you stop making us drag it out of you? Did you or didn't you ride the Van Express?"

"The Van Express? What is this, high school?" It certainly reminds me of the days when we used to go on dates and then tell each other all the gritty details—the good, the bad, the ugly, and the disappointing.

"Stop evading and answer the damn question," Allie demands.

"Am I on speakerphone?" The last thing I want to do is tell everyone in town about last night's sexcapades.

"Yeah, but we're inside my house," Tawny assures me. "No one can hear you except me and Allie . . . and my cat, Narbles, but your secret is safe with her since she can only communicate in high-pitched yowls."

"I did ride the Van Express. More than once, actually."

"Yes! I knew it! You owe me twenty bucks!" Tawny's shrill voice forces me to pull the phone away from my ear.

"You two made a bet?" I chuckle.

"As if you're surprised. I figured you wouldn't make it past third base; obviously you've changed since high school," Allie mutters, clearly annoyed that she didn't win.

"Are you slut shaming me?"

"What? No! Of course not. I'm just saying, you made Tucker wait forever before you let him get past third base."

"He was relentless, and not worth losing my virginity to."

"But this sex was good?" Tawny shifts the topic back to Van, probably because talking about Tucker always put me in a sour mood back in the day, and nothing has changed.

"Mind-blowingly fabulous, actually."

"Does this mean we're getting together later tonight so you can share all the juicy details then?"

"Uh, detail sharing will have to wait; I'm having dinner with Van tonight."

"Like a date? Is he taking you out somewhere? Are you going to the Pearl Tavern? I hear they have amazing steak, but it's, like, sixty dollars for a tiny little piece. I mean, it's wrapped in bacon, but they apparently don't even have barbecue sauce or A1 either."

This time when I laugh, I snort.

"Seriously, Allie?" Tawny chastises. "Everyone knows if the steak is really good, you don't even need the barbecue sauce."

"Well, obviously I've never had steak that good, so excuse me for liking it with barbecue sauce. At least I don't use ketchup!"

I hear the sound of shuffling in the driveway and peek out the window. I catch a shadow, but whoever it is disappears around the side of the house. I worry it's one of Billy's friends. I haven't seen my brother at all since last night, and I have to assume that he's sleeping off his hangover. "Hey, can I call you back? I think there's someone here."

"Tomorrow night you have plans with me and Allie—seven o'clock, drinks at my place."

"Tomorrow at seven. Got it."

"And there will be details. We'll be worse than the football team after a keg party."

I make a fake gagging sound. "I sincerely hope not. Those guys were always gross times a million after one of their postgame keggers. Talk to you tomorrow."

"Have fun tonight!"

I end the call, smiling to myself. It's nice to have Tawny and Allie back in my life. They were always such great friends. Even when I decided to go away to college, they were supportive of my decision.

I fling open the door to the trailer, intent on checking on Billy and getting ready for my date with Van, when Tucker, of all people, comes staggering around the side of the house. I used to think he was so gorgeous. Everyone did. He was a classic all-American football player who got good grades and was prom-king material, went to college upstate, and came home all the time to brag to his friends about all the fun he was having, and yet he still ended up back here. Ended up with my frenemy.

Except maybe appearances are far more deceiving than I first believed them to be.

"Hey. I was looking for you. No one answered the door, and now I know why." He jams a hand in his pocket and weaves two steps to the right before he overcorrects and stumbles on a divot in the grass.

I cross my arms. "What're you doing here, Tucker?"

His gaze slides over me, not quite tracking, and he smirks. "I came to see you. What else would I be doing here?"

"Are you drunk? Did you drive here?" I glance behind him, looking for a car, but there isn't one.

"I walked with my friend Johnnie." He pulls a flask from his pocket and shakes it around. It doesn't make any sound, which tells me it's empty.

I sigh, annoyed that he's drunk and obviously here to stir up shit. "Why would you be here to see me when you have a baby and girlfriend at home?"

He runs a hand through his hair. "The kid's not mine."

"What does that mean?"

He unscrews the flask and tries to take a sip but discovers what I already know: there's nothing left. He sighs and gives me a wry smile. "I'm shooting blanks."

"I'm sorry. What?"

"I can't have kids. Got tested a while back, after Sue got pregnant, 'cause the dates didn't line up."

"Should you be telling me this?"

He shrugs. "You'll find out eventually. Everyone will, 'cause Sue is sleeping with Sterling. Has been for a while now. Based on our kid, for at least a year."

That's what Tawny and Allie were saying last night at the beach party, but sometimes gossip is fiction, not fact. That doesn't seem to be the case here. "Geez, Tucker, why are you telling me all this?" I don't want this kind of information. This is one of the reasons I wanted out of here when I was a teenager. I'm happy in my bubble, one that doesn't include Tucker and his messed-up relationships.

He lifts a shoulder and lets it fall. "I fucked up, Darlin'. With you, I mean. I didn't realize what I had until I lost it."

"You cheated on me all the time or called breaks when you wanted to rub your hookups in my face, and then you ended up with freaking Sue."

"I know." He hangs his head. "I made so many mistakes. I thought . . . I don't know. I was mad that you were leaving."

"And you thought cheating and hookups would somehow communicate that to me?"

"If you knew, why didn't you say anything? Why didn't you ever call me out on it?"

"What would it have changed? The damage was already done, Tucker. I'm not saying this to hurt you, but I was biding my time. We weren't meant to have a forever, but we were too connected by all of our friends to break up and it not be awkward. I didn't want my last summer to be ruined. Should I have called you out? Probably. But I can't go back and change things."

"You're here now, though." He rocks back on his heels.

"I didn't come back for you, Tucker. I came back for my family."

"Word has it your boyfriend dumped you, and now you're hooking up with your neighbor."

"This freaking town and the gossip mongering is ridiculous," I mutter. "My ex-boyfriend and I split amicably because he wanted to move to Connecticut for a job and I wasn't interested in following him."

"So you just came back because of what happened with Billy?"

"And because my dad needed my help."

"There's no chance for us, then, huh?"

I blow out a breath, frustrated, but aware that this is a conversation I should have had years ago. "There wasn't a chance for us the second you started sleeping with people who weren't me when we were still dating. Or calling a break and hooking up with people in front of my face."

"I just wanted you to stay."

"No offense, but that was a stupid way to show me you wanted me to stick around."

"My ego got in the way back then."

"Does Sue know that you're aware of what's going on?"

He shrugs.

"Does Sterling?"

"I think he thinks he's been all sly about it." He hangs his head. "I wanted you to come back and be jealous, but it's pretty much the other way around now, isn't it?"

Despite all the crap he put me through, I feel bad for him. He might have hurt me back then, but I let him get away with it, which probably didn't help things. And then I disappeared. Neither of us ever got the closure we needed.

"I should probably go home, but I can't."

"Because Sue will be upset that you're drunk."

"Nah, she won't care about that. I drove by the house earlier this afternoon and saw Sterling's tow truck parked two streets over. I don't want to go home and smell him all over her."

I sigh. I would like to get ready for my date, but at the same time, sending Tucker home in his state probably isn't the best idea.

"Why don't you come in? The trailer's not in the best shape, but I can make you something to eat so you can sober up and get a handle on yourself before you go home."

"Why are you always so good to everyone, even when they screw you over?" He stumbles forward a couple of steps.

"It's a personality flaw." I take him by the elbow and lead him into the trailer. He almost hits his head on the top of the door but manages to duck just in time. "Do you still like peanut butter and honey, or have your taste buds matured since high school?"

"I still like peanut butter and honey. You got the clover stuff?"

"Is there any other kind?" I pull the peanut butter and honey and bread out and set them on the tiny counter as Tucker slides onto the bench and folds his hands on the table.

He looks so broken and defeated, like life has beaten him down. It makes me sad to see Tucker like this, the creator of his own demise, unable to break the cycle he perpetuates. A victim of his own making.

CHAPTER 17
ECHOES

Van

Dillion should be here soon, and I have zero chill, so I head outside to check the truck and make sure I haven't left a bunch of take-out cups on the floor. Grammy Bee couldn't stand garbage in the truck. When I was a teenager, if I left so much as the corner of a wrapper on the floor, she'd make me scrub the whole thing by hand as punishment.

I consider, for half a second, taking the BMW instead. It's a much smoother ride, and a nicer car, but Dillion is as impressed with material things as I am with soggy breakfast cereal. And I'd rather drive the truck anyway. It might not have the best shocks, but it fits in better here than a sports car. Also, the front seat is a bench, with no center console, which means no physical barriers.

I find an empty coffee cup in the holder on the dash, but otherwise it's clean. I toss it in the garbage and hear the sound of Dillion's trailer door spring shut, indicating that she's probably on her way over. Dillion is nearly silent when she's coming through the path, and half the time she magically appears at the edge of the property line and scares the crap out of me. But this time I catch the loud crunch of gravel and what sounds like someone dragging their feet. It's followed by mumbling.

Unless Dillion has suddenly come down with some kind of illness that causes her voice to drop two octaves, a dude just left her trailer.

I catch movement between the trees and someone heading down the driveway. And that someone happens to be Tucker the Fucker.

He doesn't appear to be moving very quickly, so I walk to the end of my own driveway and cut him off before he can reach the end of Dillion's. I slip one hand in my pocket, aiming for nonchalant. "Hey, Tucker."

He startles, his attention having been on his feet. His gaze is slow to meet mine. "Oh, hey, Van."

"What are you doing here?" I flip my keys around on my finger.

He glances back over his shoulder, like he's not quite sure where he is. "Nothin'. I'm not doing anything."

"That sounds like a load of bullshit, considering you came from Dillion's trailer." I didn't *see* him leave the trailer, but I heard the door close and he's walking away, so I'm assuming he was in there. With her. Alone. While I'm not particularly worried about Dillion's ability to take care of herself, I also remember what he said to me about her when I first met him. "So why don't we try that again. Why are you here?"

"It's none of your fuckin' business," Tucker mutters and then takes an unsteady step to the right, trying to get around me.

"Are you drunk?" I move closer and get a whiff of whiskey and . . . peanut butter?

"Nah, man. I'm fine."

"Really? Because you smell like you bathed in a bottle of booze. Don't be comin' around here messing with Dillion. Especially in this kind of condition. Get yourself together, Tucker, and figure out your shit. She's moved on, and so should you."

"With you?" He spits the words.

"With her life. Doesn't this town already have enough to gossip about without you dragging Dillion into your crap too? She doesn't need your drama; she has her own stuff to deal with."

He sags, like an air mattress with a hole in it. "You're right. I know that. I just thought . . . I don't know. She was always good at forgiving."

"She doesn't do much forgetting, though." I pull my phone out of my pocket. "I'm going to call you an Uber."

Tucker shakes his head. "You don't need to do that; 'sides, it'll take forever for them to get here. I can walk. I'm only a couple miles down the road."

"I'd feel better if I knew you made it home okay." I place the order and wait with him at the end of the driveway for the car to arrive. Of course it's someone he knows. He gets in the front seat instead of the back and gives me a wave before they head toward town.

I make my way down the driveway, toward Dillion's trailer. I'm about twenty feet away when she opens the door and tips her head to the side, looking confused about why I'm coming from the top of her driveway.

I thumb over my shoulder. "I sent Tucker the Fucker home in an Uber."

"Oh." She crosses her arms and bites her bottom lip. "That was good of you. I probably should've thought of that."

I stop a few feet away, assessing her posture and how tense she seems. "You okay? He didn't do anything to make you uncomfortable, did he? Because I can go kick his ass if he did."

Dillion chuckles and drops her arms. "No, he didn't try anything, and I don't honestly think it would be a fair fight, since he's still half-hammered."

"He smelled like whiskey."

"That's because he polished off a flask on his way over." Dillion exhales loudly and rubs the space between her eyes.

"You want to talk about it? He seemed like he was pretty beat down."

"Basically his life is a mess. His girlfriend and I used to be friends in high school." She makes a face. "Not really friends. More like frenemies.

171

Anyway, she had a thing for him back then, and I guess she never stopped having a thing for him. They got together at a party a couple years ago, and now they have a baby. I don't know all the details, but from what he said, she's been cheating on him for a while and the baby isn't even his, so it's kind of a cluster and he's right in the middle of it."

"Wow."

"Yeah. Small-town drama is real." She twists one of her curls around her finger. "Anyway, I'm running behind because I was dealing with his meltdown. I need to grab a shower before dinner, if you're still up for it."

"Absolutely." I take another step forward, and she takes one back.

"I don't smell all that fresh."

"I don't mind if you don't." I link my pinkie with hers and step up so I'm in her personal space. And that's when I get a full view of the inside of the trailer. "Holy shit, Dillion, it looks like it rained inside here last night."

"I left the windows open, and there are a few leaks. It could be worse, though."

"Not by much." The mattress isn't even on the bed, and there's a huge watermark on the wooden platform. It also smells dank, like old wet stuff. "You can't stay here."

She waves her hand around in the air, like it's not a big deal. "I'll sleep in my brother's old room until it dries out."

I point to my chest. "I happen to have a great bed that I'd be willing to share."

"Oh yeah?"

"Absolutely. It even comes with orgasms. And postorgasm spooning." I waggle my eyebrows, hoping it will make her laugh.

She chuckles. "Orgasms and spooning? What more could a girl ask for?"

An hour later Dillion has moved her toiletries and a few outfits over to my place, citing that as soon as the trailer is dried out and she's patched all the holes, she's moving back to her place. I leave her to shower on her own, aware that she'll be sleeping beside me tonight, and I've already promised orgasms and spooning, so there's no need to rush things.

She pulls on a pair of jeans and a loose tank, and we climb into Grammy Bee's old truck.

It takes a few tries to get the engine to turn over. "Any suggestions as to where we should eat?"

It's not as though we have a huge array of choices. She taps her lip, thinking for a moment. "How about Casual Affair? It's a couple of steps up from the diner and has better food than the bar. Everything is homemade, so the options are limited, but if you're into home cooking, it's honestly the best place in town."

"I'm game."

I'm more than happy to try something new. I don't have a ton of memories of my mom, but she used to make me breakfast every morning and always made fun dinners, like homemade mini pizzas, since my dad often worked long hours. After she passed, our nanny took over making meals for us. She made sandwiches on some ridiculously healthy whole grain seed bread that was gluten- and basically taste-free. I'm hoping this will be different. And better tasting.

When we arrive at the restaurant, we opt for a table on the outdoor patio. It's a seat-yourself establishment, so we head for the side with the water view. The breeze coming off the lake cuts the heat, and the backdrop of thick green forest is gorgeous.

Dillion stops to say hello to nearly everyone in the place and introduces me as her friend and Bee's grandson. Each time, I hear a story about my grandmother and how much everyone loved her and misses her. And although the circumstances for my being here aren't ideal, I feel like I'm exactly where I'm supposed to be.

We finally spot a two top near the back of the patio. I move my chair so I'm sitting kitty-corner to Dillion, and our knees bump under the table.

"I thought this was supposed to be a no-contact dinner."

"Since when?" I stretch one leg out under both of hers.

"Since this morning, when we discussed the whole PDA limitations of this date."

I scoff and scoot my chair even closer. "I wasn't even fully awake and was probably talking out of my ass. Nothing I said this morning counts."

She laughs and shakes her head. "You're really looking to get into the small-town gossip circuit, huh?"

"News headlines seem like something to aim for." I lean in and nuzzle her neck, nipping at her skin.

She lets out a small very non-Dillion shriek and covers my entire face with her hand, pushing me away, her eyes darting around the restaurant while her face turns scarlet. "Seriously, Van! You just love being an instigator, don't you?"

I lean back in my chair, grinning. "Only with you, since you're so easy to rile up."

The server comes over, her face matching Dillion's in color. She can't make eye contact with me, and of course, Dillion went to school with her older sister, so that turns into a conversation.

Dinner is full of interruptions from locals who want to talk to Dillion. Between catching up with people she went to high school with and clients of her dad's, we barely get fifteen minutes to ourselves, and I have no more opportunities for embarrassing PDAs. But watching Dillion in her element is enthralling. She's charming, charismatic, and nothing like the riled-up woman I was dealing with until last night. She's fascinating.

After we finish stuffing our faces—Dillion was right, the food is amazing; it's like a barbecue cookout, but better—she suggests we take a walk on the beach. We're on the southeast side of the lake, not far from where the beach party took place.

I thread my fingers through hers, and we stroll close to the shore. "So how do you like working for your dad?"

"It's actually been really good. I sort of expected there to be an adjustment period, being family and his daughter, but it's been nearly seamless."

"That's great. Is it the same thing you were doing in Chicago?" I realize I don't even know what Dillion's job was, or is.

She nods. "Project management, yeah. It's similar, just on a smaller scale. I used to manage projects for a pharmaceutical company. It was pretty impersonal, but the money was good, and at the time, that mattered."

"Because rent in Chicago isn't cheap?" I ask.

"Exactly. I actually like this better in a lot of ways. I get to help make connections with other small, independent companies, and I know most of the people who run the businesses in town. It's great to be able to work with other local businesses instead. Sure, I'm still look-ing for the best deal so we can keep costs down, but the bottom line isn't always the most important thing in a place like this." Dillion motions to the line of shops and restaurants behind us.

"It'll be harder to find a job like that when you go back to Chicago, won't it?"

"Probably, yeah." Dillion has an odd look on her face, but I can't quite read it. It's a mixture of hesitation and deep thought.

"I don't know that it's going to be much different for me."

"How do you mean?"

"I took a job for a company that specialized mainly in skyscrapers because I loved designing and the company offered me a great salary. I enjoyed what I did, and the money was a serious perk, but I don't know that I'd be in love with it the same way I was before I came here."

Dillion tips her head to the side. "What's changed for you?"

"I don't know exactly. Nothing and everything, I guess. It's just . . . different. It makes me question what the hell the point is when all I'm doing is working to live, rather than living to work. If that makes sense."

Dillion nods. "I know exactly what you mean. I realized that my whole world revolved around work and work people back in Chicago, but here it's not the same. There's something about this place—I don't know what it is, but aside from the gossip, it's hard not to love it here."

"I completely agree. And I'm loving working on Bee's garage, finding a way to take the existing structure and turn it into a functional living space."

"You should talk to Aaron or my dad about looking at your plans before you start on that. They'll be able to make sure you're adhering to the bylaws."

"I talked to Aaron about it at the beach party." The beach becomes progressively more overrun with weeds the closer we get to the beach party's location. "Why doesn't this get the same treatment as the beach on the other side of the lake?" I thumb over my shoulder.

"Because the other side is where all the summer homes are. They generate income for the town, so they put more effort into maintaining the beach there."

Here the tree line isn't interrupted by as many huge homes and docks with boathouses. "But this side is gorgeous. If the beaches were better taken care of, wouldn't they be even nicer?"

"Maybe. Probably," Dillion agrees. "But the locals worry the north side people would take it over like they've already done on the other side of the lake."

"So it's partly intentional?" I press.

"Yes and no. Obviously we'd love to have a nicer public beach, but it's what we're used to, and we can't afford another marina on this lake, which is probably what would end up happening. It's just too much pollution, you know? This lake used to be pristine, but as soon as they added the marina on the north side, it changed the entire ecosystem.

The town tried to fight against one on the other side of the lake, but obviously we lost. They had the money to make it happen, and they have the money to keep the beach clean and family friendly, so that's where they put it."

"Do you think they'd want to use this beach when they already have their own?"

"We just don't want it to catch anyone's attention. The summer home boundaries are already creeping to the east and west. We don't want to lose the entire lake. It's about maintaining balance. So much of the town is based on tourism, and of course we want to keep that thriving, just not at the expense of the entire community."

"Is there a way to do that? To maintain the beach on this side of the lake without making it too appealing?" I stop to pick up an empty beer bottle and toss it in the trash.

"I don't think anyone has tried too hard. Bee was vocal at town-council meetings back in the day, but no one else has stepped up to the plate. Besides, there's a hefty price tag attached to that kind of thing. Maintaining the beach costs man-hours, and that's not in the town budget."

"It should be equitable, though, shouldn't it?" The docks on this side are falling apart, whereas the public beach on the other side has lifeguards, new floating rafts, and gorgeous sand.

Dillion gives me a knowing look. "It all comes down to the money and who's providing it. The people in this community are middle class, and most of them make ends meet just fine, but they don't have thousands to spare to pay someone's salary to maintain a slice of beach."

It's not like I don't already know this. I witnessed it firsthand every summer. While I chose to stay in Grammy Bee's cottage and spend most of my days on this side of the lake, if I'd wanted to, I could've gone to the beach on the other side, and no one would have given me a second glance, but it's not the same for the locals. Or at least that's how it seems.

There's a level of tolerance between the local community and the vacationers. But it isn't necessarily symbiotic. Especially since now, more and more of the vacation homes are becoming permanent residences, which changes the dynamic of the community. I see it more clearly now than I did when I was younger, and I can only imagine how hard it must have been for Grammy Bee when she married someone her family didn't approve of and eventually chose his world over her own.

Warning signs are posted at the end of each dock, a single flimsy chain strung across the two anchoring posts. The signs are faded and peeling, indicating that they've been in this state of disrepair for a number of years already. Their effectiveness is highly questionable, with a few hanging so low even a toddler could step over them. As if that isn't bad enough, several docks are missing boards along the way, a gap-toothed grimace of rotten wood.

It's clear that people use them all the time, though, based on the words carved into the decaying boards. Some of it looks like the work of teenagers, while others are far more sophisticated, with messages like "Protect the South Beach community." I look around the beach and notice for the first time that the mess from last night has already been cleaned up. Only a few stray red plastic cups are lingering in the bushes, and the bonfire has been put out and marked with signs so kids don't accidentally run through the ashes.

"How did this get cleaned up so quickly?"

"Usually there's a group of us who will come with a couple garbage bags to get rid of the trash and make the beach useable again," Dillion says.

"Were you one of them?"

"Not this time, but Allie and Tawny pitched in while I was at that meeting with my dad."

"If they're willing to pick up plastic cups and beer bottles, do you think they'd be willing to go further to make it safer, especially the docks? Sometimes people need to see change is possible to be compelled to help make it happen."

"They might be, but cleaning it up is one thing; fixing all the docks and maintaining them is totally another." Dillion tucks her thumbs into her back pockets.

"I can look into it," I say. "See what the town is willing to do to help out, maybe push the Grammy Bee angle, since I know it was important to her?"

She smiles. "She loved it here. More than anyplace in town, this was her favorite. I used to drive out here with her, even in the winter. It'd be balls cold, and she'd bundle up and trudge through the snowbanks just to stand on the beach until we couldn't feel our toes and the tears froze on our cheeks, thanks to the wind."

"Sounds like Bee. Did you drink hot toddies afterward?"

"First we stopped at Boones for apple fritters. Then we'd head back and drink spiked hot chocolate. It's a wonder we never ended up in a sugar coma on those days."

She used to do exactly the same thing with me, even before I was allowed to drink alcohol legally. It makes me wonder how many of our experiences with Bee echo each other's, and if she hasn't been working her magic from the other side by threading our lives together, without us even realizing it.

CHAPTER 18
THE NEW NOT QUITE NORMAL

Dillion

As amazing as sleeping next to Van is, I move back into my trailer after a few nights. He insists that I can stay with him as long as I want, and while the comfort of his bed and the company are incredibly appealing, I cite early mornings and my middle-of-the-night thrashing as reasons why I should stay at my place most of the time.

But the real reason is . . . I'm starting to like him. A lot. And as fun as he is to spend time with, I don't want to lose sight of my own goals. It would be easy to get caught up in a summer romance, one that invariably has an end date attached to it, and that date is likely going to be sooner rather than later.

Since I've been back, I've been undecided on what my next move will be. I've been looking at positions for project managers in Chicago and checking out rentals that have a half-hour commute or maybe even less. I want to have options once I'm no longer needed here, but none of the positions have been all that appealing so far. With all the reno projects this winter, it seems like my dad is going to be on-site more and in the office less, so no matter what happens, I'll likely have to train someone to take over for me when the time comes.

I'm also aware that there's a possibility Van will eventually decide his best option is to sell Bee's property. And it would be hard to fault him, if that's what he ends up doing. With everything hanging over his head and no job, it may be the only thing he can do. So I'm reluctant to let my heart get all soft over him.

Not that I'm having much luck in that department. Everything he does makes me all melty like a toasted marshmallow.

"Hey, Dee, you in there?" Aaron snaps his fingers and gives me a wry smile.

"Huh? Oh, hey. Just lost in thought. What do you need?"

"You feeling okay?" His brows pull together.

"Yeah, of course. Why?"

He adjusts the brim of his hat and rubs the back of his neck. "Uh, I called your name three times before you snapped out of your trance."

"Oh." I touch my cheek with the back of my hand. "I'm fine. I just . . . have a lot on my mind. Anyway. What can I help you with?"

"I need to check the loft plans for the Bowmans' 'garage' and the kitchen reno for the Kingstons." He makes air quotes around the word *garage*. It's one of the ways the north side folks get around some of the tricky building permits. They'll build a one-and-a-half-story garage and put a loft on the second floor.

"Right. Yeah. Is everything okay?" Both of those projects are extensive and aren't slated to start until later in the summer, after the official beginning of hockey season, when most people have gone back to the city, or farther south if they're intent on avoiding the snow as much as possible.

Aaron raises both hands in the air, a motion meant to be calming. "Everything's fine. Mrs. Bowman wants to look at a few more options for the garage, and they're wondering if they might be able to put an extra bedroom in the pool house. They're putting in one of those swim-spa things, and those pool guys from the city are always slowing us down."

"We need to find someone local who installs pools."

Aaron nods. "There's a couple in Lake Geneva, but they're all booked up until next summer. Anyway, if you have the plans handy, it'd be great if we could take a look at them. I want to see what all I'll need to be able to tie into the existing plumbing, and I think there's a chance we'll have to upgrade the septic with the additional bathrooms they're planning to put in."

"Will you need to visit the property again to assess that?"

"Definitely, but I figure it's best if I go over the plans first and make sure everything is doable. You know what those architects are like. Sometimes the ideas are great but the execution isn't actually possible."

I spin around in my chair, open the filing cabinet holding all the current and upcoming jobs, and find the files he's asking about.

"Do you want to do that on your own, or would it be better for me to hang around and make notes?"

"If you have time for that, it would definitely cut out a few steps later." He nods to the stacks of paperwork on my desk. "But I understand if you're busy."

"I'm always busy, but in the interest of making less work for myself later, and you having to explain all this stuff to my dad, and then him having to explain it to me, and all of us having to explain it to the Bowmans, it sort of seems like it makes better sense for you and me to go over this stuff together?" I pose it as a question.

"Makes sense to me."

"Great. Let's do it, then. I'll make a fresh pot of coffee." I abandon the invoices I'm currently working on, grab my things, and follow Aaron to the break room so there's enough space for us to spread out.

Half an hour later I have a purchase list, a revised potential cost list, hourly rate subtotals, and bullet points to go over with Mrs. Bowman. I fire off an email to her and ask if there's a date and time that will work for her to get together to review the revisions. Her husband's response to almost every email we've sent is "Whatever Lainey thinks is best." It's kind of cute.

"These mansion renovations should set us up for the entire winter." Aaron leans back in his chair and sips his coffee.

"I think that's what we're all hoping. It's why I'm spending so much time making sure everything is managed efficiently where they're concerned, you know? We need great customer service so they tell all their friends about how awesome we are."

He nods his agreement. "You think maybe you want to stay on past Christmas?"

I shrug. "Billy will probably be back by then."

"Yeah, but he works on the projects, and these big ones mean either John or your dad needs to be on-site to help manage them. It's not like the small stuff we do for the local businesses that take a couple of days, or a week, and don't need extra supervision. And lately the projects have been more involved on my end. I'm not complaining, but it means we need all the manpower we can get."

I focus on my coffee mug, tracing the design on the front. "Do you think Billy will be okay working on these bigger projects?"

Aaron lifts his ball cap and runs a hand through his hair before replacing it and bending the brim. "Hard to say. He can be a real asset or a real liability. Depends on what he's been up to the night before."

This is the stuff I've been trying to get out of my parents ever since I've been back here: I want to know what the situation is with Billy and whether the DUI charge was a random accident or something more. "How many days a week would you say he was an asset?"

Aaron is silent for a few moments, weighing his response. "Maybe half and half just before he had the accident. Before that it was most of the time, but I don't know, Dee . . ." He looks around, not wanting to be caught gossiping. "He's changed in the past year. Something is just . . . off, I guess? He was always into mischief, but it was basically harmless when we were kids. Now, not so much." He takes another sip of his coffee. "I don't want to throw him under the bus or anything, but recently, like say maybe the past six months, I haven't been hanging out with him all that much."

"I noticed he was with the Wallace boys at the beach party."

"Yeah. He's been spending more time with those two, and they're nice enough guys, but they're not all that motivated. Mostly all they do is drink beers and drive around on their ATVs. And maybe that was fine when we were teenagers, but we're adults. I guess I'm looking to settle down, and he's still partying like it's senior year."

"I'm worried about him," I admit.

"Honestly, me too. I've messaged him a bunch of times since the accident, but he hasn't had much to say other than the painkillers they've been giving him kick some serious ass. Last week he asked if I had his journal from high school, though, which was weird."

"I didn't even know he had a journal."

"Me either. He doesn't seem like the type to put his feelings on a page. I chalked it up to the painkillers and left it at that." Aaron gives me a small smile.

"Maybe that's all it was, some kind of dream thing?" But I'm not sure I buy that. Billy has always been different, but this is more than that. I don't know how to broach this with my dad without him going on the defensive, but I don't feel like I can ignore it anymore.

As a teenager I used to get so annoyed that we always had to be home to have dinner as a family. It didn't matter if I was halfway across town with my friends, usually Tawny and Allie, sometimes Tucker—I'd jump on my bike and pedal my butt home. Sometimes the ride would be fast and reckless as I cut through the paths in the forest because I didn't want to be late and end up on dishwashing duty. But lately I find myself looking forward to family dinners, even with Billy's unpredictable moods.

"Where's Billy?" I ask as I set knives and forks on top of the napkins. That's one thing my mom always had: pretty napkins. Most of the time they were one season out of date because she always bought them on sale, so in the winter we'd have fall and Thanksgiving themes, and by spring it was snowmen and holly. Currently the napkins we're using have an Easter theme.

"Still in his room, I think. I knocked on his door a few minutes ago. When you're done setting the table, could you knock again, please?" She tastes the potato salad, her expression contemplative, before she turns back to the fridge, grabs a jar of pickles, and pours in extra dill juice for flavor.

"Sure thing." Once the salt and pepper are on the table, I head down the hall to Billy's room and knock, calling out, "Dinner's ready."

I listen for the sound of the bed creaking, or the computer chair rolling across the floor, but all I'm met with is silence. I knock again. "Hey, Billy, you in there?"

When I don't get an answer, I open the door, thinking maybe he's wearing headphones. But he's not. He's fast asleep, drooling on his pillow. His bedroom smells like stale farts and beer. A stack of empty bowls sits on his nightstand, and empty beer cans peek out from under his bed.

I cross the room, stepping on a discarded chip bag, which crinkles loudly, and poke him in the shoulder. When that doesn't rouse him, I give him a solid shake. He groans and flings his arm out. I'm agile enough to get out of the way before he can accidentally smack me. But he hits the can sitting on his nightstand and it tips over, brown liquid splattering the tabletop, his pillow, and the side of his face before I can right it.

"What the hell?" He scrubs a hand down his face and blinks a few times.

"It's dinnertime. I knocked a bunch of times and so did Mom, but you didn't answer. Have you been up at all today?"

"I couldn't sleep last night." He throws off his covers and swings his legs over the side of the bed. He's shirtless, exposing his torso. Billy has always been lean, wiry even, but he's exceptionally thin right now. So much so that his collarbones are sharp points, poking at his skin, and I can practically count his ribs. "Can you pass me that shirt?" He motions to the one hanging over the back of his computer chair.

I toss it to him, and he gives it a cursory sniff before he pulls it over his head. "I can help you clean up in here after dinner." I open the window to let in some fresh air.

"Don't do that!" he snaps.

"It smells like a frat house. You need some fresh air, and probably a little sunshine, unless you're trying out the whole vampire vibe."

His eyes flare and he looks around the room, as if he expects one to appear. "That window needs to stay locked, otherwise people can get in."

I can't tell if he's still half-asleep or if he's making a joke.

"Based on the smell in here, I'm confident you're not going to have any unwanted or wanted midnight visitors." I pick up the stack of dishes and the mostly empty pop can, give the nightstand a quick wipe with a few tissues to soak up most of the mess, and follow him back to the kitchen. The charred crutch has been replaced, but the new one is old and looks like it needs to be adjusted. I'd ask where he got it from, but I worry that in his current mood, all it will do is start a fight.

Billy pushes his food around his plate while Dad talks about the Bowman garage and pool house and all the amazing things that will be coming out of their place that he thinks we can probably make use of. All Billy does is grunt occasionally, and he leaves his plate half-full, says no thanks to dessert, and locks himself back in his room once dinner is over. So much for me helping him tidy his mess. I'd been hoping for an opportunity to snoop, but it doesn't look like that's going to be all that easy. Not when the only time he surfaces these days is for meals and trips to the bathroom.

CHAPTER 19
SIBLING RIVALRY

Van

My phone buzzes from the nightstand. I don't want to answer the call, seeing as Dillion is tucked into my side. She passed out right after the orgasms. We did expend a hell of a lot of energy, and she's been working long hours, so I get it, but sometimes she gets chatty after sex, and I learn new things about her, like her favorite food is popcorn and she has every single seasoning flavor under the sun, but the maple bacon is the one she can't get enough of.

Or she'll tell me stories about growing up in Pearl Lake and how the high school is an hour-long bus ride away, and in the winter they stayed home almost once a week because of all the snow. They would spend those days tobogganing. I wonder if I'll still be around by the time winter hits, or if I'll have found a new job in Chicago. The idea of not being here, with Dillion, hits me for the first time. I can't say I like it much.

I pick the phone up with the intention of sending the call to voice mail, since it's already after ten, but it's Frankie, so I hit the green button and bring the phone to my ear, answering with, "Hold on a sec."

I throw off the covers and grab my boxers from the floor, pulling them up my legs as I make my way across the room. I close the bedroom door behind me and pad quietly down the hall to the living room.

"Hey, you there?" I ask, my voice still low and hoarse.

"Yeah, man, why are you whispering?"

I clear my throat. "I'm not."

"Did I wake you up?" Frankie sounds surprised, which would make sense. When I lived in the city, I was never in bed before midnight. And even that was on the early side for me.

"Not really. Anyway, what's up? Chip break it off with Monica?"

"We should be so lucky. Although I will say, she's been around a lot less. He wasn't impressed with her behavior when we came to visit you. Girl is more high maintenance than a Kardashian." It's good to hear Frankie take my side on this, and by association Dillion's, even if he doesn't actually know her.

"You think he's starting to see the light?" I can only hope he cuts her loose before she persuades him to put a ring on her finger. If that happens, we might have to stage some kind of intervention. I take a seat on the couch, facing the fireplace. The porch light is on, illuminating the area around it, but beyond is a black abyss. That's probably the hardest thing to get used to out here: the only sounds are crickets and the rustle of critters skittering across the forest floor. Combined with the lack of light pollution from high-rises, it's impossible to see more than a few feet in front of you if it's cloudy and there's no moon or stars.

"Keep your fingers crossed, my friend."

"Will do. I'm guessing you didn't call to talk about Monica."

"You would guess correctly. I don't know if you've been keeping tabs on what's going on with your family over the past couple of weeks or not . . ." I can sense his unease, and it makes the hairs on the back of my neck stand on end.

I've been wrapped up in emptying out the garage, cold-calling companies about job opportunities—which hasn't proven fruitful so far—and Dillion. "I've talked to my sister and my dad, and I've messaged my brother, but you know what he's like. Those conversations are about three lines long. Unless something has changed in the last forty-eight hours, all arrows are still pointing at me."

"That's true for the most part, but you know how the media likes to blow things up whenever they can."

I sit up straighter. "Yeah. Why? What are they saying?"

"They're going after your family now. It's not great, Van. You know what your dad is like, always living the high life. Driving flashy cars, wearing expensive suits, outfitting Teagan in head-to-toe Prada."

"Yeah, but what does that have to do with the missing money? Especially when everything already points to me."

"It makes for a good story, though. Like the family who set up a foundation to benefit underprivileged children, only to shelter money and steal it all back because they were in hock up to their eyeballs."

"Ah fuck." I let my head drop back against the couch cushion. "Because my dad has loans out the ying-yang, and somehow they know that?"

"Yeah. Looks like someone might have leaked some information."

"Do I need to come home? Is there anything I can do?"

"No, man, I think you need to stay where you are. If you need to borrow money or anything, I can help you out, interest-free."

"Shit. It's that bad?" Frankie loaned his sister twenty grand once and charged her interest at 0.1 percent less than the bank rate, so him offering to help me out with no interest is a big damn deal.

"It's just media digging around. So as long as you don't have anything to hide, it's gonna be fine, but clearly something shady is going on. I wouldn't be surprised if the board hires someone to investigate it further because they're worried that you didn't do it alone."

"I didn't do it at all," I remind him.

"I know that, but they don't. I think they're drinking the Kool-Aid, and they believe your dad was in on it. They suspended him from the board of directors until they've completed a full audit of the books for the last seven years."

"Well, that's not good. When did all this go down?"

"It all kind of came to a head today. So don't be surprised if you get a call from your sister tomorrow."

"Okay, thanks for the heads-up. What about my brother?"

"It's business as usual there. You know how he is—unaffected by pretty much everything. If you're still good where you are, I suggest staying there."

"Yeah. Of course." I hadn't planned on coming back to the city anytime soon anyway, but it sucks to have the option taken away. I'm worried about Teagan and how she's really dealing with all of this. She's always been on the sensitive side, so this can't be fun for her. And my dad's go-to response to stress is always to spend money, which in this case isn't going to help things.

Calling Bradley to ask for an update is basically useless, since the media drama isn't likely to faze him, unless it affects his ability to access five-star restaurants and hotels.

"Chip and I will come up and visit again in a few weeks. I'll update you if there's more news, and let me know if you need anything: money, supplies, whatever. I can have it sent to you if I can't get it there myself."

"Thanks, man. I appreciate it."

"Talk soon."

Frankie ends the call before I can respond, which is his way.

A tiny part of me wonders if there's any merit to what the media is saying. But then I consider how my dad's been acting since everything happened. Like Frankie, he's been adamant that I stay here, that it's better for me if I don't come back to Chicago, where the media is likely to bombard me. That he's taking care of things and he'll get it all sorted out. My dad is a lot of things, and admittedly not the best parent or financial manager, but he wouldn't sell me out to absolve his debt. I'm being paranoid.

I grab a glass of water and pad back to the bedroom. Dillion has moved into my empty spot and is hugging my pillow. She looks like a fallen angel when she's sleeping. Blonde curls everywhere, pouty lips parted, long lashes brushing her cheek.

I slide back into bed beside her, trying not to move her around too much since she can be a light sleeper. But she's not leaving me with much in the way of room, so I stretch out along her side.

She makes a contented noise, and her palm lands on my chest and slides down. She nuzzles into my neck and murmurs, "You're cold."

I'm not convinced she's entirely awake, so I slip my arm under her and try to relax, but my brain is going a million miles a minute. It's been both a blessing and a curse to be able to turn a blind eye to the mess that is my life and escape up here. But reality is going to come crashing back down eventually, and I need to prepare for that inevitability.

Dillion rolls into me, throwing her leg over mine and nuzzling closer. Eventually I match my breathing to hers. It lulls me to sleep, but it's not peaceful.

Dillion is gone by the time I get my ass out of bed the next morning. She left a note on my pillow saying she'll message later, and she hopes I slept okay. I also have a call from my sister.

I listen to the message and realize right away that things are not okay. Her incoherent sobbing tells me that. Which is a shocker, because Teagan doesn't cry very often. I call her, and she answers on the second ring. I spend the next ten minutes trying to calm her down enough to be able to understand what she's saying.

"Can I come out and stay with you for a few days? I j-j-just need to get out of the city. I can't handle this r-r-right now."

I'm assuming "this" has to do with whatever is going on with the investigation into the missing money and all the society gossip. "Of course you can. Do you need me to come get you?"

"N-no. Bradley said he would drive."

"Bradley? Our brother?" Neither of us know another Bradley, so it's a stupid, unnecessary question. Things must be particularly bad for

191

Bradley to agree to drive her, since he thinks Grammy Bee's cottage is worse than camping in a tent. Which he has never, ever done.

"Y-yes." She sniffles. "I tried to tell him I was okay to drive, but he said he needed a break from all the city drama. I guess yesterday he took a client golfing, and he treated him like a criminal. These people are a bunch of assholes."

"I'm sorry, Teag. I wish this wasn't such a nightmare for everyone."

"It's not your fault. I know it wasn't you who took that money. It's just such a mess here. And Dad went out and bought a freaking new Porsche. As if that's a good idea when we're in the middle of all this crap. Hold on." She blows her nose. "Sorry about that. My friends haven't been very understanding. But none of them are nearly as bad as Troy."

"What happened with Troy?"

"I'll tell you when I see you. I don't want to start crying again."

I have to guess that it's bad if my sister is at risk of shedding even more tears. "Okay, we'll put a pin in that conversation until you get here. When are you planning on heading this way?"

"Bradley is getting his hair cut, and then I think after that. Do you need me to bring you anything? Food? Supplies? Money?"

"No, I'm okay. Just bring yourself."

"Not even something from Hoopla's? I'll pick you up a treat."

"You don't have to do that. It'll be out of your way." Hoopla's is one of my favorite bakeries in the city. They make the fanciest decadent desserts, but they don't hold a candle to the stuff they carry in Boones, which has become my new addiction.

"I don't mind. I'll see you soon. I love you, Donny."

"Love you, too, Teag. See you soon. Tell Bradley to drive safe."

I'm actually excited to see my sister. It's been weeks since we've spent any time together.

I decide it's a good idea to tidy up and get the guest bedrooms ready. I've just finished putting fresh sheets on the beds in the spare room and Grammy Bee's room when I get a call from Dillion. "Hey, beautiful, what's up?"

"Are you breathing heavy?"

"I was moving some stuff around."

"Uh-huh, I'm sure that's all you were doing. Have you even gotten out of bed yet?"

"I got up nice and early, you know, so I can make good use of daylight hours. I have this neighbor who likes to ream me out if I'm too loud past ten at night."

"Your neighbor sounds like a problem."

"Nothing I can't handle. Besides, I have other things I like to do after ten that are way more fun, especially since it's my neighbor being loud, not me." I lean against the doorjamb, my gaze catching on the patched drywall behind the headboard.

"I'm not loud!"

"You're not quiet, either, and that's a good thing, Dillion. I'm a big fan of the sound of your orgasms. In fact, I can't wait to hear them later." I cringe when I remember that my sister and brother are going to be here tonight, sleeping down the hall from me. Which means those orgasms I'm getting all excited about aren't going to happen. "Actually, I might have to take a raincheck on that. My sister called and asked if she can come up and visit for a couple of days."

"Is everything okay?"

"Yes and no. I think something might have gone down with her boyfriend, but I'm not sure what. She said she'd tell me when she gets here. My brother is driving."

"Oh no. Well, you'll obviously want some family time."

"You can still meet them, though? You could come for dinner?" I can count on one hand the number of times I've invited a woman to meet my family. I definitely like her enough to stage an introduction. The fact that Dillion can cook doesn't hurt, either, especially since my sister makes salads, and baked goods she rarely eats, and Bradley's skill set ends at dialing for takeout.

"Do *you* want me to come for dinner?"

"I always want you to come. And I love eating you for dinner, but it might be awkward with my family there."

She snickers. "Oh my God, you're the worst. Maybe it's better for me to skip family dinner."

"Don't skip dinner. I'd love for you to meet Teagan and Bradley." My brother is high on the pretentious side, but hopefully he'll be on his best behavior with Dillion present.

"If you're sure."

"I'm sure."

"Okay. Should I pick anything up? A bottle of wine? Something for dinner?"

"I was thinking I'd make it easy and grill burgers." Mostly because it's the only thing I can make that I don't mess up. Even my grilled cheese sandwiches end up burnt most of the time.

"You can't just have burgers, Van. I'll make a salad. Oh, and potato salad. Or loaded double-baked potatoes."

"Loaded double-baked potatoes?"

"Yeah, you bake them, then scoop out the insides and mix them with butter, sour cream, bacon, chives, and cheese and bake them again."

"Those sound heavenly and like they require a workout afterward. The naked kind."

"Well, that's not happening with your family visiting, since as you mentioned before, I'm not very quiet. Looks like you'll have to go for an after-dinner run. Speaking of running, I've got a meeting in twenty. I'll see you later tonight."

She ends the call before I can fire off a snarky comeback.

CHAPTER 20
BROTHERLY NO LOVE

Van

Bradley and Teagan don't arrive until almost five. I'm guessing my brother is the reason for the delay. They're also driving his lemon-yellow Porsche convertible. Bradley always likes to make a statement, and his car certainly does that. It screams rich, entitled, and ostentatious. At least my BMW is black and less in your face. Subdued pretention, if you will.

"Wow, this place is . . . more of a heap than I remember." Bradley slams his car door shut and looks around, cringing when he eyes the pile of trash bags I have yet to take to the dump. They're leaning against Billy's car graveyard. Apparently, he has plans to fix them all up. I'm not sure there will actually be anything left of them by the time he gets around to it other than rust and dust, but they're not on my property, and I honestly don't care either way.

Teagan gets out of the passenger side. I smile at her outfit. It's definitely her version of dressed down. She's wearing a pair of high-top rhinestone-encrusted running shoes—likely bought as a gift from my dad because she said they were fun—camo-print capris, an artfully torn tank top that probably cost a small fortune, and Gucci sunglasses. Her hair is pulled up in her definition of a messy ponytail.

She runs over and throws her arms around me. "Don't listen to him. He's in a mood because he had to drive on a dirt road, and he's worried about chips in his paint. I've missed you. I miss Sunday brunch and cocktail hours and sane conversations."

I return the embrace, inhaling the familiar scent of Chanel No. 5, her favorite perfume, which also happened to be what our mother wore. Which means in two minutes or less she's going to be swarmed by mosquitos and a whole host of other bugs that will find her amazingly delicious.

"Why don't I grab your bag, and you can come inside. We can start with cocktail hour."

"You have no idea how badly I need a drink."

I grab my sister's hot-pink metallic cheetah-print suitcase from the trunk and leave my brother to manage his own bag. It's funny to watch him struggle with dragging it across the pebbled driveway.

"The deck looks new."

"It is. Leveled it all and rebuilt it myself. Figured I had the time, and it wasn't in very good shape."

She threads her arm through mine. "Look at you being all handy! It looks great."

"I don't know why you'd bother to replace anything. Looks like a bonfire waiting to happen," Bradley grumbles from behind us.

"Bradley, don't be such a grump." She squeezes my biceps. "I love this place. It's so . . . rustic and cozy. I can't believe I haven't been here since I was a teenager." She opens the door for me. "Oh wow. I don't think it's changed one bit."

"That's a pity," Bradley sighs.

I arch a brow. "Dude, are you trying out for the morose emo teenager role in some community production, because if you are, you have it nailed. Rest assured you'll get the part."

He gives me an unimpressed look. "Ha-ha."

"Seriously, go take a nap and hit your reset button. No one is forcing you to be here or wants to listen to you bitch about the lack of five-star accommodations. If it bothers you so much, you can take a drive to the other side of the lake and knock on some doors. Maybe someone will adopt you for a couple of days."

"Oh, now that's an idea. I heard there's all kinds of retired hockey players with places out here now. Do you think any of them have college-aged daughters who are looking for a mature, employed date this weekend? Or just a hookup." I'd laugh, but by the look on my brother's face, I think he's being serious.

"Do you think hooking up with the daughter of a former professional athlete is a good idea? Also, this seems premeditated, which means you've actually thought about this. Probably in more detail than is reasonable."

"Of course I've thought about it." My brother drops his bag on the floor and doesn't bother to take off his shoes as he walks across the carpet, surveying the cottage with mild disgust. "Have you seen the cribs these guys have? Top-of-the-line everything. And I'm a good catch. I have a job; I have a nice car; I'm nice to look at. What more could a woman want?"

"Someone with an ego that isn't the size of Canada."

"I'm just stating facts, Van. It has nothing to do with ego. Don't be sore because you're unemployed and I'm better looking than you. Imagine marrying into a family like that. The wedding present would probably be a house. Maybe one on this lake." He grins, likely enjoying my irritation. Bradley is very good at pushing my buttons.

Teagan rolls her eyes. "You're not better looking than Van." She turns to me. "He talked about this the entire time we were in the car. He tried to rent a party barge on the way here so he could hatch his master plan, but since he doesn't have a boater's license and there's no trailer hitch on the Porsche, he couldn't."

"You can't tell me it wasn't a good idea. Party barges are all the rage. Everyone has one. When you have a job again, you should definitely get one."

"I'll put that right at the top of my list." I barely resist the urge to roll my eyes. "You guys want to settle into your rooms and then we can get on making cocktails?"

"I get dibs on the blue room." Teagan grabs her bag and rushes down the hall to the room Bradley and I used to share when we were kids. It has two single beds and is still decorated to suit a teenage boy, but I'm guessing she knows I've already taken the other bedroom.

"Where should I sleep?" Bradley eyes the floral-patterned couch from the eighties.

"You can take Grammy Bee's room."

Bradley crosses his arms. "Oh, hell no. It's probably haunted. And that mattress has to be the same one Grammy slept on when Grampy was still alive. Why should I have to sleep in the haunted room? Why don't you take that room and I'll take *your* room?"

I mirror his pose. "Because the room isn't haunted, and the mattress in there is new." This is a bald-faced lie, but he doesn't need to know that. "And I'm not changing my sheets. Plus, all my stuff is already in the spare room. If you don't like it, you can book yourself a room in the closest motel. There's one outside of town."

Bradley looks absolutely horrified. "I'm not staying in a *motel*."

"Then I guess this is going to have to do, unless you want to use the pullout couch." I thumb over my shoulder. "But those are your options."

Bradley huffs a sigh. "This is the thanks I get for coming to visit. You're turning into a real barbarian, you know that, Van?"

"I'll take that as a compliment."

He waves me off and heads down the hall to Grammy Bee's bedroom, grumbling the entire way.

I leave him to it and go in search of Teagan, who I find standing between the twin beds, head down, her hands on her hips.

"You okay?" I lean against the doorjamb.

She startles and gives me a small smile, but her chin trembles. "I'm sorry about Bradley. He's more temperamental than a cat." She takes off her sunglasses and tosses them on one of the beds. And I finally see the reason she's been wearing them. Her eyes are red and puffy.

"Teag? What happened?"

"Troy broke up with me." Her smile dissolves, and she tips her head back, trying to keep the tears from falling.

"He what? Why?" I like Troy about as much as I like mosquito bites on my nuts, but they've been together for four years. While I don't care for him, at least he seemed to love my sister, so I kept my opinion to myself.

She dabs at her eyes with the hem of her tank. "Last week he said he couldn't handle it anymore. My family drama was impacting his social status, and he couldn't be associated with thieves."

"Are you serious? That douchebag. I'm so sorry."

"It's not your fault, so please don't blame yourself. I honestly should've seen this coming. I mean, fifty percent of the reason I was dating him in the first place is because Dad approved and thought he'd be good 'marriage material.'" She makes air quotes around the words *marriage material.*

"It doesn't make it hurt less."

"No. It really doesn't."

I open my arms and she steps into them, allowing me to fold her into a hug.

"I miss you, Donny."

"I miss you too. I feel bad that I'm leaving you to deal with all this crap on your own."

"I'm not alone. Dad and Bradley are there."

I release her and step back, arching a brow. "No offense, but that's about the same as being alone." I wish she could come here and escape, too, but I know she won't leave Dad on his own. It must suck to be twenty-six years old and unable to move on with her own life because our father refuses to move on with his.

She chuckles wryly. "It could be worse." She pats my chest. "Come on. Let's make a nice stiff drink, and you can tell us all about your projects and what you've been doing."

"For sure." I run a nervous hand through my hair. "I should tell you that my neighbor is coming over to have dinner with us. If you're okay with that."

"Why wouldn't I be okay with that? And which neighbor?"

"Dillion, the one Grammy Bee called Lynnie. I don't know if you remember her from when we were kids. She didn't really come around, but sometimes she'd be on the dock next door or whatever." I rub the back of my neck.

"Wait. Donovan Ferdinand Firestone, are you and your neighbor a thing?"

"I wouldn't exactly call us a thing—"

"Your face is so red right now! You are totally a thing. This is so, so cute. I love it." She claps excitedly.

It's followed by a knock at the door.

Her eyes light up. "Is that her? It's totally her!" She takes one step toward the door, but I catch her by the arm.

"Please, for the love of God, Teagan, have some chill. She's low key, and we are not making a big deal out of this, so you can't either."

"Right. Okay. Find some chill." She closes her eyes and breathes in and out. "It's just so damn cute. And swoony."

"*Swoony* isn't a word."

"Van? You here? Did you know there's a yellow clown car in the driveway?" Dillion calls out.

"I love her already." Teagan slips out of my grasp and skips down the hall.

Bradley appears behind her and gives me an arched brow. I say nothing. His car is douchey and he knows it. He shoulders me out of the way and makes it to the living room before me. He also skirts around Teagan and reaches Dillion, whose eyes are wide and her cheeks red.

"Here, let me help you with those." Bradley swoops in and grabs the bags she's carrying, depositing them on the kitchen counter. "And I told my sister we should take the SUV since it's more understated, but she likes to drive with the top down, so I indulged her." He takes Dillion's hand in his. "I'm Bradley, Donovan's younger, better-looking, more successful brother. And who might you be? Other than an angel fallen from heaven."

"Uh, I'm Dillion." She looks from me to him and back again. "And I'm far from an angel. Also, not to make it awkward, but I'm sleeping with your brother, so this flirty business should probably end here."

Teagan giggles. "Oh my God, I really, really love her now."

"I should also let you know that of the two of us, I'm more gifted below the belt."

"That's untrue." I cross the room, heading straight for the two of them.

"Van's a liar and very sensitive about the subject, as you can tell." Bradley winks at Dillion.

"Not sensitive at all." I elbow Bradley in the ribs and get between him and Dillion. "Don't mind him; he likes to push my buttons."

She smiles knowingly. "Well, that's karmic, isn't it?"

I cup her face in my hand and tip her chin up, planting a kiss on her lips that lingers far past anything appropriate with my family in the room. But my brother is a shameless flirt and needs to get a clue.

Teagan giggles and Dillion pushes on my chest. "Okay, stake claimed. Everyone gets the point." She swipes across her mouth with the back of her hand and offers the other one to Teagan. "Hi, you must be Teagan. Van has told me so much about you."

Teagan ignores her outstretched hand and pulls her in for a hug. "It's so great to meet you! Van's been keeping you a secret, and I think it's awesome that you two are a thing." She slaps a hand over her mouth. "Sorry. I was supposed to be chill."

Dillion throws her head back and laughs. "I feel like I'm going to learn so many things about Van tonight."

"Absolutely. Let's have drinks!"

I sit back—since there really is nothing else I can do—and let Teagan and Dillion girl bond. I can't deny it's nice to see them getting along.

Bradley follows me outside when I put the burgers on the barbecue. He swirls his scotch—he's not excited about the fact that it's less than twelve years old—and leans against the railing. "So you're shacking up with a local, huh?"

"Dillion lived in Chicago until recently, but yeah, she's local. I know you have something to say; just make sure it isn't going to get you punched in the face."

"Are you falling for her?"

"I like her." I slap several burgers on the grill.

"She lives with her parents? Works for her dad?"

"How would you know that?"

"She mentioned it to Teagan while they were making drinks."

"Yeah, she works for her family's business and lives with her parents. It's temporary, though. She has plans to go back to the city eventually." Although she hasn't said anything about it recently.

"'The city'?" He arches a brow.

I roll my eyes. I guess maybe I'm a local now too. "Chicago. You know I mean Chicago."

"Mmm." He swirls his scotch again.

"Mmm, what?"

202

"Mmm, nothing. Wasn't she the executor for the will? Or am I getting the name wrong?"

"She's the one. Why?"

"Right. So you're not worried about her wanting what you have?" He motions to the cottage.

I give him a look. "You said yourself it's a heap. What exactly do I have to offer?"

"You're an architect, and at some point you're going to have a job again. And this place, as run down as it is, has potential. Her dad runs the only construction company in this town, and she's his employee."

"Since when did you become so jaded? Dillion isn't like that. She's honest and loyal, and she came back here to help her family out."

He raises both hands in the air. "Okay, okay. Sorry. It's been a rough few weeks, is all. It's hard to know who you can trust. I'm just looking out for you. No offense meant."

"I get it. But I like her, so no inquisition, okay?"

"I'll be on my best behavior."

An hour later we're stuffed full of burgers. Teagan even tries Dillion's loaded double-baked potatoes, which are to die for, despite her usually avoiding carbs like the plague. Once dinner is over, Dillion excuses herself, citing an early morning because she has to work.

I walk her back to her trailer and kiss her good night. When I return to the cottage, Teagan is making drinks.

"Where's Bradley?"

"In the bathroom. He's probably going to be a while." She arches a brow.

"Why? Is he feeling okay?" Most of the time I like him, when he's not being a pretentious ass. He's ridiculously pampered and entitled. Teagan and I make a game out of poking fun at him because of it.

"The Starbucks drive-through line was long, so he made me go in and get him a latte. I might have forgotten to ask for lactose-free milk on purpose."

I make a face. "Well, I guess it's good he has his own bathroom, then."

"Yup. Sure is." She looks over her shoulder before she grabs her purse and rummages around in it, producing a bottle of pills. She unscrews the cap and shakes two pills into her palm. She grabs a cutting board and a spoon and crushes them into powder.

"What are you doing?"

"Bradley is three drinks in; you know how he gets when he's sauced. He goes on these ridiculously long tirades about nothing, and you can't get him to shut up until he passes out. I'm just speeding the process and saving us from an evening of boredom." She dumps the pill powder into a lowball glass and adds some scotch, then passes the glass and the spoon to me. "Here. Stir that."

"What is this stuff?" I mix up the concoction.

"It's a sedative."

"Is it safe?"

"Totally. He'll sleep like a baby. I do it all the time when he goes on one of his tirades and won't shut up."

"Do you take these?"

"Every night." She smiles up at me. "It's okay, Van. I'm okay. I just needed something to help calm things down." She taps her temple. "Sometimes our family is a lot to handle. The therapy sessions weren't cutting it, and I wasn't sleeping well, and now I am. And I'm coping better too."

Bradley returns from the bathroom, rubbing his stomach. "I bet that coffee wasn't lactose-free. Those baristas never listen."

"Here." Teagan passes him the drink. "I made you a manhattan. I think you'll like it, and it'll settle your stomach."

"Thanks." Bradley takes a tentative sip. He smacks his lips a couple of times before he goes in for another one. He picks out the skewer of cherries and drains his drink in one long gulp.

Teagan and I exchange a wide-eyed look before we both school our expressions.

"Do you want another?"

I'm not sure he should have another one, but I can't communicate that to her with him looking right at us.

"Yeah. Sure. Why not?"

He sets the glass on the counter, and Teagan goes about making him another manhattan, this time not spiked with drugs. Bradley makes it three-quarters of the way through it before he spills the rest of it down the front of his shirt. I manage to grab the glass before he drops it, and then he quite literally passes out, full-on drooling.

Teagan cringes. "Hmm, we probably could have gotten away with one instead of two."

"Ya think? How long will he be out for?"

"Roughly six to eight hours, at least. Maybe more?"

"Wow. Okay." I scratch the back of my neck. "Should we lay him down? Maybe we should put him in Grammy Bee's bed?"

"Do you think she'll be mad that we drugged him? What if she haunts us because of it?"

"She's not going to haunt us, Teag."

"How do you know?" A branch scratches the window, and she jumps. "Did you hear that? She's in the walls!"

"She's not in the walls. I've been here for weeks; there are no ghosts, and Bee would not waste her time haunting us over knocking out Bradley."

"You're sure?"

"Positive. She's probably chilling up in heaven with Grampy, drinking heaven wine and laughing right now."

She nods and gives me a small smile. "I wish I'd spent more time with her. You always seemed to have such a good time when you were with her."

"I did." I poke my brother in the shoulder, testing his responsiveness. "Hey, Bratty Bradley, you down for the night?"

He mumbles but doesn't otherwise move.

"Wow. That must be some powerful stuff. And you take it every night?"

"I have a lot of stress. It's hard to live up to everyone's expectations."

"Maybe you should focus on your own expectations for a while." Teagan has been stuck in the middle for a long time.

"Yeah, probably." She sighs.

"Let's move him to the bed so he doesn't wake up in the morning with a crick in his neck."

"Good call. You take the top half, I'll take the bottom?"

After five minutes of grunting and maneuvering, we finally get him into the bed. By the time we're done, we're both sweaty and breathing heavily, but at least he's out of the way.

Once we have him settled in bed, my sister and I each grab another drink and take them outside to the front porch.

"So you and Dillion, huh?"

"Yeah. I mean, for now anyway. I don't think she has plans to stick around here once her brother is back on his feet, and I honestly have no clue what I'm going to do."

"Would you stay here?"

"Indefinitely? I don't know. I'm not sure there are all that many job prospects for me."

"You'll find something that works for you. You're too talented for this one little thing to get in the way indefinitely."

"Three million little things, you mean?"

"I'm obviously downplaying it because I'm sure you're already worried enough. But eventually the truth has to come out, right? And anyway, I like you with Dillion. You two work, even if maybe you shouldn't. I don't know if that makes sense. I really like her, though. You know, when we were kids, I wanted to be friends with her, but she was a couple years older and never around. Grammy Bee once tried to set up a playdate when I was little, but it didn't work out all that well."

"Why's that?"

"She wanted to catch frogs, and I wanted to play Barbie."

I laugh. "Sounds like Dillion."

She leans back in her chair. "I'm glad you have her here. It's good that you're not alone."

"Thanks. And me too. I'm sorry about Troy. I feel bad that this happened because of me."

"This isn't on you, Donny. You were the excuse he used to end something that should've been done a long time ago." Teagan sips her drink.

"You don't have to talk about it if you don't want to."

"I'm okay to talk about it. I probably should have expected it. I mean, his family is so influential in our circles, and with all the stuff going on, there was too much negative attention on him, so he ended things. Of course, he only told me that after I caught him cheating on me." She wipes away fresh tears.

"That dick. Ah shit, Teag, I'm so sorry. I would kick him in the balls if I could."

She gives me a small, tremulous smile. "Thanks. But that's actually not the worst part."

If she tells me he gave her an STI or, worse, got her pregnant, I'll kill him. Although she's been pounding martinis like a frat boy tonight, so I'm going to guess the pregnant part isn't an issue. "What else happened?"

"He cheated with Portia. And now they're dating."

"Portia Loewen? Your best friend?"

She nods, and tears slip out and track down her cheeks. "I actually think it's been going on for a long while, and this was the excuse he was looking for. I'm just so embarrassed, Van. I should've seen it. I should've known what was going on and I didn't, and now I'm the one everyone is whispering about. And all my girlfriends have ditched me and taken Portia's side. I feel like a joke."

"You're not a joke, Teagan, you're awesome. And Troy doesn't deserve you. Portia is a bitch, and she was always a crappy friend. You know, if it's too much to handle, you can come stay with me. I'm planning to convert the garage to a one bedroom."

She gives me a sad smile. "I appreciate that, but with my job and Dad . . . it'll be fine. I just need to wait it out. It'll all blow over. Once your name is cleared, it'll all go back to normal. Minus Troy. We'll get through this."

"We will. I'm here. Whatever you need, Teag."

It seems like out of all of us, Teagan is the one who has to suffer the most for sins she didn't commit. I can't help but wonder if normal is what we should be striving for—that maybe this is the universe's way of telling us it's time to make a change.

CHAPTER 21
THE RUSE

Van

I hate that my sister has to go back to the city. I don't want her to have to face all the crap on her own. With the breakup and her shitty superficial friends, this can't be easy for her. I wish I could convince her that it's not her job to make sure Dad is okay. We all lost Mom, and yes, that absence never goes away, but living in the past isn't really living at all.

The day after Teagan and Bradley go back to Chicago, I get a call from Bernie. Nothing seems to happen quickly around here, but I'd like to get everything in order and in my name, for peace of mind.

"Hey, Bernie, how's it going? You need me to come in and sign some more documents?"

"Well, I'd like to say yes, but we have a bit of an issue."

I flip a pen between my fingers to keep my hand busy. "What kind of issue?"

"I'm not sure what to make of it, but it looks like someone is trying to contest the will."

"Contest the will? Why?" It's been months since Bee passed. It doesn't make sense that someone would contest it now.

"Basically, this person is calling into question whether or not Bee was capable of making the decision to make you sole beneficiary of the estate."

I run my fingers through my hair, gripping the strands at the crown. I don't understand who would want to take Bee's cottage. A couple of months ago I would have been able to fight a legal battle over it without an issue, but with only Bee's random stacks of cash to live on, I'm not in any kind of position to put up a financial fight. The thought of losing all the memories associated with the cottage and Bee is inconceivable. "Do we know who it is?"

"Not yet, but I'm sure we'll find out soon enough. Is there anyone you can think of who might be unhappy that you're the sole beneficiary?" he asks.

"I don't know. I'm going to make a few phone calls, though, and ask some questions."

"Okay. When you have some time, it might be a good idea to come by the office."

"Sure, yeah. Is this afternoon okay?"

"Anytime is good. Just tell Darla that I asked you to stop by."

"Sure. Thanks for letting me know."

I end the call and exhale a breath, hoping to find some calm, but it's not working. Maybe my dad has gotten himself into more financial trouble than he can handle. But would he even think this place is worth anything? I don't want to believe that he could do something like this behind my back, but I need to at least find out if he knows anything about it.

I pull up his contact and hit the call button.

"Donovan, it's good to hear from you, son. How are things in Pearl Lake?"

"They're okay." They're not really, but I'm warming up to that.

"Good, good. I'm glad to hear that. Teagan said she had a wonderful time with you. She misses you, though. She told you about her and Troy falling out?"

"I miss her too. And yeah. She did."

"Mmm." I hear tapping in the background, signifying that he's probably answering emails while on the phone with me. "It's unfortunate. They seemed so well suited. And he's doing very well in finance. He would have been a stable partner for her."

"Yeah, well, his lack of loyalty sure did show his true colors, so I'm going to say she's better off without him. Anyway, I wanted to check in with you, see how things are going. Have we made any progress on the investigation into the missing funds?"

"I have a forensic accountant looking into things for us. I know you must be eager to get back to Chicago and return to the twenty-first century." He chuckles, and I am reminded of how much of a snob he can be. Even when my mother was alive, he would rarely, if ever, come stay in Pearl Lake.

"Thanks, Dad, I appreciate that. Look, I know this might be an odd question, but you wouldn't happen to know anything about Grammy Bee's will being contested, would you? You know if there are financial issues, you can always tell me."

The sound of typing stops. "I'm sorry, what?"

"I just got a call from the lawyer. The will is being contested, but he doesn't know by who yet. I've been working on having everything switched to my name, but that can't happen until this is sorted out."

"Well, I have to admit, Bee leaving everything to you and only you was a bit unfair."

"Unfair? Teagan and Bradley both got checks out of the deal," I snap. "Neither of them wanted the cottage. I'm the only one with an attachment to this place, and it was Bee's decision."

"There's no need to get worked up about it, Donovan. It's not going to change anything. I'm just saying that it isn't surprising that someone is contesting it. Although I honestly don't understand why they would bother. That cottage is falling apart, and the land it's on isn't something anyone can develop, especially on that side of the lake. Not without red tape and years of battling the town for permits. It's more of a headache than it's worth. Bee made sure of that," Dad grumbles.

"Right. Yeah. Did Mom have any relatives who might think it's worth something?"

"It's possible. Bee had a sister, but she's long passed, and I don't think Bee's nieces and nephews had any real connection to the place. I can look into it on this end if you'd like, son. I know you've got more than enough on your plate already. I'm sorry you're dealing with this too."

"Yeah. Me too. I'll let you know if I get any more information on the who and why."

"I'll do the same on my end. We'll get it all figured out. I promise."

"Thanks." I end the call more confused than ever.

I head over to Bernie's to sign what he needs, and I berate myself for not acting sooner. Bee's wishes would've been honored had I not delayed doing this.

On the way in I run into Billy. "Hey, Billy, how's it goin'?" I hold the door open for him and glance around the parking lot, searching for Dillion or a familiar car, but I see neither.

His brows furrow in confusion. He tips his chin up, eyes narrowing. "Who're you? How do you know my name?"

I've only met him a couple of times, and once he was so drunk he couldn't see straight. "I'm Van. I live next door to you, in Bee's cottage."

"Oh, yeah, right. You're Dillion's friend." He nods once and glances around, eyes narrowing again. "What're you doing here? Dillion didn't send you, did she?"

"Uh, nope. I'm just taking care of my grandmother's will. I'm not sure how long I'll be, but if you want to wait, I can give you a ride home."

"I'm okay," he says quickly. "I got it covered."

"If you're sure."

"Yeah. Thanks, though." He crutches past me and tosses them down the short flight of stairs, then grabs the railing and hops down after them.

I'm not sure how he's planning to get home, but I doubt he's going to crutch back. It's more than two miles, and half of that is dirt road. He takes out his phone once he's at the bottom of the stairs, so I assume he's calling a ride. I leave him to it.

Forty-five minutes later, I leave Bernie's office with all the papers in order, but no more information on who's contesting the will, or how much leg they'll have to stand on.

Both Dillion and Bernie can attest to the fact that while Grammy Bee was definitely eccentric, she was of sound mind when she had the will drafted.

When I get back to the cottage, I sit down and review all the documents again, trying to figure out what exactly is happening and if it's possible for someone to take this place away from me. I don't want to lose the last connection I have to Bee. I have far too many great memories tied up in this place and this town, both past and present.

Dillion messages around six, asking if we're still on for dinner. I've completely lost track of time. I fire one back telling her I absolutely want to see her, but we might have to do takeout of some kind. She shows up at my door five minutes later laden with grocery bags.

"Hey!" Her wide smile falters. "Wow, did you get into the sauce last night?"

"Are you telling me I don't look runway fresh?" I motion to my jogging pants and ratty T-shirt attire. Which incidentally is what I wore to Bernie's office this afternoon.

She sweeps her thumb gently across my cheek, her gaze moving over my face. "You have circles under your eyes, and it looks like you've been trying to rip your hair out. Is everything okay?"

I run my fingers through it, hoping to tame it. "Bernie called today to tell me someone is contesting the will."

She frowns as she sets the bags on the counter and then turns to me. "What? How can they do that? Hasn't it already been put into probate?"

"I signed the remaining paperwork today, but none of it has been filed, so technically it's still contestable."

She takes my hand and leads me over to the couch, where she pulls me down beside her. "Who would do that? Not Teagan?"

"No. Definitely not Teagan. She'd tell me if she had a problem with the will." Grammy Bee left my brother and sister each a sealed envelope that had a cashier's check in it. Teagan said it was fifty grand, and neither she nor my brother seemed upset at the time. I'm sure Teagan invested hers and Bradley spent his, since they didn't have to wait for probate to cash it.

"I figured that was the case. She doesn't seem like she'd go behind your back. She adores you. What about your brother?" She shifts and pulls her knee up, her shin resting against the outside of my thigh, and runs her fingers through my hair, maybe trying to tame it, or soothe me.

"Unlikely. That's a lot of effort, and the only thing he likes to expend that on is golf or meeting women."

"Right. Okay." She continues to run her fingers through my hair. "Is there anyone else you can think of? Some distant relative?"

"Nope. None that I know of anyway. I called my dad, and he has no idea. I'm guessing it's only a matter of time before we find out who."

"I'm so sorry, Van." She links the fingers of my free hand with hers. "This is the last thing you need right now. What can I do? How I can help?"

"I don't know that there's anything to do. I've been through the will so many times my eyes are crossing."

"What if we go through Bee's files? We might find something."

"There's a whole wall of filing cabinets." Everything feels overwhelming. My head is spinning, this day having taken an unexpected turn. I don't know who to trust or believe anymore. That Dillion is here, willing to drop everything and do whatever she can to help, is almost more than I know what to do with.

"I know it's daunting, but it'll be easier if we do it together. And if you don't want to tackle it now, that's okay too." She runs her thumb down the back of my neck, as if she's trying to relieve the tension there. "Whatever you want, Van, I'm here for you. Tell me what you need."

"I don't want to lose this place." And not just because of the memories.

"I know you don't." Her smile is soft. "And neither do I. We'll fight whoever it is. You're not going to lose more than you already have."

And it's right now, in this moment, that I realize there's more at stake than this cottage and the memories. And it took everything falling apart again, and Dillion being here to help keep me together, for me to see it.

Because in such a short amount of time, I've fallen for Dillion. And I don't want to lose her either.

CHAPTER 22
EXPECT THE UNEXPECTED

Dillion

The anxious look on Van's face shifts to surprise, and then shock, or fear maybe, before it turns hot. And then he's on me. He cups my cheeks in his wide palms and tips my head back, mouth slanting over mine. I gasp and then moan as his tongue strokes inside. He pulls me to straddle him on a groan, and then we're frantic hands, tugging and unbuttoning, pulling and pushing. He nearly knocks the lamp off the side table trying to get my shirt off, and I nearly face-plant into his chest when I shove my shorts down my thighs and kick them off. He slides forward, and I climb back into his lap, letting him arrange me how he wants. He kisses his way up my neck, and then our mouths are fused once again.

He fumbles around with his wallet. I grab the condom as soon as he frees it, tear it open, and push him back enough that I can roll it on. And then he's inside me in one deep thrust that makes my toes curl. His head drops to my shoulder, his back expanding and contracting with deep breaths. "Fuck, I love this feeling," he mumbles against my throat.

I loop my arms around his neck. We move together, a push and pull, fill and retreat that gains speed and vigor until we're both panting and sweaty, battling our way to orgasms. I fall first, thankfully, and as soon I start contracting around him, he hisses a triumphant *Yessss* and pounds his way to his own climax.

It lasts all of fifteen minutes, but my heart is slamming in my chest and I feel like I've just run a marathon. He flops back against the cushions, eyes closed, and exhales several long, slow breaths.

"What the heck was that about?"

He cracks a lid, and a sheepish grin tips the corner of his mouth. "Stress relief?"

I snort a laugh, and his eyes crinkle at the corner. "One second we're talking about the will, and the next we're naked. Seems like a classic avoidance technique to me."

He looks away for a second, maybe embarrassed about being called out. When he turns back, he's smirking, but worry lurks behind his eyes. "You call it avoidance, I call it stress relief, but it was an excellent distraction, even if it didn't last very long."

I run my hands through his hair, smoothing it out. "Should we do something constructive? Look through Bee's files and see if we can't find something that might help?"

"It's probably a good idea. I don't know how much I processed after Grammy Bee passed, you know? And just when I was ready to deal with everything, the money went missing from the foundation, and I lost my job."

"It's a lot, isn't it? Why don't we make dinner first?" I ask.

"Sure. That sounds good."

We get dressed, and I wash my hands before I pull things out of the grocery bags. Van and I fall into a familiar routine, standing side by side at the kitchen counter.

"I'm sorry you keep getting thrown curveballs."

"It's okay. I mean, it's not actually okay, but I can handle it. And it's not your fault. I feel like I'm at a crossroads in my life. Grammy Bee always believed things happen for a reason, but this whole thing—her dying; me being given this cottage; everything that happened with the foundation; coming here, getting to know you, and believing it's possible to have a fresh start, and then being told it might all be taken away—I just want to know what message the universe is trying to send me. Let go? Hold on? I'm an asshole? I just don't know."

"Well, I can tell you that you're not an asshole."

"Thanks, but you know, when I really look at the life I was living, I honestly don't think I was doing any of it for the right reasons. I liked my job, but I didn't love it. It was more about the paycheck than it was about the gratification of a job well done. I should have found it rewarding, but I didn't. This"—he motions to the cottage—"being here, working on the garage, fixing this place up like I'd talked about when I was younger . . . this is the stuff that actually means something, you know? This is what matters: making memories worth holding on to." He shucks a cob of corn, getting silk all over the counter and the floor. "I'm starting to sound like a freaking Hallmark movie, and I'm at risk of having to hand over my man card if I keep it up." He shakes his head, as if clearing the heavy subject matter. "Is everything okay with your brother? I saw him today at Bernie's."

"You did? I didn't think he had an appointment. Or not one anyone told me about. Was he with my mom?"

"No, he was on his own. I offered to drive him home, but he said he was fine, and he called someone to pick him up."

"Huh. I honestly don't know what that would have been about. I think there's a lot going on with him, and while he's always been the kind of person to dance to his own beat, he's been doing some strange things lately." I shake my head. "Ugh. You know what? Let's not talk about this either. Oh, and about the garage, I know you know what you're doing, but you can always talk to my dad about the renovation. I'm sure he'd be happy to help out."

"I keep meaning to have Aaron come by, but he's been busy. I'm going to give it a go on my own, but it's good to have backup if I run into any snags along the way."

"Makes sense. How was the rest of your day? What else is going on? Make any new discoveries since your brother and sister left?"

"Actually, I found a stack of ones in the old butter dish in the china cabinet."

"Really? I thought you couldn't find the key for it."

"I couldn't. I used a bobby pin to get it open."

"Ah yes, the old bobby pin trick! I bet Bee has a million of those hanging around. She was forever wearing her hair up."

"Oh yeah, there was an entire basket full of them in the bathroom medicine cabinet."

"It blew my mind that she could put those in without even looking at her reflection, and her hair was always perfect." I pull three sheets of aluminum foil free, then drop a dollop of butter on each and a sprinkle of salt before I add a cob of corn and roll them up.

"She wasn't big on pampering, but she hated when her hair didn't look good."

Van and I talk about Bee while we prepare dinner. Once the corn and vegetables are on the barbecue, we pull out the will and estate documents. There's an older version where the cottage was supposed to go to Van's mother, but that obviously was updated after she died.

Three hours and a mountain of scoured files later, we're still in the dark. Van is frustrated and discouraged, so we call it a night, and I take him to bed. I might not be able to solve the problem for him, but at least I can provide a distraction.

I get the answers Van is looking for the following night, when I come home from work to find a rented black SUV parked in front of my trailer with windows tinted so dark I can see nothing but my reflection in them. For a moment I wonder if my dad and my uncle have gotten themselves into financial trouble without my knowing. These

McMansion renos can be expensive, and a few years back my uncle took out some loans that weren't from the bank. It was right around the time they almost went bankrupt. And it didn't help that my uncle took some of the money to the slots to see if he could make a little extra on the side. Luckily we survived that mess, and quietly too. No one knows about it, and I'd like to keep it that way.

I look around, for what I'm not sure. Backup, maybe?

The driver's side door opens, and a head appears, followed by a body. It takes me a moment to recognize Bradley, Van's brother. He's wearing dark sunglasses and a full suit. It happens to be over eighty degrees today, so it's a lot of heavy fabric.

"Hey, Bradley. Is Van not home? Is he okay? Did something happen?" Panic hits, fast and hard, making it feel like I'm choking. My heart clenches, and I realize that I'm genuinely afraid. If something has happened to Van, I'm not sure I'll be okay, because the feelings I've been trying to ignore have only grown stronger the more time I spend with him. I glance toward the trees, but they've filled in with the summer heat, so I can't see much except for the roof of Bee's cottage.

"He's fine and not home. I'm actually here for you." He smiles, but it's stiff. "Do you have a minute to talk? I need your help with something."

"Oh, like a surprise?" I have no idea when Van's birthday is. I hope I haven't missed it.

He smiles again, wider this time. "Come, let's have a chat, Dillion." He moves toward the trailer, which I don't bother locking since the only thing of value in there is usually a six-pack of beer and occasionally my laptop, but mostly where I go, it goes.

He opens the door for me and follows me inside. Bradley seems like a pampered, spoiled younger brother, based on my impression from last weekend. I don't dislike him, but he's hard to get a read on. I can't tell if he was joking about being the better-looking brother, or if he actually believes it.

I can see the similarities between him and Van. They're definitely brothers. But where Van has a square jaw and slightly more rugged features, his brother is . . . softer, maybe more refined. He wears the suit like he belongs in it. Whereas Van looks best in a T-shirt and ripped jeans.

"Can I get you something to drink? I only have beer or water, but we have other stuff in the house." I thumb over my shoulder.

"I'm fine, thank you." He looks around the trailer, and I can practically feel the judgment oozing out of him. "So, this is where you live, Dillion?"

"For now, yup."

"Dillion's an interesting name."

"It's androgynous." Might as well state the obvious.

His gaze moves over me. I'm still wearing a polo with the company logo—the ones in my size finally came in—and a pair of jeans and flip-flops. I leave the work boots at the office. "There's certainly nothing androgynous about you, though, is there?"

"Okay, if you can dial your creepy back a few notches, that would be great. I'm not sure if you need a reminder, but I'm dating your brother, so this, whatever this is"—I fling a hand in his general direction—"needs to stop now."

"I thought you were just sleeping with him."

"We're a thing. Which means we're doing more than sleeping together."

Bradley chuckles. "I can see why my brother likes you."

"Why exactly are you here, again?"

He slides onto one of the bench seats and motions to the bench opposite him. "Have a seat."

"I'm good standing, thanks." I adopt a casual lean next to the door, both so I have an escape and because now I don't trust Van's brother. At all.

It's about a thousand degrees in here, and I can feel the sweat dripping down my spine.

He makes a noise that sounds halfway to a laugh. "You're the executor of my grandmother's will."

It's a statement, not a question, so I don't bother with a response.

He nods once and folds his hands on the table. He also tries to cross his legs but ends up hitting his knee on the crossbar. "She seemed to put a lot of responsibility in your hands. Especially for someone who wasn't family."

"I've lived next door to her my whole life. She was like family to me."

"Mmm, yes. So I've been told. It must bother you that you had such a close relationship with her, close enough that she made you the executor of her will, and yet she didn't leave you a damn thing."

"She didn't need to. And like you said, I'm not her family, so whatever she had wasn't mine to claim. Where are you going with this, Bradley?"

He chuckles. "So impatient and unrefined. I bet you're a lot of fun, aren't you, Dillion? You sure you picked the right Firestone brother to get between the sheets with?"

"Good lord. You are a sexual harassment case in the making. Keep it up, and I'm going to show you how unrefined I am."

He holds up his hands. "No need to get violent. Come on, Dillion, you and I know the real reason you're with Van."

"Which would be what?" I've about had it with this guy.

"Van is sitting on a gold mine, but you already knew that, didn't you? Which is why you're with him. You already knew what Bee's place was worth, and now you're trying to edge your way in and take what should be mine." He jabs his own chest.

"You hate it here."

"Not the point! The cottage should have been divided equally among the three of us, and it wasn't. All I got was fifty grand, and Van got everything else. There are acres of land waiting to be developed."

I laugh humorlessly. "You're living in a dream world if you think you're going to convince the town to let you subdivide Bee's land and sell it off in parcels. Besides, you'd have to have the will reversed, and that is highly unlikely." In that moment I realize Bradley already knows that. "Which is exactly what you're trying to do."

Bradley smiles brightly. "Wow, smart and beautiful. Now I know why Van is occupying his time with you."

"I know what you're trying to do here, but it's not going to happen. I have things to do that don't include listening to this crap. It's time for you to leave." I step out of the trailer and head for the house. My brother will most definitely be home. He's not particularly threatening, but at least I won't be alone with this asshole.

"Your father runs Footprint Renovations," he says to my back.

I keep walking. It's not like this isn't common knowledge. Everyone knows who my dad is, and all he would've had to do is look him up on the internet or ask someone in town, and they'd tell him that.

"I hear his business has been doing well lately. Profiting off the wealthy. Making a real name for himself. Big difference from a couple of years ago, when he almost went under."

I'm halfway to the house when I falter. I can *feel* the threat in his tone. I spin around and fight the urge to cross my arms, aware it's a defensive maneuver that will paint me as weak in his eyes. I stalk back over and stop a few feet away. "Get to the point."

His smarmy smile widens. "We could have a mutually beneficial relationship." He nods once but doesn't speak right away, baiting me, keeping me waiting. "I've heard he's looking to expand the business. Seems risky, given everything that's happening in your family."

I bite, even though I don't want to. "What are you talking about?"

"He's working on the Bowman place right now. Everyone in town is talking about it. Lots of pull that family has. Lots of friends high up there too. Big opportunities for a small-town company, unless, say, something happens to tarnish his reputation. I mean, come on, you've got a brother with a DUI charge; who knows what other dirt someone could dig up with that kind of history. Like, say, perhaps the nasty gambling problem your uncle had . . ." He shrugs and arches a brow.

I cannot believe this guy. My uncle only had that one slipup a few years back, and since then he's been in Gamblers Anonymous. Besides, he doesn't touch the financials because of it. But the fact that Bradley knows about it shows that he has resources. Everyone has skeletons in their closets. "Is this blackmail? Extortion? What do you *want*?" I'm so frustrated and, frankly, starting to panic.

He thumbs over his shoulder.

"You want my trailer?" Obviously, I'm being cheeky.

He narrows his eyes. "I want what Donovan has."

"Regular mind-blowing sex with someone he doesn't have to pay to pretend to like him?" I'm probably going to regret saying that, but man, it was a good one.

"Oh, sweetheart." He tsks and shakes his head. "Do you honestly think whatever is going on between you two is going to last?" He leans down, and I try to back away, but I'm trapped between him and his SUV. "Do you know why my brother has a thing for women like you?" He fingers a curl, and I bat his hand away. "Because it makes him feel better about himself. He likes projects, and you're his newest one. What do you have to offer him, other than the obvious? You come from nothing, and if you don't do what I want, I'll destroy your family, and you'll only have yourself to blame."

"I can't do anything to help you with the will even if I wanted to, which I don't."

"But you can say that Bee wasn't in her right mind when she wrote it." He pulls an envelope from his pocket. "You think you know this family, but you don't. One way or another, I'll find a way to get her will reversed."

"Let me ask you something. Let's say the will is invalidated. You'd only get one-third of a share. Minus what Bee already gave you. How does that help you?"

"My brother has nothing but this cottage; he'll need the money. I can buy him out. And my sister." He smirks. "You've met her. Do you think she wants this place? So you can either be on the right side of that deal or the wrong one. It's up to you, but the wrong side will come with consequences you don't like."

I tip my chin up, defiant. "I'm on whatever side you're not."

He smiles, and his fingertips trail down my arm. I bat his hand away and suppress a shudder. He forces the envelope into my hand. "You should think good and hard before you say no. I'm only offering the opportunity once; after that, every loss is on you."

Real fear settles under my skin, making it pebble. "What is that supposed to mean?"

"I can either help you or hurt you. Don't take what I'm offering you, and I guess you'll find out. I'll be in touch soon."

I crumple the envelope in my fist, and he backs off, finally allowing me to step out from between him and the car.

I want to knee him in the nuts, or slap the smug holier-than-thou look off his face. "I'd suggest not randomly showing up here again. Unless you're interested in being used as target practice."

He laughs as he rounds the hood of the SUV, opens the door, and lowers himself inside. The engine rolls over with a low purr, and he peels out, narrowly missing my foot on the way.

I wait until he's gone before I let my shoulders sag and give in to the urge to rub my temple. I can feel the headache knocking behind my eye.

Billy appears on the deck, one crutch perched under his arm, hair a mess, sleep lines on his face despite it being the dinner hour. "Who was that? One of those hockey player guys?"

"I wish," I mutter, not because they're all built like Adonis and have that rough-and-tumble kind of look about them, but because they're nicer to deal with than potential blackmailers. "Just some asshole looking to buy up some land that isn't available."

Billy nods solemnly. "Lot of that going on around here lately. I think the whole town is corrupt. It's a conspiracy, you know?"

"What kind of conspiracy?"

"The north side is keeping us under their thumbs. They run the town, even though they only live here a few months out of the year. You know Bernie lives right on the edge, between the north and south side, and he fakes having our best interest in mind because he's playing both sides."

"How do you know this?"

"I worked on his house last year. I see things. And people talk. Last night I heard them down at the lake, talking about expanding."

"How did you hear them?"

"My window was open, and I have good hearing. Great hearing." He tugs on his earlobe. "I'm hungry. I'm going inside. We probably shouldn't talk about this out here." And with that he turns around and hobbles back into the house, leaving me baffled, worried, and anxious.

I smooth out the envelope and look around, paranoid. I shake my head at myself for allowing my brother's conspiracy theories to affect me. Still, I head back to my trailer before I open it up. Inside is a check for ten grand and some legal documents. They look official, and they state that Bee was incompetent at the time she changed her will. There's a space for my signature.

There's also a list of the projects my dad and uncle have worked on in the past year, and one in particular is highlighted. There was a dispute regarding inflated charges, but I know it was resolved and was a simple misunderstanding. On top of that are reports on my brother's DUI charge and all his misdemeanors and run-ins with local law enforcement from when he was a teenager. It's not much, but it's enough that I can see where Bradley is going with this.

I need to talk to Bernie and see what recourse we have. If any. So much for Van's brother being unmotivated. It looks like he just needs the right thing to light a fire under his ass. Like blackmail.

My phone pings with a reminder that I have a dinner date with Van. I run my hand down my face and sigh. I don't know how I'm going to get out of this situation without someone getting hurt in the process.

CHAPTER 23
PARANOID

Van

I'm standing at the edge of the trees that separate my property from Dillion's, trying to understand what I've just seen. Dillion with my brother. It doesn't make sense. I try to keep from overreacting. Maybe he tried to stop by and see me, and I was down at the lake so he checked in with Dillion.

Maybe the way he was in her personal space was nothing. Maybe I'm making things up in my head, but I don't understand why he would be back here so soon after coming for a visit. Especially since he complained the entire time. Apart from when he was drugged, anyway.

Dillion's brother comes out of the house, so I head back to the cottage, still searching for a way to rationalize things. I pace the length of the living room, my gaze landing on a framed photo of Bee and Dillion. They're sitting on the front porch peeling peaches, likely for some kind of pie, since that was Grammy Bee's specialty. And tarts. God, I miss those.

My phone rings, and I nab it from the kitchen counter. My stomach flips as my brother's name appears on the screen. I answer the call, unable to keep my cool. "What are you doing back in Pearl Lake?"

"I had a little business with your girlfriend. She's quite the little firecracker. I can see why you like her. You were always a fan of the ones who needed taming."

"What business could you possibly have with Dillion?"

"Clearly I'm the one who got the brains in this family. I'm the one contesting the will, genius."

"Why would you do that? You don't even like it here." But even as I ask the question, I already know the answer.

"Because it's an investment property, you idiot. And because you got more than you deserve. That cottage was supposed to be split three ways, and because you're the suck-up, she gave you more than your share. I've done some research, brother, and those big mansions on the other side of the lake go for millions. Once the will is reversed, I'll have the property reassessed, and then I'll get what's rightfully mine."

"Well, good luck with that; you'll never make it happen." But on the off chance he does, it's going to be a challenge to find the money to buy him out, especially if he wants to sell the property off in pieces. "And I don't understand why you didn't come out and tell me you had a problem with the will instead of going behind my back."

"I knew you'd never agree to sell, so what was the point? I realize your work ethic and mine differ, but I'm of the mindset that less is more. Why should I have to work my ass off for money when it's sitting there, ripe for the taking? And the best part is, your girlfriend is going to help me."

"Why the hell would Dillion help *you*? That doesn't make sense."

"Doesn't it, though? Come on, Donny, do you really think she's that into you? She's been living next to a gold mine her entire life. She lives in a fucking trailer. She knows exactly what Bee's property is worth. Imagine how much her family will benefit if that land is developed? All those homes being built. Her dad's company would be set until he retires. It's never been about you, Van. It's about what you have and what she can get out of it. She's trailer trash, looking for a way out."

"That's bullshit."

"Is it, though? Not that it matters, because I have a backup plan. She's pretty loyal to her family. Moved from Chicago to come help out with the family business after her brother got a DUI. Which isn't all that desirable when you're counting on someone to run heavy machinery, is it? If I were to expose some family secrets, it wouldn't bode well for business, now would it? Really think about it, Van. Do you honestly believe she'd side with you over her family on this? Anyway, it's been nice chatting with you, but I have a meeting with my lawyer. Enjoy your evening."

I sit there, staring at the blank screen, trying to figure out if Bradley has lost his mind. Or if I've lost mine.

Dillion shows up half an hour later, freshly showered, hair still damp. "Hey. How was your day?" She dumps a bag of groceries on the counter. "I thought we could have jerk chicken and corn for dinner. Does that sound good?"

I scan her face for signs of unease, but she seems fine. Not like she's been scheming with my brother behind my back. If I hadn't seen it with my own damn eyes, I'd think my brother was playing mind games with me. "Sure. That sounds great." The words sound hollow.

She smiles and kisses me on the cheek as she passes, but she doesn't make eye contact as she heads for the fridge. "You want a beer or anything?"

"I'm good, thanks."

"We should shuck the corn outside, so there's less of a mess to clean up afterward." She grabs a beer and the tinfoil, and I follow her outside to the front porch.

"How was your day?" I take the cob of corn she passes me. I feel like I'm underwater, being dragged farther down the longer I sit here, waiting for some honesty from Dillion. My brother can't be right about her. But then, he's been sitting on a pile of resentment for God knows how long, biding his time and waiting for the opportunity to take me down. I don't know who I can trust anymore.

She pats the chair next to hers. "It was okay. How about you?"

"Just another day. I talked to Bernie again. He still doesn't know who's contesting the will, but I guess it's a matter of time before we find that out."

She fumbles her cob of corn, and I catch it before it can hit the ground and pass it back to her. "Thanks." She gives me a small, tremulous smile. "Bernie will help sort everything out."

I wait for her to say something as we prepare dinner, but she doesn't. Instead she talks about the Bowman reno and how he and his friends all do these intense workouts in the lake.

She's about to pull the corn off the barbecue when I lose my shit. "You wanna tell me why my brother stopped by to see you?"

This time when she drops the foil-wrapped corn, I don't catch it. "What?"

"I saw you with him today. Just before you came over here, actually. Interesting that it wasn't the first thing you mentioned."

She turns off the barbecue and turns to face me. "Whatever you're thinking, Van, you're very, very wrong."

The paranoia that's been weighing me down for weeks is too much to handle. The missing money from the foundation, losing my job for something I didn't do, and now my brother trying to cash in on Bee's cottage by using the one person I felt like I could truly trust against me. "Really? 'Cause that's not what it sounds like."

Her eyes flare with panic. "I was going to tell you. I was waiting for the right time."

"Really? When exactly is the right time to tell me you're screwing me over?" I go off, unable to keep a lid on my frustration. "After I fucked you tonight? Would that have been an appropriate time to tell me you're scheming behind my back with my *fucking* brother?"

Dillion's jaw tics. "That's not what's going on. At all. And I'm pretty damn offended that it's the first place your head went."

"What the hell am I supposed to think, Dillion? You've been here for half an hour. You've had plenty of opportunity to tell me, and you didn't take it." I gave her the benefit of the doubt, but it's only now, when confronted, that she's come clean.

She leans against the deck railing. "I wanted to talk to Bernie first."

"I bet you did. So you can see how many options you have." I pace the length of the deck, stopping a few feet away from her. "Bradley called right after you two had your little visit. Don't bother lying to me. I know he's paying you off to help get the will reversed."

Dillion's lip curls. "Do you honestly believe I would screw you over like that? Go against Bee's wishes? Listen to what you're saying. How does it even make sense?"

I run my fingers through my hair, tugging roughly. "It makes perfect sense to me! You already know everything about Bee's finances. You sure as hell know more than me." I poke myself in the chest unnecessarily hard and then jab my finger in her direction. "You've been talking about all the McMansions on the other side of the lake and how great it's been for your dad and his business. If this place gets chopped up, it'll be just another project for your family to cash in on, won't it?" Ever since the beach party, I've put my trust in Dillion, believing she's been on my side. I needed a buoy, a lifeline to hold on to when everything else in my life is up in the air.

She crosses her arms and takes a cautious step toward the porch steps, away from me. "How can you believe that I'd do something like that to you? Or to Bee, for that matter? When have I ever done anything to make you feel like I'm not on your side?"

I take a breath; maybe I am going off the deep end here. I have no idea who or what to trust anymore. I want to believe Dillion wouldn't do anything to me or to Bee, but I also never thought my brother would stoop to such lows for financial gain. All the things he said are bouncing around in my head, making it impossible to remain rational.

"This whole thing is messing with my head, and maybe I'm jumping to conclusions, but tell me, Dillion, honestly"—my voice is lower, calmer—"if you had to choose between protecting your family and me, even if it meant lying about Bee, which would you choose?"

She opens and closes her mouth a few times, a pleading, hopeless look in her eyes. "I . . . I can't answer that right now. It's why I wanted to speak to Bernie."

I don't know what I expected her to say, or if the question was even fair, but this doesn't make me feel any better. "Well, I think I have my answer."

"It's not even a reasonable question, and you know it." She steps down off the porch. "I don't need this shit."

"Of course you're gonna leave. Don't want to face the fact that you're going to screw me over." I recognize that my brother's put her in an impossible position, but I hate that she wasn't honest with me. There's no way out of this that isn't going to end up with one of us getting hurt.

"Your brother came to my house and threatened my dad's business if I didn't help him get the will reversed. He also seems to think he can put up a bunch of huge homes on the land back there and he won't run into any roadblocks along the way, which either means he's delusional or a complete narcissist, or both. I basically told him he could screw himself, but he felt that I needed to hear him out, because otherwise I'd regret the consequences. I planned to talk to Bernie first to make sure that the information Bradley had about my family won't affect their business and livelihood. I would never betray Bee, not for anything. But I want to make sure Bradley's threats can't hurt my family. And at this point, I'm starting to think he's done me a favor, since your true colors are shining through, and they look like bullshit to me. *My* brother is losing his mind, *your* brother is trying to blackmail me, and now you're accusing me of . . . what? Commiserating with the biggest asshole on the face of the earth—aside from yourself, that is?" She flips me the bird and heads toward the path, shouting over her shoulder, "Fuck you very much."

Now that I'm hearing it from her side, I'm aware I've overreacted, much like my brother might do if he can't get the exact table he wants at one of his favorite restaurants.

"Dillion, wait."

She shakes her head and tromps through the bushes.

Awesome. And now I've pushed away the one person I felt I could trust.

CHAPTER 24

BAD TO WORSE

Van

After some time to think and calm down, I realize that I've made a grave mistake with my accusations. And I've taken out my frustration on the wrong person. I send apologetic messages to Dillion for overreacting and being a jerk that, no surprise, go unanswered. Then I apologize for my brother trying to blackmail her. I'd say that whatever he's planning won't work, but I'm unsure if that's true or not, because I'm still finding it hard to believe that he's the one masterminding this. I didn't even think he had the drive or motivation to blackmail anyone, let alone figure out how to do it. Obviously, he has piss-poor judgment in who he chooses to try to blackmail, but that he tried at all is ballsy. And, frankly, shocking.

As if Teagan has some kind of sixth sense—which I would never say to her, for fear she would take me seriously and believe she can predict the future—she calls me.

"Did Bradley come see you today?" is the first thing out of her mouth.

I hate that in my current frame of mind, I even call into question whether I can reasonably trust my sister anymore either. "Uh, no. He did not."

"Really? Are you sure, because I have him on my Life app, and his phone was in Pearl Lake today—not *in* the actual lake, but in the area."

"That's because he went to see Dillion."

"Why in the world would Bradley go see Dillion?"

"Because he's contesting the will, and he wants Dillion's help to get it reversed." Just that statement alone is enough to make my head pound.

"You're kidding me. Well, that was stupid of him," she says, sighing. "There's zero chance of Dillion ever doing something like that."

I rub my temple. "And if Bradley was threatening her family's business?"

"Please tell me this is your idea of a bad joke." Her disbelief is slightly reassuring.

"I wish I could."

"He is such an ass. What in the world was he thinking?"

"That he could use Dillion to help him cash in on Grammy Bee's cottage."

"Well, there's no way Dillion would give in to him. It doesn't matter what he offered her. I might not know her very well, but she doesn't seem like the kind of person who would bend to blackmail."

"Yeah. I wish I'd had this conversation with you before she came over for dinner."

"Why? What happened?"

"I might have accused her of going behind my back and conspiring with Bradley to have the cottage taken away from me."

"Oh no. Why would you do that?"

"I was paranoid, which I think I have a right to be, all things considered. I saw her with him. At her place. And then she came over and pretended like everything was okay and that he hadn't even been there, so I called her out on it, but not in a nice way." I explain how things went down, and Teagan sighs.

"Well, you f'ed up royally, didn't you?"

"Yeah." I knead the back of my neck. "I don't know how I'm going to fix this. And now I have to deal with Bradley contesting the will. The guy does the bare minimum at all times; since when does he engage in blackmail tactics?"

"I don't know, but I had a feeling he was up to something. I just didn't know what. If he's contesting the will, he's probably already spoken to a lawyer. Do you think he's done any research on what it's going to take to get the town to allow him to subdivide the lot and put up a bunch of houses?"

"That's debatable, but possibly?"

"It's going to cost a lot of money to fund a project like that, and he spends his paychecks faster than he earns them."

"Like father, like son," I mutter. "So how is he going to fund something like that unless—fuck." I drop down in the chair and bang my head against the back of it. "I can't believe it's taken me this long to figure it out."

"Figure what out?"

"I know what happened to the foundation money. Or at least I think I do. Bradley has to be the one who took it."

"But how?"

"I don't know, but I'm guessing he got ahold of the bank information and moved the money little by little without any of us knowing. Maybe he forged my signature, maybe he posed as me, but it had to be him. Who else would it have been? What's his mantra? 'Work smarter, not harder'? It's all about the money. That asshole. I can't believe he's this big of a dick."

"What're we going to do? How are we going prove it was him?"

"I don't know. Get him to admit it? Find out what he's done with the money and out him? But let's not tell Dad. Not until we're sure. Or at least until we have the proof we need. Damn that asshole. This is such a mess."

"We're probably going to need some serious therapy after this, aren't we?" Teagan muses.

"It's possible." Probable even. Being blackmailed and defrauded by your own sibling seems like grounds for some serious therapy. "I need to apologize to Dillion. Again."

"Yeah, you do, and I need to go because Bradley just got home. I'm going to make him a special cocktail and see if I can't do some recon on my end."

"Okay. Be safe. I love you, Teag."

"Love you too, Donny."

She ends the call, and I stare at the ceiling, trying to absorb it all. I can and can't believe my brother has done this. It's shocking, because he expends the most energy on shopping and perfecting his hair. He's always been a pompous jerk, but this is way beyond anything I can comprehend. And honestly, it's not something I ever would have thought him capable of. Not to mention I've screwed up with Dillion, and now she's ignoring my messages. Which is completely understandable.

I push up off the couch and head for the front door. I'm considering doing something I normally wouldn't: groveling. I'm not sure what else I can do other than serenade her, or skywrite a message, but neither option seems like something she'd find all that romantic. Also, skywriting is expensive and seems like a waste of financial resources.

When I knock on her trailer door, I don't get an answer, so my less-than-awesome groveling plan is thwarted. The truck she drives is missing, so I'm guessing she went out. I could drive around town and see if I can find her, but that's a level of desperate I'm not sure she'll appreciate. I also don't think she'd be all that keen on a public apology.

Based on the stars, the rain they were calling for isn't coming, which means her trailer will be dry tonight and she won't have a reason to come knocking on my door. I'm probably her very last resort at this point, maybe just above making a deal with the devil and hugging a grizzly bear.

I spend the next two hours thinking of creative ways to make my brother pay for the shitstorm he's turned my life into.

Eventually I get sick of being alone with my thoughts, so I step outside, wanting to clear my head. The sun has long set and it's a clear night, but it's cooler than it has been. I remember how quickly the weather would turn in August. One night it would be sweltering and the next I'd be in pants and questioning how soon it would be before I needed a fire in the evenings to take the chill off. I grab a flashlight and head down to the dock so I can look at the stars and figure out tomorrow's get-Dillion-to-forgive-me plan. While drinking beer.

The path to the lake is winding, and little lights are set into the ground at four-foot intervals, like permanent fireflies guiding my way. I grab a chair and check for dock spiders before I sit. I remember as a kid freaking out the first time I saw one. Dock spiders are no regular spider—with a body the size of an Oreo cookie and a leg span that could fill the entire palm of a basketball player's hand, there is no way I want to share a chair with any of those beasts.

Also, there's a picture floating around on the internet of a guy's ridiculously swollen junk after he got bitten by one. I can't unsee that, and every time I catch a glimpse of one of those spiders, I get an uncomfortable twinge in my balls, like they're trying to climb up inside my body and hide from the potential for damage.

When I determine the chair is spider-free, I turn off the flashlight and drop down into it. I'm there for all of five peaceful minutes when I hear the rustle of bushes close by. I freeze and hold my breath—not that it will help me at all if there's a bear out here, looking for a snack.

My panic is short lived, though, because the noise is followed by grumbling and the sound of something hard hitting the dock next door. For a moment I think I've lucked out and that Dillion has done the same thing as me: come down to clear her head. At least until I realize the voice is way too deep to be hers.

"Fuckin' watchers . . . bugs in the shower." Dillion's brother, Billy, clomps across the wooden slats, his lantern swinging from one of his crutches. He sets it on a chair, and his crutches clatter to the dock. The sound echoes across the lake, like we're sitting in a fishbowl.

He pulls his shirt over his head and tosses it at his feet, then hops uncoordinatedly to the edge. I haven't seen him since the last time I ran into him at Bernie's. From what I've witnessed, he seems like a recluse. I imagine that getting a DUI and taking out your neighbor's mailbox in the process might make someone decide to hermit for a while.

It's cool just in my shorts and T-shirt, and he's almost painfully lean, so it can't be all that warm for him. Apart from the moon, there isn't much light to provide visibility, and the water is as black as the sky, dotted with pricks of starlight.

Lily pads float close to Dillion's family's dock; the water around here is marshy. The only way to combat that is to bring in sand, but it looks like it's been a few years since anyone has done that. It used to be my job as a teenager to bring wheelbarrows of it down every time I came for a swim so we could wade in and not get tangled up in the weeds at the bottom, or end up with a foot covered in leeches.

I don't have a chance to make my presence known before he does a graceless belly flop off the end of the dock, but the second he hits the water, I'm already out of my chair. I'm thinking night swimming alone while wearing a cast is not a good idea.

"Ahhh! What the fuck? Stop touching me!"

My beer bottle clatters to the dock, the remaining liquid foaming and sloshing across the boards. I flick on my flashlight and rush to the narrow path worn between the two docks. I nearly trip over his discarded crutches.

"Billy? Man, you okay?"

"Who's that? Who's there?"

Billy flails around in the water, his head going under, and he does the windmill, his panic obvious when he comes back up, sputtering and coughing. He's only a handful of feet from the edge of the dock, but with the weight of his cast, it would be a challenge to swim. I'm also unsure if it's waterproof.

"It's your neighbor, Van. I'm a friend of Dillion's. Grab the end of this, and I'll pull you back in!" I hold out his crutch as he continues to flail and struggle.

I don't want to jump in after him. Not because I care if I get wet, but Billy's too frantic for me to get in the water with him without some kind of floatation device. It's about twelve feet deep at the end of the dock, which shouldn't be an issue, but I don't want to get dragged under by him and end up drowning ten feet from a dock.

I'm grateful when he finally manages to grab hold of the crutch.

But as soon as he's close enough, he clutches my arm and nearly pulls me in with him. I end up having to shimmy along the edge until the water is shallow enough for him to stand. Even then, he struggles, likely because he's trying to walk on a casted leg and the bottom of the lake is full of rocks and sticks.

"I'm gonna get in and help you back to shore, okay?" I kick off my shoes and pull my shirt over my head before I join him in the water. The temperature has definitely dropped over the last few days, both in and out of the water, and goose bumps break across my skin as I sling his arm around my shoulder. He leans on me for support, and by the time I finally get him out of the water, he's shivering.

I force him to sit down so he doesn't do any more damage to himself.

"What the hell were you thinking? It's dark, you can't see a damn thing, and you have a freaking cast!" My shorts are suctioned to my legs, and the cool breeze coming off the water sends a shiver down my spine.

"I needed to shower, and I can't use the one in the house," he mumbles.

I can smell the alcohol on his breath. "Why? Is it broken?" I nab my T-shirt from the dock and pat his shoulders to dry him off.

"Might as well be. They're planting bugs." The words are hard to make out because they're slurring together and he's mumbling. "I saw that man in the driveway this afternoon, talking to Dee. He must be a fed or something. He's been watching me. They all have."

"He's not a fed; he's my brother and an asshole. Raise your arms, please."

"Why? What are you going to do?"

I hold up his discarded shirt. "You're cold, and it doesn't look like you brought a towel down with you, so you should put this on."

His teeth clack a few times before he finally lifts his arms in the air, allowing me to pull his shirt over his head. It hangs off him, his collarbones poking out like hanger wire.

"He's still probably working for the feds, though. That's what they do. They make you think they're just your family, and then they sell you out. Dee lived in the city for years. She has to have connections. She might not even know she has them."

I'm struggling to understand what he's talking about. I have to wonder if he's been smoking the reefer in addition to whatever he's been drinking. "Why would Dillion have connections to the feds?"

"It's all connected. Everything is. They brainwash you and make you believe they're good, and they're not. Even my mom is working for them. The diner is a cover."

Dillion mentioned being worried about her brother, and now I have to question if she's right to be concerned. Nothing Billy says makes sense, and most of it seems to be rooted in paranoia.

Something I'm familiar with.

Thankfully not at this level, though.

"We gotta get you back up to the house, Billy."

"Nope. No way. It's bugged. They're watching me. They can hear my thoughts."

Not for much longer if he pulls another stunt like this and drowns in the freaking lake.

CHAPTER 25

OH, BROTHER

Dillion

"What do you mean he's not in his room? Where would he go? Did one of his friends pick him up? Did you try his phone?" I'm grabbing a drink with Tawny and Allie when my mother calls me, frantic because she can't find my brother.

"He said he was going to take a shower, but that was more than an hour ago," my mom says, her voice wavering. "I thought maybe he was planning to see friends, but we called everyone, and no one has heard from him. I called him, but he's not picking up. Maybe he's hanging out with someone we haven't thought to call."

"I'll be home in ten." I throw a twenty on the table and grab my purse. "I gotta go, Billy's missing."

Allie tries to hand me back the money. "Did one of the guys he hangs with pick him up?"

I shake my head, both to taking the money and the friend situation. "None of the guys have seen him. He said he was going to take a shower, and now they have no idea where he is."

"Is there anywhere you want us to look?" Tawny asks.

"Maybe the beach? Although I don't know how he'd get there unless someone is covering for him. I can't see him getting very far with a freaking cast. I'll call you if I find him."

"And we'll call you if we hear anything from anyone."

"Thanks." I rush out of the bar and hop into the truck, putting it in gear before I even have my seat belt fastened. I take the roads faster than I should, terrified that something has happened to my brother. He's been home for weeks, and other than Bernie's, he's only gone to the beach party and the bar. Both times he got passed-out drunk. He hasn't been seeing friends at all, come to think of it.

My heart is in my throat the entire drive home, and when I get there, both my mom and dad have their phones to their ears. I make a beeline for Billy's room and nearly gag when I open the door. It smells like body odor, cheese, feet, and stale beer. There's a black garbage bag beside his bed, and if I had to guess, I'd say that's most definitely the source of the stale-beer smell.

I grab a corner of his sheet and tug, pulling it free from the mattress. Underneath are a whole bunch of nudie magazines and used tissues, which is gross, but what's more worrisome are the books on spy theory. Billy has always been fascinated by conspiracy theories, but lately he's been more paranoid than I remember him ever being before. I'm starting to wonder if there's more to it than just the books he's reading.

I scan his room and finally find his phone, lying on the floor, half under his bed. I pick it up and hit the screen. He has a ridiculous number of missed calls and messages, many of them from the friends we've tried to call tonight.

I punch in the number one four times in a row and smile briefly at his predictability before I start scanning the most recent messages. The more I see, the more worried I become, because that paranoia that I've noticed is in full effect in his messages with his friends. And they've been reaching out while he's been staying quiet, saying he can't message because everyone is watching him.

A knock at the front door has me dropping the phone on the bed and rushing back out to the living room. I prepare myself for the worst-case scenario, like the sheriff coming to tell us he's in jail or, worse, that they've found his body.

I throw the door open and suck in a relieved, albeit confused breath when it's not the sheriff at the door, but Van and my brother.

Billy's shoulders are curled forward, his head down, and his teeth chattering. It's not particularly cold, but the nights are cooler these days, and the water temperature is dropping along with it.

"Where the hell have you been? We've been worried sick! Why are you both wet?" I shoot an accusatory glare at Van.

"Billy was down at the lake, going for a swim."

"What in the world would possess you to go for a swim at night with a freaking cast on? It's not even the waterproof kind! You could've drowned! Mom!" I shout over my shoulder. "Grab me some towels." I usher my brother inside. "Jeez, you're freezing."

"I'm not that cold." His teeth clack together.

"Really? Because the teeth chattering tells a different story."

Mom appears with a single towel. "Oh!" She glances between Van and Billy. "What happened?" She rushes over and drapes the towel around Billy's shoulders.

Van is wet from the waist down, and shoeless. "Did you go in after him?"

"Yeah." He nods once, and another wave of goose bumps pebbles his skin.

"I'll go get more towels." I leave Van dripping in the middle of the kitchen and grab a stack from the linen closet.

Mom flips into hyperdrive and runs to the laundry room, gathering fresh dry clothes. It occurs to me that Van could go back to his house and change, but he graciously accepts the sweats and T-shirt and heads down the hall to the bathroom.

My parents help Billy to their bathroom, since Van is in the one my brother would typically use. I'm hopeful it's not completely disgusting. I grab a stack of clean clothes from the top of the dryer and follow them inside.

Billy grumbles about being fine, but my dad ignores him and takes the fresh clothes. Based on the state of his cast, he'll need to have it replaced. I leave my parents to manage him like a grumpy oversize toddler and return to the kitchen. Needing to do something with my hands, I put on the kettle and then take out the double boiler so I can make some hot chocolate. Van opens the bathroom door and steps out into the living room. The sweats are my brother's. They're way too long, but Van's thighs are thicker and his waist isn't nearly as narrow. They're stretched tight, and so is the shirt. His hands are strategically clasped in front of him, covering his junk.

I'd think it was cute if I wasn't so pissed off at him.

"Can I make you some tea or hot chocolate?" I don't want to be nice to him right now, but considering he saved my brother from potentially drowning, I feel compelled to at least make him a warm drink.

"Hot chocolate would be great, thanks. Where's Billy?" Van crosses his arms over his chest, not defensively, more to warm himself up, or at least that's my impression, based on the way he fights another shiver.

"My parents are getting him warm clothes. If you're still cold, there are blankets in the living room." I motion to the couch on the other side of the open-concept room. The kitchen, dining room, and living room are all one big space. I shouldn't be embarrassed by my family's home. It's modest and quaint and a mishmash of other people's secondhand things, but it's where I grew up and holds mostly fond memories. Still, I'm self-conscious having him in here, which is ridiculous, considering my current living arrangement is a trailer and he's now the owner of Bee's semi-hoarder-style cottage.

"I'm okay. I wasn't in for very long. I'm sorry about what happened earlier and what I said. I just . . . I saw you with my brother, and then he called and told me he was contesting the will and that you were going to help him declare Bee as incompetent. It was one more thing on top of all the other stuff I'm dealing with, and I overreacted."

"So you took him at his word rather than asking me my side?" I set the kettle on the stove, happy I have something other than Van to focus my attention on.

"I thought you would tell me, but then you acted like everything was fine. What was I supposed to think?" His voice is softer now, holding none of the accusation it had earlier.

I reduce the heat on the burner and turn to face him, seeing his point, even if it still hurts that he assumed the worst. "I called Bernie as soon as your brother left, but I didn't have any answers. And honestly, look at what's happening right now in this house. Since I've been home, I've been trying to tell my parents that there's more going on with Billy than they're willing to admit, and tonight he almost drowns. And probably would have if you hadn't been there. I was worried that you wouldn't see what I saw, or believe that your brother could do something like that. Or maybe wouldn't want to." The end of my nose tingles, and I pinch the bridge as a distraction, aware I'm on the verge of tears. Which I hate. "Maybe I should have said something right away, but I couldn't predict what your reaction was going to be. People don't always want to see the truth, Van, even when it's standing right in front of them. I've been the one trying to open people's eyes in this house, and it's exhausting. I was trying to protect you, not hurt you."

He takes a step toward me. "I'm so sor—"

I hold up my hand to cut him off, because there is more I want to say. "I know you tried to dial it back when we were having that conversation, like you knew you were pushing the limit, but you asked me an impossible question that I couldn't answer."

"I shouldn't have asked you to choose between your family and me. That wasn't fair."

"No it wasn't, but I understand why you did, and you have a right to. The answer isn't cut and dried, though, which is why I was waiting to talk to Bernie. I was trying to save us both some hurt."

Van sighs and closes the space between us. He traces the edge of my jaw with his fingertip and then takes my hands in his. "I'm sorry I doubted you, Dillion. I know you have a lot going on, maybe more than I realized, and I should have come out and asked the questions, but my head was a mess. While I love Bee's cottage, what I'm most worried about losing is you."

His expression is a mix of worry and apology. As much as it hurt at the time, I can see where it all went wrong. "I can give you a pass on this one, but next time come out and ask me, and I promise if your brother ever tries to blackmail me again, I'll let you know right away."

"I'll punch him in the nuts if he so much as looks at you the wrong way." Van lifts my hand and kisses my knuckle. "I'm so sorry. I'm a lot to deal with."

"Like I'm not." I glance around the house. "And you're nothing I can't handle." I tip my head back, meeting his warm gaze, and my breath catches.

He tips his chin down as the kettle starts to whistle. We both let out strained chuckles. Van brushes his lips against my temple and steps back so I can replace the kettle with the double boiler. I add milk to the second pot and stir while it heats, adding chocolate and whisking until it melts and turns a warm brown color. Van leans against the counter and watches me. I pour the steaming concoction into mugs, adding marshmallows and a dollop of whipped cream before I pass Van a mug.

We sit down at the table next to each other, and I glance over my shoulder to see if anyone is within earshot before I drop my voice and ask, "Can you tell me what happened?"

Van shrugs. "I don't really know, but I went down to the dock to clear my head. Billy showed up and just stripped down and jumped right in. He was talking to himself, so at first I thought he wasn't alone, but when I realized he was and that he was struggling, I rushed to help him. When I asked him what he was doing, he said he couldn't shower in the house because it's bugged and he's being watched."

"Bugged? He's never been afraid of spiders before."

"No. Not insect bugs, but like the way feds wire places in TV shows."

"So he thinks the police are watching him? Why? Because of his DUI?"

"I don't know. Maybe? He wasn't making much sense."

I rub the back of my neck. "This is worse than I thought. I think there's more going on with him than just taking too many painkillers and drinking too much."

"Do you think he's gotten himself into more trouble? Like he has a drug problem?"

"No. Well, maybe he's using the painkillers and the alcohol to self-medicate, but I have a feeling it's mental health. My great-aunt always struggled with ups and downs, much the same way Billy does. But I think back then people would call her eccentric and brush it off. Based on the stories I've heard, it was a lot more than that. She was anxious and paranoid. She was always talking about conspiracy theories, to the point of being obsessive about it. I don't know if it's hereditary or not, but if it is, Billy could be facing the same thing. He's always been one of those people who thinks everything is a conspiracy. I'm concerned he needs help, and not the kind any of us can give him."

Van flips his hand over, palm up, and I slip mine into his. "I'm sorry. I don't know what to do or say to make it better, but I'm here, and I'll help however I can."

"If you hadn't been there tonight, who knows what would have happened." My voice cracks. There's a very real possibility that Billy might not have been found until it was too late to help him.

Van puts an arm around me. "It's okay. It's gonna be all right. We'll figure it out."

When my mom comes back to the kitchen, I can practically feel her embarrassment. As it is, her cheeks turn red. "I'm so sorry, Van. Poor Billy has been having a rough time, and I think he had too many beers. I'm so glad you were down there to help him get back up."

"Me too. I would've hated for something bad to happen to him." Van kisses my temple and takes the opportunity to excuse himself so we can handle this as a family. I *need* to have this conversation with my parents. There's no more sweeping it under the rug, pretending everything is okay.

I walk Van to the door. He pulls me in for a brief hug and whispers, "Are you going to be okay? I can stay if you want."

"I'll be fine. I appreciate the offer, though."

He nods once and presses his lips briefly to mine. "I'm still sorry about the way I acted earlier. I'll be waiting for you if you need me later."

As soon as the door clicks shut, I turn back to my mom. "Billy could have drowned if Van hadn't been there to help him."

She wrings her hands and smiles stiffly. "Billy said he fell off the edge of the dock."

"That might be what he said, but that's not what happened." I fill her in on Van's version of events.

Mom sinks into a chair, fingers at her lips. "Oh, that's really not good."

I fill a mug with hot chocolate and place it in front of her, then take the seat across from her. "It's really not. He needs help, Mom. There's more going on than any of us realized."

"He's supposed to see the doctor tomorrow to have his ankle checked."

"He needs to see a doctor for more than his ankle," I say gently.

"Dillion is right," Dad says from the living room doorway. "Billy needs help."

The next morning, we take Billy to the doctor and have his ankle looked at after the impromptu dip in the lake. His cast is beat up as a result and definitely needs replacing, since it's cracked in a couple of places. He'll also need x-rays to determine whether he's done additional damage.

It's almost a relief when he has a fit against the doctor, being belligerent and paranoid, finally showing them the hurt they can't see. He's certain it's all a scam and that the doctors are in on it, and they're going to bug his cast and then they'll be able to track him wherever he goes. It gets to the point where he's so worked up they have to sedate him.

It's painful to witness, and my mom is beside herself, tears tracking down her cheeks. She dabs at them with a tissue while my dad wraps an arm around her shoulders. I fight my own tears, wanting to stay strong, but it's hard. I can't begin to imagine how they feel about this. For me it's been building for a long while, and I have guilt over thinking it was Billy being irresponsible when so much more was happening in his head. Even worse is that he didn't feel like he could tell any of us what was going on. No one should ever be that lonely.

But he's here now, and as hard as it is to watch him rail and break down, I know that we're doing the right thing, even if it hurts. I don't want him to suffer any more than he already has, and mental health isn't something you can put a Band-Aid on. In a small town, it's even more difficult, because everyone knows your business.

The doctor takes us into her office and brings along a hospital psychologist. Dr. Saleh is new to the hospital, but she has that gentle way about her that puts you right at ease. Her warm smile and soft demeanor are exactly what my parents and I need. And the reassurance that we're making the right decision. "With Billy's consent, we think it would be best to admit him, so we can perform a full psychiatric assessment. There's a possibility that he's reacting negatively to the medication, but based on what you're reporting, it could be more than that."

Mom chews on her fingernails, and Dad looks absolutely crushed.

"Do you think he'll agree? How long would he have to stay?" Mom asks.

"It could be a few days, or as long as a few weeks. It depends on how Billy responds to treatment. My concern is that the longer we leave this, the worse it will get."

My mom turns to my dad. "Whatever he needs?"

He squeezes her hand and gives her a soft smile. "We have to do whatever is best for him."

They both turn to me, and my dad asks, "Do you think that's a good idea?"

My heart breaks for them. They've always been such great parents, but this is a truth they didn't want to see, or were too afraid to. So I do the only thing I can, because I realize that they're paralyzed and can't make the decision on their own. "This is the best thing we can do for Billy and for our family. Let the doctors help him."

It's late afternoon by the time we get home. My parents are exhausted, and I keep reassuring Mom that this is the best thing we can do for Billy. I hope I'm right.

The moment I enter the trailer, I hear Van tromping through the brush. I meet him at the door. I didn't end up going to his place last night, the conversation with my parents having gone on until the wee hours of the morning.

He's dressed in a pair of navy sweats that have seen better days and an old T-shirt, but he still looks fantastic. "Hey." I step right into him, and he folds me into a warm embrace.

"Hey, yourself." He lets me hold on to him for a few long, comforting seconds before he kisses my cheek and pulls back. "How is Billy? How are you? I've been thinking about you all day."

"He's okay. Or he will be, I hope."

"That's good. Do you want to talk about it at all? Maybe you want to come back to my place? I can make up for being a jerk yesterday."

I give him a small smile. "Yeah, sure, that sounds good. Just let me grab a couple of things?"

"Of course." Van waits at the door while I shove pajamas and my toothbrush into an overnight bag. Once I have my things, I shoulder the bag, close the door to my trailer, and follow him down the path back to his place. I realize I've started to look at it not as Bee's anymore, but as his.

As soon as we're through the narrow path, he links our fingers together. "You okay?"

I realize I didn't answer that question before, too fixated on Billy and what he's going through. "I think so. I've known for a while that things with Billy weren't okay, but seeing him break down today made me aware of how hard this whole thing has been on him. He's always had ups and downs, but this is more than that. I hate that he's been going through this alone this whole time." As we step inside the cottage, I tell him about the episode Billy had at the hospital and that they admitted him.

"How did your parents handle that?" He takes my bag, sets it on the kitchen counter, and pulls me over to the couch I've sat on a million times before. Being in here feels different now. Bee's was always a haven, but this is so much more than that.

"Better than I expected. I thought my mom would put up a fight, since they've been doing a lot of brushing things off, but I realized they didn't know what to do. No one wants their kid to go through what Billy is. There's guilt attached to it, like it's somehow their fault that he's like this, and I guess genetically there's probably a link, but it's not as though they have control over it. They needed someone to say this was a good idea and that it needed to happen so they could feel okay about it, and that person had to be me."

"And how do *you* feel about that?" Van brushes my hair back and smooths his thumb down the side of my neck. "Being the one they looked to for help to make the decision?"

"We're all in this together, so that definitely makes it easier. I don't feel as though the decision rests solely on my shoulders. We made it as a family. And I know that Billy might be upset now, but I'm hoping with time and treatment he'll see that we did this because we care about him." I lean into him, letting those words sink in. "That's what it's always been like with my family. We back each other up."

"That's good. I'm glad you have that." There's wistfulness in his tone.

"Me too. I don't know if I would have been able to make that decision on my own. Leaving my brother at the hospital was so hard; I just wanted to wrap him up in love and keep him safe, but I knew I couldn't do that for him. Having my parents there as a support was a big help." I squeeze his hand, aware that our family situations are vastly different. "I'm sorry about your brother," I add. "I can't imagine how you feel, or how hard this is for you. Family are supposed to take care of each other." I tip my chin up as he tips his down.

Our gazes meet, and something shifts in the air around us. A new kind of tension sparks and crackles between us. A connection that wasn't there before, so much more intense this time.

"I could be that for you," I whisper. "The person you can count on not to let you down."

"You already are, Dillion." He cups my cheek in his palm and dips down and presses his lips to mine. "You're the best part of my day and the one person I look forward to seeing more than anyone else. I'm lucky to have you in my life."

This time when he comes back for a kiss, it's a soft lingering one that sends warmth rushing through my veins, and heat settles low in my belly, sparking need. He deepens the kiss, and when it's clear it's about to become more, he takes me to his bedroom. We undress slowly, paying special attention to each other's most sensitive spots, until we're both panting and desperate.

He settles between my thighs and enters me on a slow stroke. "I love this," he groans against my lips. He pushes up on his forearm, his eyes meeting mine, soft and vulnerable. "I love you."

My heart clenches, and my breath catches in my throat for a moment before I murmur, "I love you too."

I wrap my legs around his waist, and we move together, a slow tide rising until bliss washes over us.

CHAPTER 26

DOWN WE GO

Van

The days and weeks that follow are hectic and stressful for Dillion. Not only is she worried for her brother in the hospital being treated for a psychiatric condition, but the threat from my brother hangs over both of our heads. It makes us edgy.

While Bernie and I push back against my brother contesting the will and my father attempts to talk some sense into him—which is proving futile—Teagan is trying to hack into his email and see if she can't find information that way. She hasn't spent a great deal of time on computer hacking, though, so it's not necessarily the most effective sleuthing either of us has engaged in.

With everything going on, I do my best to be there for Dillion, aware that she's the kind of person who tends to try to manage everything on her own. But I want to give her a shoulder to lean on, as she's been doing for me.

Three weeks after they admit Billy to the hospital, they have a formal diagnosis. He has bipolar disorder, and the hallucinations were a manifestation of the combination of medication, alcohol, and insomnia. The withdrawal wasn't easy on him, but once alcohol was removed from the equation and they started him on medication (which will need to be monitored closely in the coming weeks), they agreed to release him as an outpatient. He has to attend therapy sessions several times a week, but he can sleep in his own bed. And he's excited about eating something other than hospital food.

Dillion is sitting cross-legged on the couch, hugging one of Grammy Bee's embroidered pillows. "I think we should throw him a little party. Nothing big, just a 'Welcome home' and 'We love you' kind of thing. The past few weeks have been tough, and he's worked hard to be able to come home. I want him to know we've got his back and we're proud of him, you know?"

"I think that's a great idea. Do you want it to be family?"

"And a few close friends. Aaron has been to the hospital every day since they started letting Billy have visitors, so he should definitely come. And obviously you need to be there, since you found him down at the lake."

I've been to visit Billy a bunch of times since he was admitted. At first I went with Dillion, but after a few visits I started going on my own. We talk construction and play basketball on the outdoor court. He beats me every single time. Although he does have about four inches on me.

"I can be there. Absolutely. Just tell me what you need help with, and I'll do it."

"I'll make a few phone calls, and then you can help me make a cake!" She hops up off the couch and plucks her phone from the end table. First she calls her parents, who are on board with the welcome-home party; then she calls Aaron and a couple of Billy's other friends who have been supportive over the past few weeks.

Once the calls are made and some food is ordered, she pulls out Bee's KitchenAid mixer, circa the nineties, and we get to work making a cake and icing from scratch. Three hours and a lot of me dipping my finger into the buttercream icing and getting hit with a spatula on the back of the hand later, we have a **WELCOME HOME** cake.

Dillion stands with her hands on her hips, frowning. "It looks like a pair of preschoolers decorated this."

I kiss her on the temple. "But the icing and the cake taste delicious, and that's way more important. Besides, it means more because it's homemade. He's going to love it."

Twenty minutes later she gets the call that her parents are picking up Billy and that people are on the way to their house. We bring the cake over to her parents' place and find Aaron already standing in the driveway, holding a bottle of fizzy grape juice with a bow on it and a platter of meat and cheese.

"Hey." He grins sheepishly. "I thought maybe you could use a hand setting things up."

"Absolutely! Thanks so much for being here and for being so supportive."

"Always, Dee. I feel bad that I backed off as much as I did. I should've realized there was more going on."

"We all missed the signs for a long time, but now he's on the right path, and we're here to help him stay on it. That's what counts." Dillion gives him a side hug. "Anyway, let me run inside and grab all the stuff for the picnic table so we can get things set up before my parents get home. My mom said she'd text before they leave the hospital."

She flounces up the steps to the front porch and disappears inside the house.

"Hey, man, how's it going?" Aaron jams a thumb in his pocket and rocks back on his heels.

"Good. You?" I like Aaron, and when we're talking renos, the conversation flows, but sometimes I find it hard to get a bead on him.

"Yeah. Also good." He glances at the cake. "Dillion make that?"

"She did. We did, actually." Oh yeah, the territorial streak is strong. He grins. "But she decorated it, right?"

"I think she did a great job, you know, for a nonprofessional."

"Oh yeah. She makes the same cake for Billy every year for his birthday. It's Funfetti, isn't it? Got all the little rainbow chip things in it?"

"Yeah, it does. You guys grew up together, right?"

"Yup. She's like my sister, and she looks at me like a brother."

"I wasn't . . . that wasn't . . . I wasn't trying . . ."

Aaron holds up his hand. "You don't need to explain, man. I get it. I might think of her like my sister, but I'm not blind. I know she's gorgeous and she's got a heart bigger than Pearl Lake. She loves hard. Just be good to her, that's all."

"I plan to."

"I figured." He tips his chin in the direction of Grammy Bee's. "How's the reno plans going? You still want me to have a look at the garage?"

"That'd be great. I have a few different plans already drawn up, but it would be great to have someone familiar with building code, and plumbing and electrical, to have a look at it before I submit it to the town for approval. No point going to all the trouble only to find out I can't tie into the existing septic, you know?"

"For sure. Want me to take a look after the party?"

"If you have the time, that'd be perfect."

Dillion returns with her arms laden with party supplies.

"Babe, why didn't you ask for help?" I rush over to grab some of the items perched on top.

"I got it."

I nab a pack of paper plates and a box of plastic utensils before they hit the ground. "Really?"

"You distracted me when you came running at me."

I don't say anything else, but I move the cake out of the way, and Aaron and I help her set up. There's punch and an array of nonalcoholic beverages. Bowls of chips, trays of veggies and fruit, and, in the center of it all, the cake.

We have enough time to blow up a few balloons and tape them to the side of the house and the picnic table before Tawny and Allie show up, along with a couple of Billy's more reliable high school friends.

A few minutes later, her parents pull down the driveway. Her dad jumps out as soon as the vehicle is in park, opens the rear passenger-side door, takes Billy's crutches, and helps him out of the truck.

Over the past few weeks he's put on some much-needed weight; his face is filling out, and the dark circles under his eyes are disappearing. He's without his cast now, but he accepts his dad's offer of a crutch so he can cross the driveway without difficulty.

"What the heck is going on?" he asks, face turning red.

"Welcome home!" we all shout, sort of in unison, and Aaron starts clapping, so we all join in.

"Man, if this is the kind of party you throw me for winding up in the hospital, I should consider going to college or something. I feel like there'd be a live band if I managed to graduate." While he seems embarrassed, he also looks genuinely happy.

Dillion rushes up to him and says something. Billy smiles down at her and pulls her into a hug. "I'm joking around; this is great. Thanks for sticking by me."

Everyone greets him and gives him a hug, telling him in low whispers how glad they are he's home and that they're there for him, whatever he needs. I stand back and watch, amazed by the way his family has rallied around him, and I wonder how different things would have been for our family if we'd come together when we'd lost my mom, rather than going in separate directions.

It doesn't take long before Billy is worn out from the socializing, and probably the entire day. I help Dillion clean up, and while she takes some time with her family, Aaron follows me over to Bee's so we can look at my plans for the garage and, later, once that's finished, what it would take to renovate the cottage.

"I don't think it'll be tough to get permits to make changes to the existing buildings. That's not usually the problem around here. It's more about when people are looking to build things like condos. The lake can't handle much more boat activity than it already has."

"Dillion and I talked about that. I've talked to the town council and asked about cleaning up the beach on this side."

He stuffs his hands in his pockets. "Yeah. I've heard about that. Just wanna make sure you've got Bee's best interests in mind while you're doing that."

"How do you mean?"

He leans against the side of the truck, flipping a set of keys around his finger. "You're city—you see an opportunity to swoop in and make changes—but there's always another side to it. We can fix up that beach, but someone has to maintain it, and it all costs money. And if it's too pretty, then everyone with cottages on the other side starts sniffing around, looking over here for more places to build. Bee was big on preserving the lake and the community. I hope you're looking to do the same, is all."

I don't have a chance to reply because a car pulls down the driveway. "What the heck is my sister doing here?" I mutter.

She parks beside my BMW, which is covered with flower blossoms since I've been driving Grammy Bee's truck most of the time. She barely has the car in park before she hops out. "You will never believe what I found today!" She practically bounces across the driveway, heading straight for me while waving her phone in the air. She skids to a stop when she sees Aaron leaning against the truck. "Oh! Hey. Hello! I didn't realize you had company."

Her gaze flips between me and Aaron and back again, and she changes course and makes a beeline for Aaron. Teagan has always been highly social, and very charismatic. She holds out her hand. "Hi. Teagan Firestone. I'm Van's sister. You must be a friend of my brother's."

"Aaron Saunders. I was talking to Van about his reno projects. I work with Dillion and her dad." He engulfs my sister's hand in his giant one. His is covered in little scabs and nicks and scars. She has a purple manicure with some kind of design on the nail of both ring fingers.

"You have huge hands."

Once he releases hers, she grabs his wrist and holds it up, like she's forcing him into a high five. She matches the heel of her hand with the heel of his and presses her palm to his, splaying out her fingers. Her fingertips only reach his first knuckle.

She whistles lowly. "That's just . . . wow. You should be a basketball player with mitts like these." Her gaze drops to his feet, and then she does a full-body scan, all the way from his scuffed work boots, over his ripped and stained jeans, and back to his face.

He arches a brow. "I like football better."

"There's more violence in football. All that tackling. Full-body hugging."

I clear my throat, not sure what I'm witnessing.

Teagan drops his hand and steps back.

"I should probably be heading home," Aaron says, flipping his keys around his finger. "Just shoot me a message later next week, and we can set up a formal meeting to go over your plans. I'll help you get them ready so the permits won't be a fight with the town."

"Great, thanks, Aaron. I appreciate that."

He nods to my sister. "Nice to meet you, Teagan."

"You too." Her smile is on the right side of maniacal.

I wait until he's out of hearing range before I ask, "What the hell was that?"

"I don't know. But I made that so weird, and awkward. I guess it's a good thing I don't live here, otherwise I'd have to actively try to avoid him in the future. God, he's so . . . small-town hot."

"What does that even mean?"

"Like he clearly hasn't showered, or changed out of his work clothes, but that just makes him sexier. Why is he so sexy? I mean, he hasn't shaved in at least two days. And he probably doesn't manscape at all. I wonder if he has any tattoos." She taps her lip.

"Okay. You can keep those thoughts inside your head."

"Huh?" She looks away from his retreating form. He's so tall he has to duck way down to avoid getting clotheslined by the tree branches over his head.

"Nothing. Never mind. Not that I'm not happy to see you, but what exactly are you doing here?"

"Oh! Right! I have Bradley's cloud password!" She bounces up and down excitedly. "Or most of it, anyway. Enough that I think we can figure it out."

"How did you manage to get that?"

"I drugged him again, and then I went through his desk at work, and his entire room at the house. I found some things I wish I hadn't, but you know how he has the worst memory in the world and his password is the same for every single site?"

I didn't know that, but I go along with it. "Sure."

"He has this notebook on his desk, and there was a page ripped out, but I could see the outline of words, so I did that thing where you use the side of a pencil to scratch the next page and find out what was on it." She holds up her phone and shows me a picture of the paper. "I took the actual page, too, but I figured I'd want photographic evidence. I'm crossing my fingers that once we get into his cloud, we'll get some answers."

"As long as he wasn't smart enough to delete all the trails."

"He's smart enough; I'm just not sure he'd take the time to do it."

Teagan and I grab my laptop and flip it open. We'll only have three tries before we're locked out, so we need to be smart about it.

"I think that's a hashtag after his name." Teagan points to what looks like a bunch of scratches.

"He really has the worst penmanship, doesn't he?"

"Yup. And who uses their own name as their password? How stupid is that? And is the *e* backward?"

"I think it's a three?"

"Oh! Good call. Okay. So his name is the password, plus a hashtag, and then what?"

"I'd say number one, but it doesn't look like that's what it is since it's curved and not straight."

"Unless he wrote out the number one?"

"Ooooh. That would be smart. Should we try it?"

I type in the password and cross my fingers as I hit enter. But I get the red "Wrong Password" message.

"Shit. We have two more tries. Are we sure that looks like a zero? Or an *o*?"

"I think so. God, we need to not get this wrong." Teagan taps her lip. "I have it! What's his favorite movie of all time?"

"Uh, I have no idea."

"He loves James Bond movies. He's dressed up as him every single year at Halloween since he was a teenager."

"All he does is wear a suit, though."

"Because it's easy, but also because he loves those movies. Try double oh seven."

"You're sure about this?"

"Positive. Just try it."

"You try it." I shift the computer toward her, and she types in the password.

We cross our fingers and hold our breath as she hits the enter button.

And this time we don't get the error message.

We both shout obscenities.

"Oh my God, we're in!"

An hour later, Teagan and I have found more than enough evidence to point all the fingers back at my brother. Somehow he managed to get the passwords to my bank accounts and forged a bunch of signatures. He actually was pretty good at doing it; I even believe that some of the paperwork I've seen had my signature.

"Who the hell takes this many dick pics? And who is he sending them to?" Teagan holds her hand up in front of the screen to block yet another image of our brother's penis. There are many on the cloud.

"Maybe it's his version of flirting?"

"How are we related to him?" Teagan shakes her head. "Dad is going to be so disappointed."

I hadn't stopped to think about how Dad will react to this whole thing. Having someone steal $3 million from your late wife's foundation is bad enough, but finding out that it's your own son would be a real mindfuck. "How do you want to do this? Should we tell Dad before we pass this information over?"

Teagan taps her lip and stays silent for a few seconds before she answers. "I think we call a family meeting, but we don't give Bradley time to make an escape. Right now he must think he's pulling one over on us, so we don't want to give him the benefit of a heads-up. And the sooner we do it, the better." She flops back on the couch. "I can't believe we have to take our own brother down. How much does this suck?"

"A lot."

I haven't always been my brother's biggest fan, but finding out that he's the reason for everything that our family is dealing with takes my opinion of him to a new low.

Half an hour and a short conversation with Dillion later, in which I tell her I have to go to the city to deal with a family issue and that I'll fill her in on everything when I get back, Teagan and I are headed to Chicago, with me in the driver's seat.

The landscape changes from tree-lined highways to the bustle of a busy freeway.

"Do you miss this?" Teagan asks as we get closer to our exit.

My dad lives outside the city in a massive two-story home. Teagan still lives in the main house, but Bradley took over the pool house a few years ago. I was the only one who moved out and got my own place. I don't think Teagan necessarily wants to stay in the house; it's more that she doesn't want to leave our dad alone in a huge house that's full of memories of our mother.

"Honestly? The only thing I miss about being here is you."

She nods. "I can see that. Pearl Lake is full of such good memories and great people."

"It really is." I pull off the freeway and drive down familiar streets, back to the house I grew up in. It's been months since I've been home, and I realize I don't miss this place at all. In fact, as soon as I pull into the driveway, I can feel the shackles of a past none of us can ever seem to escape locking me back in.

"You ready to do this?" I ask Teagan as I park beside my brother's ostentatious car.

"As ready as I can be. You?"

"Same."

We both sigh and get out of the car, closing our doors in tandem. We fall into step beside each other. The front door is huge and black with a wrought iron design set in the center. The redbrick face of the house is elegant and gorgeous, but even from the outside, I know it's a pretty shell without a heart.

She punches in the code and lets herself in. "Dad?"

"I'm in my office!"

We find him sitting behind his desk, bifocals halfway down his nose, a stack of papers in front of him, his computer screen glowing.

Over the years his shoulders have started to round from all the time he spends sitting behind a desk. It's nine o'clock and still he's working, and it's exactly what he'll do until he's too tired to keep his eyes open. Despite the late hour, and the fact that he's in his own house, he's still wearing a suit. His salt-and-pepper hair is cut short and styled neatly. He looks put together, but it's a veneer. I can see myself in him, and what my future might look like if I ever choose to follow in his footsteps—a sad, lonely man.

He smiles when I appear behind Teagan. "Donovan! I didn't know you were here. It's great to have you home. Are you staying for a while?" He stands and walks around his desk, pulling me into a hug.

"Uh, probably not. Is Bradley home?"

"I think so. Is everything okay?" His brow furrows, and he looks from me to Teagan and back again. "Did something happen?"

"Yeah, and I don't think you're going to be particularly happy about it."

Teagan and I sit him down and show him what we've found. The offshore accounts set up in my name, half the money from the foundation already gone, frittered away in a matter of months. The forged signatures, the fraudulent accounts.

"How do you want to handle this, Dad?" Teagan asks softly.

He leans back in his chair and scrubs a palm over his face. This conversation seems to have aged him five years in the span of half an hour. It can't be easy to be in his shoes, finding out one of his children tried and succeeded to frame his other son.

"I've bailed Bradley out more times than I can count. And maybe that was where I went wrong." He sighs. "I can't help him out of this one. He's going to have to face the consequences of his actions."

Dad reaches for his phone and calls Bradley up to the house.

He strolls into Dad's office five minutes later, dressed like he's about to hit the club. His eyes flare when he sees Teagan and me. "What's going on?"

"You should have a seat." Dad motions to the empty chair.

"I'm on my way out." Bradley thumbs over his shoulder, eyes darting back to me as he takes a cautious step toward the door he just walked through.

"Your plans for the evening have changed, I'm afraid."

Dad turns the laptop around to show Bradley what we all know: that he's a thief and a liar. Bradley's expression shutters, and he crosses his arms. "What is this?"

"Based on the number of forged checks and fake accounts, I would call it fraud." Dad laces his fingers together and folds them on his desk. "Why would you do this to your own family, Bradley?"

"Where should I start? How about when you lied and said Bee's cottage was worth jack shit and let her hand over what could be worth millions to your golden child? Or maybe we should talk about the way you've been pissing away our money ever since Mom died on frivolous purchases you don't need. The house is mortgaged to the rafters. There'll be nothing left in a decade." He flails a hand around. "Or all that money sitting in a damn foundation, and for what? A tax shelter for money we don't even have. I realized a long time ago that you're going to leave me with nothing but debt, so I took matters into my own hands. I wanted my inheritance before there wasn't anything left to inherit. Work smarter, not harder, Dad."

"You're a selfish bastard," Teagan snaps.

"And you're his damn lapdog!" Bradley says, motioning to our dad. "It's pathetic the way you're always pandering to whatever Dad wants. Taking care of him like he's already an invalid. Staying in this stupid house, and for what?" His angry gaze shifts to Dad. "It's not like any of us are going to get anything when you finally kick the bucket. You're a walking corpse. You stopped living as soon as Mom died; you just don't have the decency to do yourself in. Instead you bury yourself in work! Money is the only thing left you can give us, and you don't even have any to give."

"Bradley, you need to watch your mouth," I snap. "You've already done regrettable things; don't burn what's left of your bridges because you've got an ill-placed vendetta."

"I'm not wrong!"

I can't believe how unaffected he is by what he has done. It's like he doesn't even know that it was wrong. It reminds me of what Dillion said—that sometimes we don't want to see the truth, so we make up one that suits us better.

"But you're not right either," Dad says quietly. "Framing your brother and stealing from the foundation isn't the answer. I realize I haven't been the best role model, or even a very good father, but there's more to life than money, Bradley."

"What about Grammy's cottage? Why go after that, especially after stealing the three million?" I need an answer, even though I'm probably not going to like it, or understand his motivation.

"Everything comes so easily for you. You've always been the golden boy who can do no wrong. It doesn't matter what I do; I'll never be as good as you. Hell, I've worked with Dad since I could hold a job, and still it's you and all your successes and how much you've accomplished. Everyone fawns over you. Do you have any idea how frustrating that is? So I figured I'd take the thing that mattered most to you so you'd know what it's like to lose out."

"What you've done to your own family is shameful, Bradley," Dad says. "If your mother were still here, she would be devastated."

"Well, she's dead, and I never really knew her because of you. She's been gone for almost two decades, so how she would've felt is hardly relevant. Stop living in the damn past!"

My dad pushes out of his chair. "This isn't a good reason for tearing what's left of your family apart, Bradley. This isn't something I can fix for you. You're going to have to deal with this mess on your own." I haven't seen this version of my father in a long time.

Bradley's demeanor shifts, and he looks suddenly panicked. "So what are you going to do? Make me pay it all back?"

"No."

Bradley's shoulders sag with relief, but only for a moment.

"You're going to report yourself to the board and the police, and then you're going to deal with the consequences of your actions. And if you don't make the call, I will."

His gaze darts around the room, and his half smirk slowly fades as he takes in Teagan and me, a somber, united front against him. I see the moment he realizes Dad is serious.

"But I could go to jail!"

"You should have considered that before you framed your own brother."

There's no satisfaction in watching my brother being taken away from our family home in handcuffs. Clearing my own name lacks the kind of closure I wanted, because it shines yet another negative spotlight on my family. And all the issues my dad has been burying for years are finally out in the open. I can handle it, because I don't have to stay here and watch the fallout, but my dad and my sister don't have the escape I do, and I worry that this will only serve to tear us further apart.

CHAPTER 27
SHOULD I STAY OR SHOULD I GO?

Van

The next few weeks definitely aren't easy. People love gossip, especially the scandalous kind. I worry that my family drama is going to be too much for Dillion to handle on top of everything else she's dealing with. Especially since my dad doesn't bail Bradley out, and as predicted, he ends up in jail. Nothing says newsworthy headlines like your brother going to prison for fraud.

But Dillion stands by me.

In fact, the more drama there is, the more she and her family work to insulate me from it. I get invited over for dinners. Pies show up on my front porch. And through it all, Dillion is there, not only for me, but for Teagan as well, who has been visiting nearly every weekend.

While everything settles in the city, I decide to stay in Pearl Lake through the winter. I'm not in a rush to go back, and with the design jobs I've picked up on the lake thanks to referrals from Aaron and Footprint Renovations, I'm easily able to manage the simple lifestyle I've grown to love in Pearl Lake. I don't know if it's enough to make a career out of, but I'm getting by. And now that the $3 million in missing funds isn't hanging over my head, companies are no longer shoving my résumé aside.

It's early evening, almost a month after my brother's takedown. In order to avoid a trial, Bradley took a plea deal. He'd hoped it would reduce his sentence, but he'll be spending the next three years in prison. I'm not sure he's remorseful—more that he's pissed he got caught and has to pay all the money back that he stole.

Tonight Dillion is working late and doesn't expect to be home for another hour. I'm taking the opportunity to go through some of Grammy Bee's office files, something I've been avoiding, since there are fifty years' worth of them. There's an entire cabinet full of manuals for various appliances, many of which are so old that if they break, there's no way to fix them. I've just tossed a manual for an eight-track cassette player into the garbage bag when there's a knock on my door.

I assume Dillion got off work earlier than expected, so I shout, "Come on in!"

There's a long pause before the door creaks open—it needs some WD-40 or a new set of hinges—and I turn to find not Dillion but her mom standing in the doorway.

"Oh, hey. Hi, Mrs. Stitch."

She glances around the space and gives me one of her warm, slightly uncertain smiles. Dillion's mom is an interesting woman. When she's at work, she's bubbly and full of life, talkative and friendly; when she's not at the diner, she's soft spoken and a little nervous. Her gaze lands on the TV. "It's just Marilyn, Van. Have you eaten dinner?"

I glance at the clock. I'm not sure what time I sat down this afternoon to tackle the filing cabinet, but it's getting close to six. "Not yet. I figured I'd wait until Dillion gets home."

"She's going to be at least another hour, and they're probably feeding them anyway. Why don't you come on over? You shouldn't eat dinner alone."

"Who's feeding her?"

Marilyn smiles wider, likely at my tone, which is infused with both jealousy and a hint of suspicion. "The Kingstons. The guys just finished the pool house, and the Kingstons invited them to celebrate with dinner and discuss what they're planning next."

"Planning next? I thought they were done with this project."

"Mmm. Well, they keep adding to the list of things they want done, so they want to talk options. I expect they'll be calling you, depending on what they're tackling next. Anyway, it's just me and Billy tonight, and I made shepherd's pie. We'd love to have you join us, if you're interested."

I've had Dillion's mother's shepherd's pie before. Just the mention of it makes my mouth water. "Sure, yeah, thank you. That'd be great."

When Dillion and her dad finally roll in, we're sitting at the dining room table, dinner long finished, dessert plates set on the counter—I can't say no to coconut cream pie—and the three of us are deep into a game of Farkle. It's a dice game that's ridiculously addictive.

Since Billy's been home from the hospital, things have improved. He goes to AA meetings, and the doctors recently gave him the go-ahead to work part time. According to Dillion, he'll be able to manage his mental health, provided he continues to check in with his doctor regularly, attends therapy, and has his medication closely monitored.

It's been an adjustment, and he's slowly reconnecting with friends, making better choices, and avoiding situations that will get him in trouble.

Dillion stops short when she sees me sitting across from her brother. Her cheeks are flushed—probably because they had wine with dinner, and that's the effect even one glass can have on her.

"Oh, hey. Well, I guess this explains why you're not answering your phone."

"I got an invite for dinner, and I couldn't say no. We're almost finished here. Why don't you grab a seat and watch your brother wipe the floor with my Farkled ass."

"Oh! I love this game!"

Billy points a finger at his sister. "You can't help him."

She raises both hands in the air. "I'll be a silent observer."

She slides into the seat beside mine and checks out the scorepad. We all keep track of our own scores. And each other's. Apparently, it's the only way to keep everyone honest. When it's my turn, Dillion makes little noises, as though she disapproves of my choices.

Billy calls her out, and she gives him her innocent doe eyes. "I didn't say anything!"

"You're making noises, though. You can't do that. It's not allowed. No noises, or you have to leave."

"Geez, who peed in your cornflakes?"

"I'm one round away from winning—don't mess it up for me."

"Mom's pretty close to you; she could still turn it around." She grimaces at my score. "Wow, you suck at this game, don't you?"

"I'm not a betting man."

"Clearly."

Five minutes and three more warnings later, Billy wins the game. I thank her mom for dinner and Billy for the ass whupping in Farkle and head back to my place with Dillion.

"I can't believe my mom invited you over for dinner. I'm sorry I wasn't there. And that you got dragged into a game of Farkle. That can literally go on forever."

I usher her into my place, rubbing my hands together as we step inside. The weather has turned, with fall settling in and turning the leaves yellow and orange. "It's okay. It was fun. Billy seems to be doing great."

"He really is. So much more himself, but happier, you know? They said sometimes the medication can make people feel flat, but he's still got his personality, so that's great. And he loves being back at work. He can't do the heavy lifting he used to yet, and he can't operate the machinery, but it's a step in the right direction for him."

"I'm glad. It's like a one-eighty from how he was when he broke his ankle." I pick up the box of files sitting on the couch and catch my foot on the coffee table. I must do it at least once a week, and I have the bruises on my shins to prove it. The furniture is slightly too large and the table awkward to get around. The box tips over, and half the contents dump out onto the floor. "Ah crap."

I set the box down and push the table out of the way so I can gather up the fallen papers.

"Is that a manual for a VHS player? Those have been obsolete for decades." Dillion bends to help me clean up the mess.

"Bee kept every manual for everything she ever bought, apparently. You can toss it into the box over there. That's all for the burn pile. We're going to have one hell of a bonfire when I'm finished going through her filing cabinets."

"We can make s'mores and talk about the good old days when things didn't break within six months of buying them."

I smile, aware she was referencing Grammy Bee's irritation with our disposable society. "She registered everything she could for a warranty. I remember when she took back a set of sheets she'd had for twenty years because the seam started ripping."

"She had Tupperware from the seventies and made them replace it because the seal had gone on something! It was hilarious."

"And embarrassing if you were in the store with her and she was making a fuss."

Dillion chuckles and picks up another manual. This one for a toaster. Something falls out of it and flutters to the coffee table. "Oh man, did she even keep the receipts? I wonder what a toaster cost back in the day."

We're both laughing when her eyes suddenly go wide and she drops the manual and picks up the receipt. "Oh my gosh, Van. Look at this!" She holds it out to me.

I frown as I inspect what looks like a bond note from the sixties in the sum of $100,000. "Is this real? This can't be real."

"I don't know. That was her bank."

"Do you think it's the only one?" We look at each other and then the pile of manuals on the floor.

We abandon the box and start leafing through them, shaking them out one at a time. Each manual contains a single bond note in various sums. Some are as small as five grand; others are worth as much as a hundred thousand. When we're done with that pile, we go through the ones in the burn box and find even more.

We keep sifting through her files and eventually stumble on her stock portfolio. The most recent statement is from last year; the amount of money is staggering. We sit on the floor in the midst of the discarded papers and stare at the stack of bond notes. Some are in Grammy's name, others in mine, Teagan's, and Bradley's. It makes me sad that he's put himself in such a terrible situation when, if he'd just been patient, he would have known she hadn't left him out. In some ways, I wish Grammy hadn't made us play this game of hide-and-seek, but I understand why she did. She always wanted to bring us together.

"I had no idea about any of this. The stashes around the house, yes, but not this," Dillion says softly. "I would have said something a long time ago if I'd known."

"I know you would have. I thought the stashes around the house were going to help me clean this place up, but this could set us up for generations."

"Are you going to share it with Teagan?" she asks.

I realize then what I've said, and how in my head I've included Dillion in the *us*. It's what I want: for her and me to be something that lasts. But I don't correct her, because I'm not sure where she's at, and asking that when we've just stumbled on millions of dollars doesn't seem like the best idea.

"She deserves her share, and maybe Bradley will one day too. Now we have exactly what we need to clean up the beach on this side."

Dillion smiles. "You really want to do that?"

"All my best memories are wrapped up in this place." *And you*, I want to say, but I don't. "I want this to be a place my kids can come to, and theirs after that. If I can do things to help this community, I want to. Bee would want me to. I'm going to make some calls in the morning. See what's possible."

"After you go to the bank."

"Right. After I go to the bank."

The next morning I take the bond notes to the bank to see if I'm excited about nothing. It turns out that I'm excited for a very good reason. Millions of very good reasons.

I set up a meeting with a financial adviser for early the following week and stop by the town hall. I expect that I'll have to set up a meeting, but the town councilor invites me straight into her office. I tell her what I want to do and how I'd like to get the beach back into shape so the community on this side of the lake can have a place to take their families, just like my grandmother did. With the promise of money to help fund the project, and a consistent budget to maintain it, the councilor seems to be on board.

If I can secure all the permits for things like public washrooms and new docks over the winter, we should be able to start the project as soon as the ice melts off the lake.

I don't think it's possible for anything to spoil my good mood. And then my phone rings.

I check the caller ID.

It's my former boss.

CHAPTER 28
STAY FOR ME

Dillion

The office door swings open, and Van walks in. He's wearing a pair of faded jeans, a pale-blue T-shirt that has seen better days, and a black jacket. His hair is windblown, and his cheeks are flushed. Fall has settled over Pearl Lake, turning the leaves the color of fire.

My gaze finally meets his, and my smile drops. His eyes are wide, slightly manic. "Are you alone?" He closes the door behind him, a gust of crisp autumn air making the papers on my desk ruffle.

"Yeah. Everyone's out on a job. Why? What's wrong? Did something happen? Please tell me the bond notes weren't fake."

He gives his head a quick shake. "They weren't fake. And something happened."

"Something bad or good?"

"The CEO of my old company called."

"Okay." I can't read his expression, which makes me nervous.

"They offered me my old job back."

I lean back in my chair, and it rolls a couple of feet away from my desk. "Oh. Wow. And how do you feel about that?"

"Good. I think I feel good about it. They offered me a promotion, a change to a new department where I'll get to work on restoration projects. They even offered me a raise, and an apology."

"Are you going to take it? Do you want to?" *Are you leaving me?* is the question I don't ask.

He drops into the chair on the other side of the desk and runs a hand through his hair. "I don't know. At first I was like 'Fuck no,' because I was fired for no valid reason, but they've offered me my dream job. And I know I don't *technically* have to work any kind of job if I don't want to, thanks to Grammy Bee, but retirement seems like something I should think about twenty years from now."

I smile. "Well, that makes sense. I can see retirement before thirty being premature."

He runs his hands down his thighs. "They offered to double my salary. And I'll be able to keep an eye on Teagan and my dad. It seems like a smart move?" It comes out more question than statement.

I don't want to rain on his parade, or his good news, or make this about me. If I were in his position and my former company offered me my job back at double the salary, and an opportunity to be closer to my family again, I'd probably be inclined to take it. Van is close with his sister, and since all the crap that's gone down with his brother, Van and his dad have gotten a lot closer. While there are still limits to that relationship, I would never want to stand in the way of his rebuilding a connection that's long been broken. "When would you start?"

He drums his fingers on the arm of the chair. "In a couple of weeks."

"So you'll be moving back to the city?" Just saying it out loud makes my stomach twist uncomfortably. From the moment Van moved into Bee's cottage, I knew it was temporary, that eventually he would go back to the city, because that's where all the great architecture jobs are. But I didn't expect the news to hurt as much as it does. And that's just the idea of it, not his actually moving.

"Come with me," he says. "I know maybe you can't do that right away because of your dad and working for his company, but once things are under control here, you can move back to the city with me. I'm sure I can pull some strings and get you an interview at my company. You'd be a fantastic fit. You're already staying with me most of the time now, so moving in together wouldn't even be much of a transition. And we could work in different departments so we're not in the same space, if you don't want to make it weird or anything."

His excitement makes me giddy, and my immediate gut reaction is to say yes, because I don't want to lose this man. Over the past few months, I've fallen undeniably, hopelessly in love with him. As much as I want to be with him, I worry that following him back to the city will be trading one kind of happiness for another.

"I love you," I say gently.

"I love you too." He swallows thickly, his smile uncertain.

"I came back to Pearl Lake because I felt an obligation to help my family." I look around the office, at the space I've made my own over the past several months.

"I know. And you've been amazing. Footprint Renovations has never done better."

I nod, although I'm not the reason for the success; I'm just part of the package. "Now that I've had a chance to spend some time here and rebuild all the relationships I let languish when I moved to the city, I've realized that it wasn't the town that was the problem. It was me and the situation I put myself in. I wanted out because I didn't know how to fix the mess I'd made, and now things are different. *I'm* different."

"You don't want to leave anymore." His voice is laced with sadness and understanding.

I shake my head. "I understand that you need to do what's best for you, and if that's taking your old job back, then that's what you should do. I want to be with you, Van. I love what we have, but this is my home. My heart is yours, but it belongs here."

CHAPTER 29
I MISS YOU ALREADY

Dillion

The first month is a rough transition. Midweek visits are basically impossible as Van dives headfirst into his new job.

I end up going to Chicago for the first weekend instead of him coming home to Pearl Lake, but it wasn't at all what we expected. He worked most of the weekend, leaving me to entertain myself and solidifying my resolve that I'm done with living in the city. But I'm determined to make our relationship work, because I love him more than I thought possible.

Tawny and Allie turn Wednesdays into a girls' night to break up the week. We hang out like old times, and I tell them all about the hockey players on the other side of the lake while they share the town gossip. I find out that Tucker and Sue finally broke things off, only after a paternity test proved that the baby wasn't his. Sue ended up moving to the next town over, incidentally where Sterling happens to live. As bad as I feel for Tucker, he made his bed, and now he has to lie in it.

Even with the girls' nights and all the dinners with my family, I've gotten used to having Van around all the time, so scaling back to two days a week is an adjustment, and not a great one. Especially when he has to cut the next weekend short because of a project he needs to finish. One night with him out of fourteen isn't sustainable.

We talk every night on the phone, but he's always tired by the end of the day, and it isn't the same as having him next to me. He's offered to let me stay at Bee's, but it feels weird without him. Far lonelier than my trailer.

Finally, six weeks after he takes the job in the city, I get him for a three-day weekend. He's due home in a couple of hours, so I shower, shave, do my hair, and even put on makeup before I head over to Van's and start preparing dinner, wanting to be there when he finally arrives home.

At six thirty I give in and message, asking about an ETA. It takes half an hour for him to message me back, and when he does, it's with a "Sorry, had an impromptu dinner meeting," and he's just leaving now.

I stand in the kitchen, staring at the chopped veggies and the dressed chicken while fighting tears. I'm not a crier—I never have been—but the past several weeks have been hard without Van, and instead of things getting easier with time, everything's grown increasingly more difficult. Long-distance relationships are tough, and I've always been a proximity person.

I put all the food away, saving it for tomorrow night, and make myself a grilled cheese instead. By the time Van gets home, it's nearly eight thirty. He drops his duffel bag at the door, and I don't even have a chance to pull my depressed ass off the couch before he's straddling my lap, one knee sinking into the cushions on either side of me, hands in my hair, thumbs under my chin, tipping my head back.

"I missed you so much." His eyes search mine for a moment, hot and needy and desperate, before he slants his mouth over mine.

We don't make it to the bedroom, instead frantically stripping in the middle of the living room. The coffee table gets shoved out of the way. We nearly break a lamp, and the couch creaks ominously beneath us, but we both seem to need the connection in a way that defies logic and reason. Also, the couch is seven million years old and probably needs to be replaced.

Half an hour and two orgasms later, I'm wearing Van's dress shirt and nothing else, and he's in boxers and a pair of sweats. It's too cold to go shirtless, so eventually he pulls on a Henley, and we snuggle on the couch.

"I'm sorry I was so late getting home." He kisses my temple.

"It's okay, I know it's been busy."

"Mmm." He plays with my fingers. "It has been. Busier than I anticipated, really. I actually had a meeting with my boss this evening about my contract."

"Oh?" I tip my head up to meet his gaze.

He seems nervous. "I showed him some of the designs I was working on while I was here this summer. They wanted to shift me into lead architect for one of our big clients."

My stomach twists uncomfortably. "That sounds amazing. What exactly does that entail?"

"I'd be the lead for an entire project. So if a client wants a new green space designed, I'd oversee everything from an architectural standpoint. I'd have a team working under me and everything."

"That's incredible." I know from my time doing project management that managing a team is a huge job, especially in a big company. He'll have to work longer hours and be in the city probably more than he already is. I want to be happy for him, but I don't know what that means for us.

"It is, but I said I couldn't take it unless they gave me flex hours."

"Flex hours? Why?"

"Because I decided I don't love long-distance relationships or being away from you for five days at a time. So I said I'd take the position, but only if they cut my in-office time to three days a week."

"What did they say?" My heart is in my throat, and I try to tamp down my hope.

"That they would do their best to accommodate my request, and I'll still get the raise. There will be times when I'm needed more, but usually I'll only need to be in the city a few days a week at most. I can supplement with virtual meetings when they're necessary."

"And this is what you want?"

"Absolutely. There are things I want to do here, like getting the garage loft finished, starting the cottage renovations, and cleaning up the beach come spring. If I'm in the city most of the time, I won't be able to tackle any of those things effectively or efficiently. Besides, I love you more than I love this job, and I don't want anything to jeopardize that."

"What about your family? What about Teagan and your dad?"

"I'll still see them when I'm in the city, and they're not far. I want more days with you than without you. I want to put down roots and build a life, and I want to do that here, with you."

EPILOGUE
MATCHMAKER IN HEAVEN

Van
Six months later

It's a work-from-home day, and I've already tackled all my calls and emails early this morning, leaving my afternoon free. Three days a week in the city is turning out to be the perfect arrangement. There are times when I have to pull long days to make it work, and in the winter months I make sure all three days are back to back so I can make long weekends a regular thing. It's been a juggling act, but it's absolutely worth it.

Because it means I get to do the thing I love and be with the person I love more than I'm without her.

"Do you have another box? I've already filled this one." Dillion folds the flaps over and scrawls the words FRAMED PHOTOS across the top of it.

"Yup, got another one right here." I pass her the empty box and take the full one, moving it to the porch.

We're getting ready to paint, which means we have to take all the photos off the walls. And there are a lot of them. Probably close to a hundred. As soon as the ice was off the lake, we started preparing the cottage for renos. Over the winter we renovated one of the bathrooms, and we tackled the kitchen this spring. We've also started on the garage, which meant ripping off the roof and building up, so we could turn it into a loft apartment and still keep the storage space under it. Dillion's brother and Aaron are doing all the work according to my specs, and so far it all looks fantastic.

With the kitchen taken care of, we're moving on to the painting and freshening-up stage. And it doesn't matter how thorough we think we've been; we're still finding stashes of money hidden in the house. Just like Dillion said, it's an Easter egg hunt that keeps on giving.

Teagan has been coming up to visit frequently, and I expect that will only increase once the garage is finished. Bradley's incarceration, and our dad's unwillingness to call in favors to lighten his sentence, means the next few years are going to be rough for him.

Also, Dad's finally moving on. He's going for therapy to deal with his guilt over the loss of our mother, and he recently started dating someone. I think Teagan comes here so she doesn't feel like she's intruding.

When I return to the cottage, Dillion has already managed to fill half the box. I reach over her head for the photos that are too high for her to get without a step stool. I lift a picture of me with Grammy Bee from the wall, inspecting it. It was taken in town and shows me helping her out of her ancient truck. Her smile and mine say everything about who we were to each other.

Dillion rests her cheek on my biceps. "Every time you came to town with Bee, you'd always hop out of the truck as soon as you had it in park, and you'd run around to the other side before she could open the door."

"That door stuck all the time. I didn't want her to put a shoulder out."

"I know." She smiles. "She was forever trying to WD-40 the hinges, but she could never get it to open easier. You'd have to yank so hard on that door, and then when you'd finally get it open, you'd look so relieved, and she'd be so happy. I loved those moments you two always shared, so I captured this one."

"I didn't know you took this picture."

"Mmm. I had it framed for Bee's seventy-fifth birthday."

I turn it over and slide the backing out, aware that Grammy Bee always dated the pictures on the back. My name and age are scrawled neatly on the back, and along with it is a note.

I set the picture down and unfold it.

Dearest Donovan,

If you're reading this, it probably means that I'm gone. I hope you've found all the treasures I've left for you, and that you're making the smart choices I know you're capable of. You were always a wonderful young man, and you've only gotten better with age, much like a good scotch ;)

If all has gone the way I hoped it would, you and Lynnie will have found your way to each other. I'll never forget the way you always headed for the food truck, even though you can't stand hot dogs. Or the way she'd ask about you as if she was being sly back when you were teenagers and still too obtuse to see what was right there in front of you.

If I'm right about the two of you and you have managed to open your gloriously big hearts to each other, then I'm sure I'm sitting up in heaven smiling down on you.

When you're ready to make her yours forever, you'll find what you need in the top drawer of the china hutch in the right-hand corner. Don't wait too long on that, either, because she's not one you want to lose.

Love and best wishes for a bright and wonderful future,

Grammy Bee

"I'd say I can't believe that she'd do this, but it's exactly like Bee to play matchmaker, even from heaven," Dillion says.

"It really is." I set the note carefully on top of the picture and head for the china hutch.

Just as she promised, there's a small black-velvet bag in the back of the right-hand corner. I slip the small box out. I don't need to open it to know what's inside.

I turn to Dillion, standing in the middle of the living room, surrounded by boxes and pictures of the life and legacy Bee left for us, and drop to one knee. "You're my person, Dillion. You gave me a reason to put down roots. You make this place home. You're my summer love that turned into forever. Be mine, Dillion. Marry me."

I flip open the box to reveal Bee's engagement ring. It's simple and elegant and exactly right for Dillion.

She smiles and nods, eyes bright with unshed tears. "You brought the magic back to this place for me, and you made it impossible not to love you. Of course I'll marry you. My heart is yours."

I slip it onto her finger and rise. Taking her face in my hands, I press my lips to hers.

A gust of wind makes the chimes tinkle outside, and I know that we'll always be watched over with love.

ACKNOWLEDGMENTS

Nearly fifty years ago, my parents and my aunt and uncle invested in a little chunk of forest on the water in Ontario, four hours from their home. They helped each other build cottages next door to each other, and as a child I had the amazing privilege of spending most of my summers up there. Over the years the cottages had little facelifts, but they're still very much a reflection of the seventies, when they were built, and the fact that they haven't changed is one of my favorite things about the family cottage. It's a home away from home, serene and calm, with terrible internet access. There are more than a hundred stairs from the cottage to the lake, so you'd better not forget anything when you head down to the dock.

Thank you, Mom and Dad, for giving us such a great place to create memories. The cottage was, and always will be, one of my favorite places to be.

Husband and kidlet, I'm so lucky to love you and be loved by you. Thank you for always standing by me.

Pepper, one day I will get you to the cottage, and we will moan about the stairs to the dock together.

Kimberly, thank you for your endless cheerleading and always knowing exactly what I need to hear and when I need to hear it.

To my Montlake team, thank you so much for making this such a wonderful experience. It's an honor and a pleasure to work with all of you.

Sarah, you're a true friend, and I'm lucky to have you.

Hustlers, I couldn't ask for a better book family. Thank you for all the years of love and friendship.

Tijan, you're such an amazing human being. Thank you for sharing your friendship with me.

Sarah, Jenn, Hilary, Shan, Catherine, and my entire team at Social Butterfly, you're fabulous, and I couldn't do it without you.

Sarah and Gel, your incredible talent never ceases to amaze me. Thank you for sharing it with me.

Beavers, thank you for giving me a safe place to land, and for always being excited about what's next.

Deb, Tijan, Leigh, Kelly, Ruth, Kellie, Erika, Marty, Karen, Shalu, Melanie, Marnie, Julie, Krystin, Laurie, Angie, Angela, Jo, and Lou, your friendship, guidance, support, and insight keep me grounded. Thank you for being such wonderful and inspiring women in my life.

Readers, bloggers, and bookstagrammers, your passion for love stories is unparalleled. Thank you for all that you do for the reading community.

ABOUT THE AUTHOR

New York Times and *USA Today* bestselling author Helena Hunting lives on the outskirts of Toronto with her incredibly tolerant family and two moderately intolerant cats. She writes contemporary romance ranging from new adult angst to romantic comedy.

LINKS

Website ⇨ http://www.helenahunting.com/

Amazon ⇨ http://amzn.to/1y6OBB7

Twitter ⇨ http://bit.ly/HelenaHTwitter

Facebook ⇨ https://www.facebook.com/helena.hunting69/

Pinterest ⇨ http://bit.ly/1oQYRVN

Instagram ⇨ http://instagram.com/helenahunting

Goodreads ⇨ http://bit.ly/GoodReadsHH

Newsletter ⇨ http://bit.ly/HelenaHnewsletter

Bookbub ⇨ http://bit.ly/BookBubHH

The Beaver Den ⇨ http://bit.ly/TheBeaverDenHH